LUCIFER

Book Three of The Redemption Series

S.J. WEST

Sandra J. West

LIST OF BOOKS IN THE WATCHER SERIES

The Watchers Trilogy

Cursed

Blessed

Forgiven

The Watcher Chronicles

Broken

Kindred

Oblivion

Ascension

Caylin's Story

Timeless

Devoted

Aiden's Story

The Alternate Earth Series

Cataclysm

Uprising

Judgment

<u>The Redemption Series</u>

Malcolm

Anna

Lucifer

Redemption

<u>The Dominion Series</u>

Awakening

Reckoning (Spring 2016)

OTHER BOOKS BY S.J. WEST

<u>The Harvester of Light Trilogy</u>

Harvester

Hope

Dawn

<u>The Vankara Saga</u>

Vankara

Dragon Alliance

War of Atonement

Lucifer

CHAPTER ONE

Sometimes your heart makes decisions that your brain doesn't agree with. When that happens you can either trust your first instinct or spend precious moments debating with yourself as to which course of action is best. I've always been one to trust what my heart tells me to do. It's never let me down before, and I hope it hasn't sent me on a wild goose chase for answers now.

I need to find out what Lucifer knows about my future. What is he trying to warn me about? My heart is telling me that his true motives fall on the side of wanting to protect me more than they point towards him simply wanting to bolster his own position of power on Earth. I can't just dismiss what I see in his eyes every time he looks at me. He cares for me, possibly even loves me, in his own peculiar way. I know he loved my mother more than he loved anyone else in his life… And, because of that once in a lifetime love, I know he will never intentionally harm the last remnant of his soulmate.

As I stand in Lucifer's domain, I begin to question my rash decision to follow him to Hell. My heart aches with guilt because I know Malcolm will be upset that I didn't wait to speak with him before I left. Nevertheless, I couldn't afford to have Lucifer's phase trail close and shut me off from the answers I so desperately need. I hope Malcolm will be able to understand that I've done this for the sake of our future together. We need to know what Lucifer knows. Yet every time my biological father warns me to stop seeking the seals, he phases to Hell like he thinks it will shelter him from the storm of my questions. He needs to learn that he can't keep coming here to hide from me.

I look around at my surroundings and find them…not quite what I was expecting.

Snow falls all around yet never seems to reach the ground. The scene set before me is absent of its presence, and I notice the flakes which fall never land on me either. They simply disappear, not leaving a trace of their existence.

I find myself standing in front of a mammoth building constructed from blocks of limestone. The branching network of structures on either side makes it apparent that additions had been built on over a span of years. The main building has six floors, and cornered with turrets with conical copper roofs, which have long since turned green with age. I look up at the sky but only see an unending darkness. There's no sign of clouds, which makes me wonder what the origin of the phantom snow is.

"You shouldn't have followed me here," I hear Lucifer say behind me.

I turn completely around to meet his disapproving gaze. He's sitting on the bench underneath the shade tree in what appears to be a replica of Malcolm's courtyard back in New Orleans. The change in scenery is disorienting. It's like half the space is occupied by the building at my back, and the other half is a reconstruction of the courtyard.

Lucifer is dressed casually in a blue turtleneck sweater and jeans. His blond hair is pulled back into a ponytail and peppered with the falling snow. I stare at him, wondering why he's the only one being affected by the snowfall.

"I had to," I tell him, crossing the short space separating us until I'm standing directly in front of him. "You have answers that I need."

"I'm under no obligation to tell you anything," he says, a scowl appearing on his face as he sits up straighter and crosses his arms over his chest. "You should leave now while you still have the chance."

"Are you threatening me?" I ask.

Lucifer shakes his head. "Still so naïve, Anna."

"Then why don't you enlighten me?" I challenge. "What is it that I'm missing?"

"Not even I can control everything that happens in Hell. If it wants to keep you trapped down here, it will. It can warp your mind to a point where you become lost in your own thoughts. You'll never quite know if what you're experiencing is real or simply a figment of your imagination. You could lose your sanity here and never know it. Is that what you really want, Anna? Do you want to lose yourself to madness?"

"Of course not," I say, "but you keep coming here like it will protect you from my questions. You need to realize that I'll follow you anywhere to get the answers that I need."

A loud, booming clang resounds in the air. It's a haunting sound like one you would hear in a nightmare, warning of impending doom. Two more deep resonating tones follow it.

"The show's about to begin," Lucifer tells me in a resigned voice. "You might as well sit down with me and watch it if you refuse to leave."

Lucifer's attention is drawn away from me to something near the building at my back. I sit down beside him on the bench, and follow his gaze to discover what has captured his interest so completely. I lift a trembling hand to my lips and feel my eyes begin to burn with tears.

My mother and Malcolm are now standing on the front steps of the building.

"Why are they here?" I ask, worried that I may have unintentionally altered their fates by coming to Hell.

"They're not," Lucifer tells me, a note of longing in his voice as he continues to stare at my mother.

I notice that the figures of my mother and Malcolm are completely still, like they're decorative statues that have been placed in front of the building.

"I don't understand," I admit, looking over at Lucifer for an answer.

"This is a memory... my memory," Lucifer explains, in such a low voice I have to strain to hear his next words. "Hell is different for everyone because we all have different triggers that truly torment our souls. For some people it's physical pain. For others it's the pain of not living when they had the chance and allowing their fear to hold them back."

"And for you?" I ask, already having a good idea what torments him the most.

"Reliving memories I have of your mother," Lucifer says, confirming what I already suspected. "It feeds on my pain by making me experience key moments of our life together over and over again. And...I let it."

"Why?" I ask quietly, not demanding an answer but wanting to understand why he would willingly allow himself to be tortured in such a way.

"Because..." Lucifer's brow furrows as he stares at the figment of my mother and I see a shimmer of tears glisten in his pale blue eyes. "Because this is the only way I can see her."

The look in his eyes and the way he made this simple statement makes my heart ache for his loss.

Lucifer's words remind me of what Malcolm said when I told him I couldn't promise I wouldn't trade in my soul if it meant I could save his life. Malcolm told me then that if I ever did that we would be permanently separated from one another after death. Heaven would be lost to me, and we would have to spend an eternity forever without one another. It saddens me to know that my parents are living through such a hell. For Lucifer that was a literal state of being.

I notice that the falling snow is accumulating on Lucifer while it still simply fades when it comes close to me.

"Why is it snowing here?" I ask, thinking it peculiar that Hell should be so cold.

"Hell has always been a mirror of my soul," Lucifer tells me, his face looking drawn with a sorrow I can't even comprehend. "Since Amalie's death I've felt dead inside." Lucifer looks over at me. "If I could I would let you kill me to take my seal and end my torment once and for all. At least an existence in the Void would numb my soul and finally bring an end to its pain."

"I don't want to kill you if I don't have to," I tell him. "I was told there was another way to take the seal from you. I don't suppose you would willingly tell me how to do that, would you?"

Lucifer stares at me, but the distant look in his eyes tells me he isn't going to give me the answers I need, at least not yet.

Another deep clang reverberates through the air like a death knell, and Lucifer returns his attention to the scene near the building.

"You should watch this," he tells me instead. "I think you'll find it interesting."

"Why are you being so stubborn?" I ask, not even bothering to hide my aggravation with him. "Why can't you just tell me what I need to know?"

Lucifer doesn't even hear my questions. His attention is locked on the scene by the building, completely lost in the reenactment of one of his memories.

Curious by what I might witness I follow his gaze and watch, too.

The figures of my mother and Malcolm finally begin to move.

"How many are in there?" my mother asks Malcolm as they walk up the steps of the building.

My mother is holding my sword in one of her hands, its blade blazing with yellow-orange flames. Malcolm is holding a broad-sword and dressed in his overlord outfit.

9

"We were told most of the staff in the hospital is changelings now."

"Why would they take over a hospital?"

"Very few people question the death of someone in such a place. I'm sure Lucifer sent them here to harvest more souls for him," Malcolm says in disgust.

"I still haven't met Lucifer yet," my mother says, as if she finds it a curious thing.

"Count yourself lucky, Amalie," Malcolm tells my mother. "I know I feel fortunate that I haven't had to deal with him for the last twenty years. Although, I guess it's about time for him to rear his ugly head and start making trouble again like a spoiled child. Let's just worry about killing these changelings for now before they cause any more damage."

Malcolm opens the door to the building and allows my mother to precede him.

The scene changes as though we're watching a movie, and I see my mother running down a long dark hallway in pursuit of a man dressed in a white orderly outfit. When she reaches him she yanks on the back of his shirt and throws him up against the side of a wall, causing him to fall backward onto the floor. My mother's hands burst into blue flames as she wraps them around the man's neck, instantly turning him into a pile of black ash. Just as she stands back to her full height, I see Lucifer phase in only a few feet opposite her in the hallway.

When my mother looks up and sees him for the very first time in her life, her lips part and there's a perceptible quickening to her breathing. Her fingers loosen on the hilt of her sword and it clatters to the tiled floor at her feet.

The look on Lucifer's face in the memory is almost a mirror of my mother's. It's one of utter disbelief.

They don't say a word to one another, but there isn't any need for them to.

I watch as a man and a woman, both carrying knives, walk down the hallway behind my mother, but she's so preoccupied with the sudden appearance of Lucifer that she doesn't notice their stealthy approach. Just as they reach out to grab her Lucifer breaks the connection with my mother's gaze to look at them. This seems to unweave the spell my mother is under. She quickly phases to a point just behind the two changelings and grabs each of them by the neck, using her power to reduce them to nothing more than ash.

My mother looks back at Lucifer and asks, "Who are you?"

Lucifer just stares at her, as if he has lost the ability to speak. Finally, he says, "Someone you don't want to know."

"How can you say that?" my mother asks, sounding hurt by his words. "I've been waiting my whole life for this to happen."

Lucifer keeps his face neutral but even I can tell he knows exactly what my mother is referring to. Slowly he begins to shake his head at her.

"You don't want me as your soulmate. You don't even know who I am."

My mother is silent as she stares at Lucifer, and I see a look of calm certainty settle over her features.

"I don't think it much matters who you are," my mother tells him. "Because whether you like it or not we're meant to be together. Why are you trying to deny it?"

"Because making me your soulmate is a punishment from God."

"For whom?" my mother asks defensively. "For you or me?"

"For both of us," Lucifer says. "You should just try to forget you ever saw me. I think we will both be better off if I just disappear and don't return until after your death."

"No."

"No?" Lucifer says, his eyes narrowing on my mother. "I don't think you're in any position to dictate what I choose to do with my own life."

"Even if you want to leave me alone I don't think you can make yourself do it," my mother tells him, with such certainty that there is no point in Lucifer even trying to form an argument. "And, besides, I won't let you hide from me."

One corner of Lucifer's mouth lifts in a small lopsided grin at her statement.

Malcolm phases in at the other end of the hallway behind my mother, but as soon as he sees she's with Lucifer he phases to her side.

"Well, look what the hounds dragged up from Hell," Malcolm says, eyeing Lucifer with undisguised revulsion. "Long time no see, Lucifer. Too bad your absence from my life couldn't have lasted a lot longer."

My mother doesn't even flinch when Malcolm identifies the stranger who is her soulmate. Obviously she knew who he really was the moment she saw him. Lucifer has an aura of strength around him that is unlike that of anyone else. I felt it the first time I saw him that night at the beach house, and I can tell my mother felt it, too. You don't have that sort of quiet strength without being someone extremely powerful.

"Malcolm," Lucifer says with the same level of disgust as he looks him up and down appraisingly. "How's the leg?"

Malcolm scowls at Lucifer at the reminder of his pain. Lucifer just grins tight-lipped, looking rather pleased with himself.

"You might as well leave," Malcolm tells Lucifer. "We've killed all of the changelings you had here. I guess you'll need to find some other unsuspecting souls to harvest."

"Who says I haven't already?" Lucifer taunts arrogantly. "You should know by now that you can never stop me. I am what our father made me into, Malcolm. In a way, you could say I'm really doing God's work."

Malcolm lets out a harsh laugh. "You can delude yourself into thinking that if you want, Lucifer. But you and I know that the only thing you've ever been interested in is gaining more power for yourself."

"As simple-minded as ever, I see," Lucifer says in feigned disappointment.

"I just see you for what you are," Malcolm replies. "Come on, Amalie. Our work here is done."

Malcolm gently takes hold of my mother's elbow, but she yanks it out of his grasp. Malcolm looks at her questioningly, but my mother's eyes haven't left Lucifer's face. Malcolm looks between my mother and Lucifer, and instantly realizes what's going on.

"Oh, hell no," Malcolm growls. "This is not happening. You're coming with me right now, Amalie!"

Malcolm grabs my mother's elbow more forcefully and phases them both away but my mother simply phases right back, giving Malcolm no other choice but to follow her.

"Amalie," Malcolm implores, "you need to stay away from him!"

My mother drags her eyes away from Lucifer to look at Malcolm. She hesitates before speaking, as if her next words are hard for her to say to him.

"I'm sorry, Malcolm. I can't do that." My mother looks back at Lucifer and a slow smile lights up her face. "He's mine."

Malcolm's scowl grows even darker. He looks over at Lucifer and demands, "What the hell did you do to her?"

"It wasn't my doing," Lucifer answers, unable to keep his eyes off my mother. "You'll have to ask our father to explain Himself if you want an answer to that question."

Malcolm turns to Amalie and grabs her by the shoulders, forcing her to look at him instead of Lucifer.

"Amalie, listen to me, please," he begs. "Whatever it is you think you feel when you look at him, forget it. Lucifer will never be able to love you more than he does himself. He isn't built to care for someone else like that. Don't give him your heart. He'll only break it in the end."

"For once," Lucifer chimes in, "I agree with you, Malcolm."

My mother looks back at Lucifer. "You can try to reject what you feel but since I feel it, too, I don't think you'll be able to deny it for much longer."

"It doesn't much matter what you feel for me," Lucifer tells her, a note of regret in his voice. "When you learn of the things I've done in my life, it will be enough to make you want to stay as far away from me as you can get."

"Are you sorry for the things you've done?" my mother asks him directly.

Lucifer is silent for a few seconds as he considers her question.

"Some," he admits reluctantly, "but not all."

"Then I refuse to believe there isn't a small bit of good left in you. Maybe that's why we've been brought together. Maybe I'm meant to remind you of that."

"Good luck finding any good left in that son of a bitch," Malcolm scoffs, releasing his hold on my mother as he turns to look at Lucifer. Malcolm points a finger at Lucifer and growls, "You keep away from her."

"Not that it's any of your business," Lucifer replies, "but that was my intention from the moment I saw her. Neither of us needs this complication in our lives. All I need is a goody two-shoes holding me back from the work I'm meant to do."

"As long as we understand one another," Malcolm says, looking satisfied with Lucifer's answer.

"The two of you are talking to each other like I'm not standing right here," my mother says in exasperation. "Don't I get a say in how my life is supposed to go?"

"No," Malcolm and Lucifer say in unison, at least agreeing on this one thing in their lives.

"Well, I hate to inform the two of you," my mother says almost angrily, "but I've never been very good at doing what I'm told, especially when I know it isn't right."

"You won't see me again after tonight," Lucifer tells my mother, with so much conviction *I* almost believe it. "I have enough self-control to stay away from you. Can you say the same, or are you going to prove to me that I've been right all these years in thinking humans are weak-willed and minded?"

"Don't do that," my mother says, shaking her head at him. "Don't try to provoke my anger to prove a point. It won't work with me."

"Stay away from me, Amalie," Lucifer tells her, a warning in his voice. "Nothing good can come from us being together."

Lucifer phases, and the scene fades away.

I look back at Lucifer beside me. The snow completely covers his sweater and hair now, almost making them appear white.

"How did she make you change your mind about being with her?" I ask him.

"By being extremely stubborn," he tells me, a small smile tugging at the corners of his lips as he fondly remembers my mother. "It didn't help that I found myself inventing reasons to seek her out. The connection between us was stronger than anything I'd ever experienced before. The only other human I ever felt connected to was Jess, but with Amalie it was…different, more intense. I began to like the person I was when we were together. She made me want to let go of my hate because her love for me was so all-consuming. Your mother never doubted for one moment that we were destined to be with each other. Even though Malcolm tried his best to warn her to stay away from me she refused to listen to him. There were times I wish she had. I knew I wasn't good enough for her yet she wouldn't listen to me either."

The blackness in front of us transforms into a mirror of the courtyard we're sitting in.

My mother is sitting on an identical bench, crying. Lucifer phases in and sits beside her. Without saying a word he brings her into the folds of his arms so she can cry against his chest. He gently begins to stroke her long brown hair.

"Amalie," he says tenderly, "why are you crying like you've just lost your best friend?"

"Because I think I have," she says, sobbing even harder.

Lucifer lets her cry for a little while longer before asking, "Can you tell me what happened?"

My mother sniffs before saying, "Malcolm and I had a fight."

"About me, I presume."

My mother nods her head against Lucifer's chest. "He even brought my parents into it this time."

"And what did they think about us being together?"

"My father took Malcolm's side."

"And your mother?"

"She just wants me to be happy. She doesn't like you, of course, but she knows I'll never truly be content unless you're a part of my life."

"Neither of them is wrong, you know," Lucifer tells her. "Malcolm is right in thinking I'm not good enough for you. And your mother is right in thinking you'll never find true happiness without me."

My mother leans away from Lucifer a little to look up at his face.

"Maybe if you removed the curse from Malcolm he would change his mind," she suggests hopefully.

Lucifer seems to take her suggestion seriously but ends up shaking his head. "I can't do that."

"You can't or won't?" she questions.

"Won't," Lucifer admits. "There's too much that's passed between Malcolm and me, Amalie. Even if I did remove the curse it wouldn't change his mind about us."

"I can't let you go," my mother says, snuggling her head against Lucifer's chest. "I'd rather be dead than live my life without you in it. Malcolm will just have to come to terms with the fact that we're meant to be together."

"I think you need to prepare yourself for the possibility that he will never accept that."

"And what about you?" my mother asks. "Are you going to stop fighting your feelings for me?"

Lucifer sighs, resting his cheek on the top of my mother's head.

"I don't think I have any more fight left in me when it comes to you, Amalie."

"Good," my mother says, Lucifer's words finally stopping the flow of her tears. "I was getting tired of trying to make you see reason. Maybe this experience will teach you a lesson."

"And what lesson would that be?" Lucifer asks, sounding slightly amused.

"That I'm always right," she replies, as though the answer should have been obvious.

Lucifer chuckles, and my mother sits back to look at his face.

"I think that's the first time I've ever heard you laugh," she says with a small smile of true happiness. "I like it. You should do it more often."

"Maybe I will," he tells her, grinning.

My mother takes a deep breath and says, "I love you."

I can instantly tell by the look of surprise on Lucifer's face that this is the first time she's said those words aloud to him.

My mother's gaze falls to her lap as he continues to stare at her after her heartfelt declaration. I know what she's waiting for. She's waiting for him to say the same three little words to her, but he simply remains silent as he continues to gape at her.

"I...love you, too," Lucifer finally tells her, the words sounding like they cost him a lot of effort to say.

"You don't have to say that just because I said it," my mother tells him, obviously hearing the same hesitation in his voice that I did.

Lucifer reaches out a hand and places it underneath my mother's chin, gently lifting her head up until their eyes meet.

"I love you, Amalie," he says, his words sounding surer this time. "I'm sorry it didn't come out quite right the first time. I've...just...never said them to anyone before now."

My mother smiles shyly, and leans in closer to Lucifer until their faces are barely an inch apart.

"Lucifer," she murmurs, "kiss me..."

Lucifer hesitates for only a second before grabbing my mother to him and kissing her passionately.

I feel Lucifer take hold of one of my hands and instantly find myself sitting on the real bench back in Malcolm's courtyard.

"Why did you bring me back here?" I ask him, feeling cheated out of seeing more about my parents' life together.

"Because what happens after that kiss isn't something a daughter should see her parents do," Lucifer says, sounding slightly embarrassed.

"Oh," I say, not needing any further explanation.

I feel Lucifer begin to pull his hand away from mine but I grab it before he can.

"Please," I beg, "tell me what you think will happen if I collect all the seals. I need to know."

Lucifer stares at our conjoined hands, his face drawn with worry.

"You'll change, Anna," he finally says, sadness at the prospect of this eventuality in his voice. "You'll become something you won't be able to recognize anymore."

"How will the seals change me?" I ask, becoming worried for the first time since my mission began that maybe Lucifer was right about my quest.

Lucifer raises his gaze and looks me straight in the eyes.

"You'll grow to be more of a monster than I am," he tells me. "Hate will fill your soul to the point where you can't be saved. If you want to stay the person you are stop trying to retrieve them, Anna. Save yourself and those who love you the pain of losing you in that way."

Lucifer phases back to Hell, leaving me with even more questions than I had before.

CHAPTER TWO

I stare at Lucifer's phase trail and know exactly why he's returned to Hell. I pity his lonely existence. He only wants to relive beloved memories of his time with my mother, allowing Hell to feed off his unending misery. Having found my own soulmate, I can only imagine the torment Lucifer is living in. If I was faced with an eternity without Malcolm, I'm certain I would either go mad or simply die from a broken heart. Unfortunately, the rift separating Heaven from Hell is a chasm no one can traverse.

I stand up from the bench and take a deep breath to help brace myself for what awaits me inside the house. I want to be with Malcolm, but I know he'll be furious with me for leaving without letting him know where I went. Then again, I can't imagine he would have simply stood aside and let me follow Lucifer to Hell. He would have done everything within his power to keep me from phasing there, even though it did end up providing me with some valuable information. I now know a small portion of what Lucifer was holding back from us. I have a feeling there is more to the story than what he told me, but at least he knows there's nowhere he can go that I won't follow to get the truth.

When I phase back to Malcolm's bedroom, I find the man I love sitting on the edge of the bed, looking completely lost. His elbows are resting on his thighs, his head hanging low, propped up between the palms of his hands. I feel an overwhelming sense of guilt as I look at him. I don't like to see him so sad, and I like it even less because I know I'm the reason for it.

As soon as I take a step forward, Malcolm's head jerks up. I'm in his arms before I can even think about taking a second step.

"Anna," he sighs with a mixture of relief and worry, hugging me tightly to him, "where have you been? Did someone take you? Are you hurt?"

Malcolm makes to lean back to look at me, presumably to make sure that I haven't been harmed in any way. I quickly wrap my arms around his waist and hold him firmly to me, needing to feel his strength.

"I'm fine," I tell him, feeling anything but after what Lucifer has told me. "Just hold me, Malcolm. All I need right now is to feel you."

Malcolm does as I ask, but I know his questions are far from over.

"Where were you?" he demands, but not harshly. "We searched everywhere we could think of but couldn't find you."

I'm silent for a long time, because I know the moment I answer his question he'll be mad. I would much rather deal with a worried Malcolm than an angry Malcolm.

After a while I hear, "Anna...tell me where you've been."

I close my eyes and breathe in Malcolm's scent, drinking in his warmth for a few more precious seconds before giving him my answer.

"I followed Lucifer to Hell."

Malcolm jerks back from me and grabs hold of the top of my arms. He looks into my eyes like he hopes to find that I'm joking. His eyes narrow on me in anger when he sees that I'm not.

"Have you lost your mind?" he demands angrily.

"We needed answers," I tell him, trying to sound reasonable.

"*You* needed answers," Malcolm corrects. "*I* wouldn't ask you to go there for anything in this world. You can't just traipse down to Hell and come back, thinking that place won't change you in some way. Once it grabs a hold of your mind, it won't let go, Anna. You don't play with something that dangerous. Look what it's done to Lucifer!"

"I'm not going to argue and say it was the smartest thing I've ever done," I admit, knowing I don't have a leg to stand on. "But I needed Lucifer to tell me what he knows about our future."

"What he *thinks* he knows," Malcolm corrects. "Our future is what we make of it. Nothing Lucifer says will change that fact."

"It might," I say, seeing my words register on Malcolm's face. "He told me what collecting the seals might do to me."

Malcolm lets go of my arms, obviously not expecting my fact-finding mission to have borne fruit.

"What did he say?"

"He said they could transform me into a monster worse than him. That they would fill my soul with so much hate I wouldn't be able to recognize myself anymore."

Malcolm's brow lowers at hearing this news, but he doesn't say anything.

"What are you thinking?" I ask, knowing he's considering my words thoughtfully.

"Do you remember me telling you the warning God gave us?" he asks. "The one about us needing to make sure your heart remained pure?"

"Yes," I say.

"Maybe this is why we were told that," Malcolm reasons. "If the seals can darken your heart then maybe there's a way to protect your soul from them."

"But how am I supposed to keep my heart pure?"

"By not allowing hatred to fill it," Malcolm says, pulling me back into his arms. "We won't let that happen to you. My father wouldn't have sent you down here just to become something worse than Lucifer. He doesn't play games with a person's soul like that. Letting people have a choice in who they become has always been important to Him. You're stronger than anyone I know, Anna. I think you were built to withstand whatever evil resides in the power of the seals."

"But what if they're stronger than me?" I ask, letting Malcolm share my worry because I need his strength now more than ever. "What if the power they carry ends up consuming my soul?"

"I won't let that happen," Malcolm says fiercely. "And I believe in our son."

I look up at Malcolm. "What do you mean?"

"Lucas has seen our future together," he reminds me. "And I choose to believe we'll live the future he's seen for us. You need to do the same, my love. Believe that we'll have a little boy named Liam and a little girl named Lillianna. Though, I've been thinking about that name..."

"Don't you like it?" I ask, smiling at the dubious look on Malcolm's face.

"Seriously, that name is a mouthful," Malcolm almost complains. "Let's shorten it to Liana. If she ever does something bad, by the time I get her full name out of my mouth I will have forgotten what it was I was going to chastise her for."

I giggle, the tension from our conversation broken slightly.

"I'm fine with Liana," I tell him, my heart swelling with love for the man and future father of my children.

Malcolm lets me go and takes one of my hands into his.

"Come on, everyone is worried about you. Next time at least leave me a note before you just disappear. Though I'm not sure how happy I would be if you wrote, 'Gone to Hell. Be back soon'."

"I'm sorry I put you through that," I tell him. "I just couldn't let him disappear again without getting some answers. It might even explain why Will had a hard time resurrecting me. Is he still here?"

"No. He isn't allowed to stay on Earth for very long after he revives you."

"I wish he could stay here with us permanently," I say. "I think I could use all the friends I can get right about now."

Malcolm squeezes my hand reassuringly.

"I won't let anything happen to you," he tells me, with so much conviction I have no choice but to believe him. "Now let's go find the others and let them know you're back."

Malcolm phases us to the sitting room, where everyone seems to be waiting on news of my whereabouts.

"Mommy!" Lucas yells, removing Luna from his lap and scrambling off his seat on the couch beside Millie. He runs to me and wraps his little arms around my hips, hugging me so tightly I'm not sure he ever intends to let me go.

Vala leaps from her own spot on the couch and comes to sit behind Lucas, an ever-faithful protector of us both.

"Where were you, Anna?" Vala asks, worry over my sudden disappearance evident in her voice.

I look around at Millie and my Watcher protectors as they all come to stand in front of us, anxious to hear my answer.

"Lucifer came to see me, and I followed him to get some answers," I tell them, not wanting to flat-out say that I traveled to Hell in front of Lucas. He was upset enough. I didn't want to aggravate the situation.

"Have you lost your mind, lass?" Desmond asks me in utter disbelief.

"My thoughts exactly," Brutus grumbles, crossing his arms over his broad chest and shaking his head in disappointment.

"Did you completely forget what I told you about that place?" Jered says, not bothering to hide his aggravation with me.

I look at Daniel and wait for him to chastise me, too.

"I don't think I have anything else to add," he tells me with a shrug. "They've pretty much said it all."

"I went because I needed answers," I tell them. "And I got a partial one from him."

Gently, I loosen Lucas' hold on me and bend down on one knee to face him.

"Lucas, would you mind going with Millie to the kitchen and getting me something to drink? I'm really thirsty."

"Ok," Lucas says, unaware that I'm sending him on an errand so he doesn't hear what I need to tell the others.

"Come along, Lucas," Millie says, holding out her hand to him. "I know just the thing we can fix for your mother to make her feel right as rain."

Lucas and Millie walk out of the room, with Vala pushing Luna along to follow close behind them. Once I know they are out of hearing range I go on to tell the others what I told Malcolm about Lucifer's warning.

"Do you trust what he told you?" Jered asks, knowing I would be able to tell if what Lucifer said was the truth or a lie.

"I…think he was telling me the truth," I tell them, only then realizing I didn't feel confident in my answer. Usually my natural sixth sense would tell me definitively whether or not someone was speaking the truth. Why didn't I feel it while I was talking to Lucifer?

"Why don't you sound sure?" Malcolm asks, looking as worried as I feel.

"Because I'm not," I admit, seeing no need to hide the fact from them.

No one says a word but they all look unsettled by this revelation.

"Do you think it's a side-effect from having two of the seals?" I ask them.

"It's possible," Jered says. "We're entering unknown territory here, Anna. None of us knows all the answers. We'll just have to deal with the consequences of you obtaining the seals as they happen."

"Let's assume for now that Lucifer was telling the truth," Brutus says. "Is collecting them really worth the risk it poses to Anna? Because I don't think retrieving them is worth losing her like that."

"I understand your concern," I say, "but Malcolm and I don't think God would send me to do something He doesn't think I can handle. We need to have faith that He knows what He's doing."

Jered sighs in resignation. "Anna's right. We need to trust that our father has a plan to keep her safe."

"I still don't like it," Desmond says, running one hand through his shoulder-length hair in frustration. "I don't like it one bit."

"I don't think any of us likes it," Daniel tells him, "but when have you known our father to do something without thinking it through? He sent Anna to this particular point in time for a reason. I think we just need to trust Him. But," Daniel looks at me, "if there comes a time when you feel like you're losing yourself, you need to say something. Don't hide anything from us, Anna. You may think it'll cause us worry but your silence would worry us even more. Promise me you'll ask for our help if and when you need it."

I nod my head. "I promise you I won't keep what's happening to me a secret. I'm going to need all of you to help me survive this."

Malcolm puts an arm around my shoulders.

"We'll get through this together," he promises me.

There's a moment of silence before Jered clears his throat to break it.

"I think we need to talk about Botis," Jered says. "And... what else might be happening."

"What do you mean?" I ask.

"We seriously doubt Botis is the only one Lucifer placed in a position of power here on Earth," Jered tells me. "I think it would be a good idea if we all split up and scouted out the other cloud cities."

"It makes sense," Malcolm agrees. "If Lucifer wants to prevent Anna from killing the princes, placing them in high-profile positions would definitely make it more difficult. Plus it would feed their greed for power and keep them happy for a time."

"Why would he allow them to have that much authority on Earth?" I ask.

"Normally he wouldn't," Desmond says. "But to protect you I guess he'll do just about anything."

Desmond volunteers to go to Stratus even though I can tell Brutus wants to be the one who goes there. It makes me even more determined to find a way to introduce Brutus to Kyna Halloran, his soulmate. I'm selfishly curious to see Kyna's reaction when she first sees Brutus. Will her face reveal exactly how she feels, just like mine did when I first saw Malcolm? I seriously doubt I'm the only one who met their soulmate and looked like a lovesick puppy afterwards.

Brutus ends up going to Virga while Daniel goes to his home cloud city of Cirro. Jered decides to travel to Alto, which leaves only one cloud city to investigate.

"I'll go to Nimbo," Malcolm volunteers.

"I can go there for you," Jered says. "You should stay here with Anna."

"It will be faster if we all split up," Malcolm says. I suspect there is another reason behind Malcolm's decision to go there, but I decide not to ask while we're still in the company of the others. "Besides, Anna needs to get some rest."

"I'm fine," I tell him, not wanting him to use my human frailties as an excuse to leave me.

"You died and you've been to Hell and back, literally," Malcolm says. "You need to try to get some sleep. I think you'll do that better if I'm not here."

"Then at least walk with me to the kitchen before you leave," I say, finding a reason for us to be alone so I can ask him his real reason for leaving me.

After everyone phases to start his own inspection of the cloud cities, Malcolm and I make our way to the kitchen, hand in hand.

"Why are you really going to Nimbo?" I ask him.

Malcolm peers over at me and I can tell he knows I can't be fooled.

"To be honest with you, Anna, I'm still angry about what you did. I need some time alone to get over it."

"You're angry I went to Hell without telling you," I say, just to make sure I fully understand the reason.

"I'm angry that you went there at all!" Malcolm says, allowing a bit of his temper to show. "And being angry with you is the last thing I want right now. Therefore, I'm going to go to Nimbo to find out what's happening there, if anything. It'll give you some time to rest and give me some time to cool off."

I stop abruptly in the hallway leading down to the kitchen. Malcolm has no choice but to stop, too, because I don't let go of his hand. He turns to face me and waits for me to say something.

"Would it help at all if I said I was sorry?" I ask.

"Not really, because that would just be you lying to me," Malcolm answers brusquely.

"You're beginning to know me a little too well," I say as I let my gaze slide to the floor, unable to look at the disappointment on his face any longer.

"I just need a little time to myself to get over it," Malcolm tells me.

"How long will you be gone?" I ask, my heart already starting to ache with just the thought of his absence from my side.

"I'll be back tomorrow," he promises me, his voice sounding gentler. "I don't want to stay away from you for very long either. Just...let me do this. Let me go blow off some steam and then come back to you with a clearer head."

Malcolm pulls me into his arms and holds me as he lets out a heavy sigh.

"I love you, Anna, but what you did was reckless and inconsiderate, not only to me but to everyone who loves you. Can you promise me you won't go there again?"

I consider lying to Malcolm, but I know he would see right through it.

"No, I can't promise you that," I tell him.

He sighs heavily once more.

"I suppose I expected that answer but I was hoping you would give me another one." Malcolm pulls back to look at me. "If you go there again don't stay long, Anna. The longer you stay, there the more of a hold Hell will gain over you. It will rummage through your memories and try to find a way to make you want to stay there."

"I promise I won't go there unless I absolutely have to," I tell him. "But I won't let Lucifer use it as an escape route from me either."

"Just be careful," Malcolm cautions. "It's the one place I can't go to help protect you."

"Why? Because of your curse?"

"Not just that. Hell feeds off your guilt and uses it to trap you there. I have enough remorse to fill a thousand lifetimes, Anna. If I ever stepped foot inside it, I would be lost forever."

"I thought God forgave you for all of that, Malcolm."

"He did. And I forgave myself to an extent. Nevertheless, I still feel shame over what I did, and I don't think that's a bad thing. If I felt nothing at all, then I would be worried. I keep my guilt close to me as a reminder of what I once was. If

I simply forgot all those people and what I did to them, I think that would be more disrespectful to their memories than anything else I could do."

I understand what Malcolm is saying, but I still wish he could forget about his past. Then again, if he did that he wouldn't be the man I love.

We continue to make our way down to the kitchen. Millie is slowly stirring something in a pot on the stove, while Lucas reaches up into a cabinet from his stepstool to bring down two glass mugs.

"We're just making you some warm milk," Millie says to me when she sees us walk into the room. "I know how much you like to drink it right before you go to sleep."

"Thanks, Millie," I tell her, taking a seat at the table.

"I should be going," Malcolm says, leaning down to give me a kiss on the lips. "I'll be back tomorrow. I might even be back before you wake up."

I nod. "Be careful."

Malcolm winks at me. "Always."

He phases away, leaving me longing for his presence almost instantly.

"Where is Master Malcolm off to?" Millie asks me, setting my mug of warm milk in front of me while Lucas comes to sit beside me with his own glass filled to the brim.

"Just a little reconnaissance trip to Nimbo," I tell her vaguely, not wanting to cause Lucas any worry over his father's absence.

"Well, drink up, my sweet. You should try to get some rest afterwards."

I lift the mug to my lips and notice, out of the corner of my eye, Lucas staring at me. I take a sip of the milk before resting the glass back on the table and looking over at my son.

"Are you all right?" I ask him, noticing him still staring at me, almost like he's looking through me not at me.

I gently touch him on the back, which seems to break his trance.

He blinks a few times then looks up at me.

"There's going to be a war," he says, his voice sounding distant.

"A war?" I ask, suddenly realizing what just happened. "Did you just have one of your visions?"

Lucas nods, his eyes brimming with tears.

I pull him into my arms and hold him as he starts to cry.

After he stops crying, I gently ask, "Can you tell me what you saw?"

"Just a lot of people fighting," Lucas tells me with a small sniffle. "But, I saw you, Dad, and the other Watchers right in the middle of it all."

"Can you tell me who it was we were fighting?"

Lucas shakes his head. "No. But there were a lot more of them than you."

"Did you see anything else?"

"No," he says, wrapping his arms around my waist. "I don't know what happens. I don't know who wins."

I hug Lucas tighter and hope it reassures him that everything will be all right... Even though I'm not completely confident it will be.

CHAPTER THREE

After Vala and I tuck Lucas and Luna into his bed, I wander back to my bedroom. The house feels empty without Malcolm's presence. On the other hand, perhaps I just imagine it's the house when it's actually my soul crying out for the return of its other half.

"Did Malcom leave because he was mad at you?" Vala asks as I open the door to my room and let her enter first.

"Yes," I admit, walking in and closing the door behind me. I lean my back up against the cool wood, and fight back tears born of guilt and a desperate need to have Malcolm by my side. "Maybe I shouldn't have gone to Hell but I didn't feel like I had a choice, Vala. I needed to know why Lucifer kept warning me not to retrieve the seals. At least I was able to learn a little bit about what the seals might do to me."

"I think intellectually Malcolm understands why you did what you did," Vala says, jumping up on my bed and lying down to face me. "He's probably more upset by the fact that you went without even thinking about what might happen to you down there. You made a rash decision that might have taken you away from him forever. I think you were very fortunate that nothing bad happened while you were in Hell, Anna."

"I don't think Lucifer would have let anything harm me," I say, pushing away from the door and starting to undress. I notice a nightgown lying on my bed, and send a silent thank you to Millie for always taking care of my needs even before I realize what they are.

"You know," Vala says, "your father told me about Hell once."

"Really?" I ask, surprised by this new bit of information. "What did he say about it?"

"He told me that Hell was a lot like me."

32

I feel my forehead crinkle, showing my bewilderment. "What did he mean by that?"

"He said in the beginning Hell was a lot like I was when I first came to you. I was naïve of the world around me, but learned how I should act and who I should become as we spent more time together. When Lucifer went to Hell to claim it as his own personal domain, it learned what it should be by observing his behavior. It began to mimic what it saw inside him."

"Lucifer told me Hell was a mirror of his soul," I tell Vala, slipping my nightgown over my head and crawling into bed, bringing the edge of the comforter up to my chin.

"Lord Andre said that, over the years, Hell has become a sentient entity. It can think for itself now without having to rely on Lucifer anymore. Your father told me he wasn't sure who the master of Hell was now: Lucifer or Hell itself."

"From what I saw down there, I would say Hell has more control there than Lucifer does at the moment. He seems so lost without my mother, Vala. I feel so sorry for him, but I'm not sure what I can do to help."

"I can understand why you pity him, Anna, but keep in mind that he's in control of his own fate."

"I know," I tell her, yawning and snuggling down deeper under the covers. "I don't like the idea of Hell feeding off of his sorrow like a leech, though. I just wish I could figure out a way to ease his pain. "

I close my eyes, realizing that I am completely exhausted, and allow sleep to drag me completely underneath her spell.

I feel someone shake my exposed shoulder, waking me before I'm ready to face another day. My body doesn't feel like it's gotten nearly enough sleep to recuperate from the previous day's events. When I open my eyes, I find Millie sitting on the side of my bed with an apologetic look on her face.

"I'm sorry to wake you, my sweet, but you have visitors."

I slowly sit up and notice sunlight is now filtering its way into my room through the windows, marking the start of a new day.

"How long have I been asleep?"

"Only a few hours," Millie tells me. "I wouldn't have woken you, but Lord Gray said he had an urgent matter to discuss with you."

"Gladson is here?" I ask, wondering what could be so important that Auggie's onetime lover felt the need to seek me out for help.

"Yes, he's downstairs in the sitting room with Mr. Stokes."

"Barlow's here, too?" I ask, but don't really need her to answer. I'm merely surprised that they're both visiting me at the same time.

I quickly get out of bed, and see that Millie has already set out a beige cable-knit sweater and grey slacks for me to wear.

"I don't know what I would do without you, Millie," I say, giving her a quick kiss on the cheek before I start to dress.

"Well, you won't have to worry about that for a long time to come," she tells me confidently.

"Did they happen to tell you why they're here?" I ask, slipping into the slacks first.

"No. They just said they needed to speak with you as soon as possible."

Millie takes my nightgown from me after I slip it off. I pull on the sweater then quickly run a brush through my hair. After I slip on a pair of black flats, Vala and I make our way downstairs to greet our guests.

I find Gladson pacing in front of the fireplace in the sitting room, as if agitated about something. Barlow is perusing Malcolm's possessions like someone who appreciates the quality of the items he sees.

34

"Gladson," I say, walking up to him and kissing him on a cheek. "What's wrong?"

Gladson lets out a heavy sigh, looking troubled. Barlow abandons his inspection of the room's contents and walks over to us.

"I need your help, Anna," he says gravely. "I'll understand if you want to refuse what I'm about to ask of you, but I couldn't think of anyone else I could come to about this."

"Gladson, just tell me what's wrong. You know I'll help you in any way I can."

"It's about Auggie's mother," Gladson says hesitantly. "I know the two of you never exactly got along, and I can't say I ever liked Catherine much either. However, Auggie loved her, and I feel like I should honor his memory by saving her."

"Saving her?" I ask, surprised by his choice of words. "Save her from what exactly?"

"My spies tell me that thing masquerading as Auggie has kept her locked in her chambers at the palace since your wedding. I was told she was being kept safe, so I hadn't been too worried about her up until now. This morning I received a disturbing report that he's become physically violent with her. My spy didn't have any details but he said Catherine could be heard screaming all through the night, yet this morning things have been eerily quiet in her room."

"Is she even still alive?" I ask, remembering Levi's physical brutality with Malcolm quite well. No human could survive such torture.

"I've been told she's on the verge of death," Gladson tells me. "I think we need to rescue her now before he has a chance to finish her off."

"What do you need me to do?" I ask not for Catherine's sake, but Auggie's. Gladson was right. Auggie loved his mother very much, even though he didn't agree with her politics most of the time. I knew he would want me to help her if it was within my power.

"Levi has Catherine's rooms shielded so no one can teleport in or out of her rooms. Otherwise I would just go grab her myself," Gladson says. "I thought maybe you could use this phasing thing you can do to get her out of the palace."

"How do you plan to keep her safe afterwards?"

"That would be where I come in," Barlow says. "I've arranged to have her taken off-world until it's safe for her to return. One of the captains of a mining freighter owes me a favor, so I called it in. He still wants to be paid for it, though. I was hoping to talk to Malcolm about his compensation, but your maid said he wasn't here."

"He had some other business to attend to," I say, not seeing any reason to tell either of them what is really going on; at least not until we actually know if there is anything to tell. "How much does the captain want?"

"He doesn't want a direct cash payoff," Barlow says. "He wants Malcolm to make his freight company the exclusive transporter of thorium off of Mars."

"Does Malcolm have the power to do that?" I ask.

"Yes, he can grant Vitor the rights," Barlow replies.

"Then tell him he will be granted what he wants," I say. "He has the word of the Empress of Cirrus."

Barlow smiles and bows slightly at the waist. "I will most certainly do that, Empress."

I see Barlow's eyes focus on the three-diamond ring on my finger.

"Well," he says, "I guess Malcolm finally manned up and asked you to marry him. I didn't think it would take very long before he came to his senses."

"You're engaged?" Gladson asks me in surprise. "Rather sudden isn't it, Anna?"

36

"Not really," I reply. "In fact, I would say our marriage has been planned for a very long time."

Gladson looks perplexed by my statement but smiles at me anyway. "As long as he makes you happy I don't care how long you've known him. Auggie only ever wanted you to find someone who would love and take care of you."

"And I found him," I reassure Gladson, knowing he's only trying to look out for my best interests. "When can this Captain Vitor have his ship ready to transport Catherine off-world?"

"He can probably have it ready to go in a couple of hours if I give him the go-ahead," Barlow says.

"Then do it," I tell him. "I'll go get Catherine and bring her back here to stay until the ship is ready to leave."

"Are you sure that's safe?" Gladson asks. "What if Levi figures out where you've taken her?"

"It won't matter," I tell them. "He isn't allowed to come to this house. You don't have to worry about our safety."

"Could you give me a lift over to the Alpha Transport Site?" Barlow asks Gladson. "Vitor's ship is docked there."

"Have you ever considered having a personal teleporter installed?" Gladson asks Barlow, holding out his hand to bring up his own holographic transport controls. "I'm sure with your connections you could find a bootleg one."

"And let Cirrus know where I am 24/7?" Barlow says with a raised eyebrow. "No, thank you. I like to maintain my privacy."

"Are you going to take Malcolm with you to retrieve Catherine?" Gladson asks me.

I shake my head. "No. I don't think I should waste time waiting for him to return. I need to get her out of there before Levi can do her any more harm. Don't worry, Gladson. I'll be in and out before anyone knows I was even there."

"Just be careful, Anna," Gladson cautions, leaning in to give me a kiss on the cheek.

"I will be," I tell him.

"We'll come back as soon as the captain is ready to disembark," Gladson tells me before placing a hand on Barlow's shoulder to teleport them both to the Alpha Transport Site.

"Perhaps you should take me with you this time," Vala says. "I seem to remember your last trip to Cirrus not going as smoothly as you planned."

"I'll just be smarter about it this time," I tell Vala, touching her head and phasing us both back to my bedroom.

I quickly change into my white leather outfit.

"Why are you changing clothes?" Vala asks.

"This outfit allows me to become invisible," I tell her, sitting to put on my boots.

"No one can see you?" Vala asks. "Not even Levi?"

"Not even Levi," I confirm. "Even if he's in her room he won't be able to see me. I just can't do anything about him knowing I've phased there, because he can still track that. With any luck he isn't watching or in her room. I'll just grab her and return quickly."

"Wouldn't it be better if you waited for Malcolm to come back so he can go with you? You're just going to exacerbate his temper by charging off again."

"Don't worry, Vala. I know what I'm doing."

I stand up and pull the zipper up on my jacket.

I silently wish myself invisible and see Vala's eyes go wide in surprise.

"Well, that was certainly impressive," she admits.

"I'll be right back," I tell her before phasing to Catherine's rooms in Cirrus.

Opulent was too tame a word to describe the chambers of the one-time Empress of Cirrus. 'A display of gratuitous wealth' was the phrase that came to mind. The floors were made of the rarest of granite. It was a mixture of blue tones with white and inlaid with streaks of gold. The walls were sheets of hammered gold, hung with decorative mirrors to give the already large space the illusion of being infinite. I walk from the sitting room over to the doorway I know leads into Catherine's bedchamber.

The room is quiet, like a tomb. When I walk further in, I see Catherine has fallen greatly from the glory she once held.

The former empress is lying on her bed, balled up into a facedown fetal position. Her hair is matted to her head, and looks like it has not been washed in days. As I approach her bed I can see her body is trembling slightly, like a frightened animal. I feel an intense anger wash over me at the pitiful sight of Auggie's mother.

"I know you're here," I hear Levi say, in a singsong voice meant to taunt me out of hiding.

I look over to the entrance and see him standing in the doorway, scanning the room, searching for me. I hold back a gasp at the grotesque sight of him. Death does not become this particular prince of Hell. His cheeks are sunken in, as are his eyes, causing the illusion of dark shadows against his pasty white skin. He looks like a ghost of the man he once was.

"Don't you want to come out and play with me, Anna?" Levi sneers. "Why are you hiding in the shadows like a coward when we always have so much fun with one another?"

"You're lucky I don't kill you where you stand," I tell Levi, knowing I probably should have remained silent but allowing my temper to get the best of me.

Levi looks at the quivering form of Catherine on her bed. A slow smile spreads his thin, sickly lips into a self-satisfied grin. The once-proud Empress of Cirrus looks trapped inside her own mad little world. She doesn't show any outward signs of hearing our conversation.

"What did you do to her?" I demand.

Levi nonchalantly shrugs his shoulders and casually leans up against the doorjamb, crossing his arms.

"A little physical torture. A little mental anguish. Nothing I haven't done to a million other victims a million times before now. I guess she's just been so pampered most of her life that she wasn't prepared for what I had in store for her."

"Why did you torture Catherine?" I ask. "What did you hope to gain from it?"

Levi smiles tauntingly. "Your anger, dear wife."

"I don't understand why that's so important to you. Why do you keep testing me in every way you can?"

"Because, my little dove, I want to hurt Lucifer, and you're a surefire way to do that."

"How does making me angry with you achieve that goal?"

"I hope to make you face who you are actually meant to become."

"And who do you think that is?"

"The true master of Hell."

Levi's answer catches me off guard. I wish myself to become visible, because I want him to look me in the eyes when he gives me the answer to my next question.

"What do you mean?"

"Don't you feel it, Anna?" Levi asks, smiling smugly at me as he pushes away from the doorframe to walk closer to me. "Don't you feel the power you're gaining from collecting the seals? I mean, you only have two of them, but surely you've already noticed the change."

"I don't know what you're talking about," I lie, knowing all too well what he's referring to but not wanting to admit it to myself much less him.

Levi laughs. "You're a horrible liar, Anna. That power you feel. That strength inside of you will only grow stronger as you collect more seals. Hasn't Lucifer told you what will happen if you gather them all from us?"

"He's told me some of it," I admit.

"Then let me tell you the rest. Do you know what the seals are?"

"Evil."

"You're thinking far too small… they're so much more than that. The seals are pure energy, my dove. Energy fueled by all the hate in the universe. Time makes them grow stronger as people become more dissatisfied with their lives and the conditions under which they have to live. Why do you think Lucifer hasn't unleashed them yet?"

"I don't know."

"Because he was waiting for the universe to reach a boiling point, where the seals would be so powerful not even God Himself could stop them from opening."

"Is there a way I can destroy the seals as I gather them?"

"Even if there were, you wouldn't want to do that."

"Why?"

"Because," Levi says, stopping just a foot away from me, carrying with him the stench of death, "destroying them would, in effect, destroy parts of your own soul."

"What are they doing to my soul now?"

"Destroying it in a different way."

"How?"

"When you kill one of us and send our soul to the Void, you sever our connection to the seal we carry. Its energy has nowhere else to go but inside you. Every time you take in a seal, its power becomes tethered to your soul. You're the perfect host, Anna. "

"I was told there's a way for me to take the seals without having to kill you."

"We can give you the seals of our own free will, but none of us will do that. We know what you would become with that much power. If you think Lucifer is a fiend, just wait to find out what you'll become, my little dove. I have to say I hope I live long enough to see it. I hope you do, too."

I'm silent for a moment. I'm afraid to ask my next question, but I know I have to.

"What's that supposed to mean?"

"You're part human, Anna. There's no guarantee your body will survive absorbing that much pure energy. Even Lucifer wasn't stupid enough to risk keeping all the seals. Why do you think he divided them among us and didn't just retain all of that power for himself? No *one* being is meant to possess that much power. If I were a betting man, I would wager that the seals will end up killing you in the end. Pity that. I do so enjoy our little conversations with one another."

Honesty probably isn't one of Levi's strong suits, but even without my ability to distinguish the truth from a lie I can see that he's telling me the truth.

I feel like I've been given way too much information at once, and need some time alone to evaluate it.

"I'm taking Catherine away from here," I tell Levi.

"Please do. She's become a bit of a turn-off now anyway," he replies, sounding bored. "All she seems to be able to do is whimper. I think I've completely broken her spirit. So, be my guest in trying to pick up all the pieces and put her back together."

I look back at the sad form of Catherine on the bed and place a gentle hand on her shoulder. She doesn't flinch away, which is something I take as a good sign. Perhaps Levi hasn't completely severed her mind from the real world, and she knows it's me touching her.

"I hope you believe what I just told you, Anna," Levi says. "Maybe you won't be so eager to kill me now."

"There's nothing that will stop me from killing you, Levi," I tell him. "You marked yourself for death the moment you took my father away from me."

"I don't know why you're going on about that," Levi says in exasperation, rolling his eyes. "It's not like I put him somewhere dangerous or even uncomfortable. He's perfectly fine where he is. I'm simply holding him over your head so you don't kill me. Can you really stand there and say that I would still be alive if I hadn't kept Andre as my hostage?"

"No. I can't. I probably would have killed you the moment I found out you murdered my best friend."

"See," Levi says, as if I just proved his point. "It was a good thing I kept Andre around then, for your sake and mine."

"I'm leaving now, Levi," I tell him. "The more I'm around you the more I want to kill you."

"Then, by all means, leave, my little dove. A permanent death is not the wedding gift I want from you."

I phase Catherine to my bed in Malcolm's home. She's so far gone mentally that she doesn't even seem to realize she's been moved.

43

"Vala, would you please go get Millie?" I ask.

"Ok, Anna," Vala says, walking to the door of my room. "Could you open the door for me?"

I turn away from the bed to do as Vala asked when something strange happens. I hear the click of the bolt slide inward just as the door swings open. I expect to see someone walk in, but the space in the hallway is empty.

"Anna," Vala says, looking back at me, "what just happened?"

I look from Vala to the open door and swallow hard, hesitant to give voice to what I'm thinking.

"I'm not sure," I tell her as my heart starts to pound against the walls of my chest. "But I think I may have just discovered a new power."

CHAPTER FOUR

While Vala seeks Millie, I attend to Catherine the best I can.

"Catherine," I say, sitting on the side of the bed and gently gliding my hand up and down her back, doing my best to soothe her, "you're safe now. No one here will harm you."

She doesn't move at all, just lies curled up, face-down and trembling.

I have no idea what I can do for Auggie's mother. I find myself in a position I never thought I would be in with Catherine. For most of my life, she played the role of authority figure, making sure I was fit to become the next Empress of Cirrus. Now our roles have been completely reversed, and I find myself at a loss to know how to help her.

I simply sit there and do what comes naturally. I begin to hum a tune Millie would often sing to me when I needed comfort as child. Eventually Catherine's trembling subsides, and I'm given a glimmer of hope that her mind is working its way out of whatever dark corner of Hell Levi pushed it into. I may not have liked Catherine very much, but being tortured by Levi was something I would only wish on my worst enemy. Unfortunately Levi *is* my worst enemy, so such a fantasy will never come to pass.

"Oh my," Millie says from the doorway before she makes her way over to the bed. "Do you have any idea what he did to her?"

I look over at Millie as she comes to stand next to me.

"Nothing good I'm sure," I tell her. "But I haven't tried to examine her yet. I just got her to stop trembling. We should see what exactly he did to her, though."

Millie places her hands on her hips and considers Catherine's state for a moment.

"Well, first things first, then; let's turn her over and see what we find. She doesn't seem to be in a state of mind to know what's going on around her anyway," Millie says.

"Let me turn her over," I tell Millie, knowing my strength will make it physically easier to handle Catherine.

I gently roll Auggie's mother onto her side, and see that her eyes are open but staring blankly at nothing. She's holding her right arm up against her breast, but it's missing something vital… a hand.

Millie gasps at the sight of the mutilation, and I have to hold back my own rage over Levi's cruelty.

"Why would he take her hand?" Millie whispers, almost as if she's afraid Catherine will hear us speaking about her condition.

"Mostly to just cause her pain would be my guess," I say, realizing I'm learning how Levi's mind works far better than I really want to. "He may have wanted to make sure she couldn't use any of her holographic controls to teleport away or contact anyone for help."

I look down the length of Catherine's body, and notice a random pattern of bloodstains on her white nightgown from the chest down. I slowly lift up the hem of the skirt to continue my examination of her injuries. A plethora of open slash marks crisscrosses her thighs and abdomen. Some of them look like they have already become infected, oozing a yellow-green puss.

"I'll get the healing wand," Millie says, sounding breathless at the sight of our gruesome discovery.

Millie runs out of the room and is back far quicker than I would have thought someone her age could move. She glides the wand over the wounds, but the magic of modern technology does nothing to heal them.

I sigh in disappointment, having already guessed this would be the outcome.

"I was afraid that wouldn't work," I say. "Levi must have used his lightning whip on her."

"Then how do we heal these wounds?"

"They'll have to heal on their own," I hear Malcolm say behind us as he walks into the room, obviously having overheard our conversation. Of anyone in the world, I know Malcolm knows the pain Levi's whip can inflict.

When I look over my shoulder and see Malcolm, I instantly feel as though the weight pressing against my chest is lifted. Malcolm comes to stand beside me and I take one of his hands into my own, desperately needing the comfort and strength I feel when we're together.

Malcolm examines the torture Catherine has endured by Levi's hands. A dark, murderous scowl contorts his features. Neither of us ever had much love for Catherine, but she's become an unwitting victim in a war very few people know is being waged right in front of their eyes.

"Desmond is downstairs," Malcolm says. "Let me get him up here to see what he can do for her with traditional medicine."

Malcolm phases away from my side, but quickly returns with Desmond in tow before I even have a chance to miss him.

We move away from the bed to give Desmond room to perform his examination of Catherine's injuries.

Malcolm takes me into his arms and I lean into him, resting my head against his chest.

"I guess I don't have to ask what you did while I was away," Malcolm says in a resigned voice.

"I had to get her out of there," I tell him. "Auggie would have wanted me to protect his mother."

Malcolm sighs, but refrains from saying anything else. I think he's coming to terms with the fact that there are certain things I have to do. He may not like them, but my conscience will always propel me to do what's right.

"Malcolm," I say, reluctantly pulling away from him to look into his deep blue eyes, "we need to have a talk."

I think the graveness of my tone tells Malcolm more than I could have said in words. I want him to be the first one to know what I learned from Levi. I need his guidance and advice before we make the information known to everyone else.

"Desmond," Malcolm says, looking over at our friend, "we'll be in my study for a little while if you need us."

Desmond nods his head, acknowledging that he heard Malcolm, but says nothing as he continues to study Catherine's wounds.

Malcolm phases us to his study. He takes a step back from me, crossing his arms over his chest.

"I take it this *isn't* going to be good news," he says, watching me warily.

"No, it's not," I admit. "In fact you might want to sit down before I start."

Malcolm takes my advice and sits down on the sofa while I pace in front of him and tell him exactly what Levi told me. I also tell him about being able to open the door by just thinking about it. I can only ascribe the ability to the power of the seals manifesting themselves inside of me.

After I'm done, Malcolm doesn't say a word. He simply sits silently and stares at me. I can't read his expression. He closes his eyes before I have a chance to decipher what he's thinking. I begin to wonder if what I said is too much for him to take in. I can't help but think he's been handed a raw deal by being made my soulmate.

Unexpectedly, I see God phase into the room. He stands between Malcolm and me, but His eyes are fixed on Malcolm.

"I'm here, My son," God says, looking at Malcolm with the compassion of a concerned parent.

Malcolm opens his eyes, and I see them shimmering with unshed tears. My heart tightens inside my chest at the sight of his distress, because I know I'm the cause.

"You need to tell us what's going on," Malcolm tells God in no uncertain terms. "I need to know if what Levi told Anna is true."

"Yes," God says, "it's true."

"Then why?" Malcolm demands. "Why are You making her retrieve the seals if You know what they'll do to her?"

God looks over at me. "Because that's what she was born to do."

"To do what exactly?" Malcolm bellows, standing up from his seat and facing his father. "To either become a monster or die? Are You telling me those are her only two options?"

"Things aren't always what they seem, Malcolm. Every situation can have a thousand different outcomes. There are simply too many variables in play at the moment to know what the result of this particular moment in history will be."

"Then there's a chance we can have the life we want with one another?" Malcolm asks, an audible yearning in his voice to hear God give him hope that our future isn't completely lost to us.

"Yes, there is a chance you can have the future you want. Never lose sight of that possibility," God tells Malcolm before looking over at me. "Anna, you have one of the most ancient and strongest souls in existence. I wouldn't have given you this mission if I thought you would fail in achieving your goals. I have faith that you will succeed, but... you always have the choice of letting things remain the way they are."

"You know I can't turn my back on what needs to be done," I tell Him, wondering why He even bothered to bring up that option. "I can't hide in the shadows and let them win."

"We've seen what Lucifer has done. He's made it almost impossible for Anna to kill the other princes now," Malcolm tells God, making me wonder what he and the other Watchers have learned from their scouting missions.

"Almost," God agrees. "But I'm sure Anna can still find a way to retrieve the seals with all of you helping her." God turns His gaze on me again. "Anna, I feel like I should caution you about something while I'm here. I realize you want to understand Lucifer better, but you should be careful about spending too much time in Hell. At the moment it's acting like a spoiled child who wants to punish its parent for ruining its life. It may try to use you to hurt Lucifer, and I'm not sure he's strong enough right now to survive losing you, too."

"I understand," I tell him. "I won't go there unless I have to."

"Then I will leave the two of you to talk now," God tells us. "I'm sure you have a lot to discuss with one another."

"Are you still coming?" Malcolm asks God.

"You know I wouldn't miss it for the world," God replies. "Simply call to Me when it's time."

"I will," Malcolm says.

God phases, and I turn a questioning gaze to Malcolm.

"What is it you want Him to come to?" I ask.

Malcolm walks over to me and takes me into his arms.

"Our wedding, of course," he replies, sounding like he thought I should have already known what the two of them were discussing.

"Are you sure you still want to marry me?" I ask jokingly, unable to prevent a nagging doubt that he still does in spite of everything we've learned.

50

"Of course I still want to marry you," Malcolm says in a slightly chastising voice. "I want our union to have my father's blessing now more than ever."

"What if…" I begin, but have a hard time finishing. "What if I do become a monster, Malcolm? What if the seals make me into something horrible, and I'm not able to control the powers I gain from them?"

"I don't believe that will happen," Malcolm says with a confidence I wish I felt. "Like Levi said, no one has ever had that much power. Therefore, no one knows what will happen to you. This could be just a lot of worry over nothing, Anna. He may not have said it in so many words, but my father thinks you can handle the energy the seals possess. Otherwise, He wouldn't have sent you down here to retrieve them. I trust in His judgment a lot more than I do Levi's or Lucifer's. Lucifer may love you and be doing what he is because of that fact, but I seriously doubt he wants to compete with his own daughter for control over Hell. I think he's done what he has so far to partially protect you, but to mostly keep his position of authority in Hell."

"I'm assuming from what you said to God that you and the others found out what Lucifer has done in the other cloud cities."

"Yes," Malcolm says with a sigh. "He did what we thought he would, and placed his people in positions of power in each one. I'm not sure how we'll be able to get to the princes now and kill them without it looking suspicious."

"Where are they and who did they kill to get there?"

Malcolm kisses me on top of the head, before letting me go and taking one of my hands into his.

"Come on. I think the others would like to tell you what they found out themselves."

Malcolm phases us to the sitting room where we find Jered, Brutus, and Daniel having a lively discussion with one another.

"I say we just let Anna kill them and deal with the political ramifications of it all later," Brutus says as he stands by the fireplace, one elbow propped up on the mantel.

"Brutus, I think you're letting your heart think for you instead of your brain," Jered chides gently from his seat on the sofa. "And I don't blame you one bit. I understand Kyna's safety is paramount to you, but we need to think about this rationally. Anna can't become known as the royal assassin of the leaders of Earth. We need to keep her sovereignty over Cirrus intact so she can remain empress after she disposes of Levi."

"I have to agree with Jered on this one," Daniel says from his chair situated between the other two. "We need to take care of the situation in a way that doesn't turn Anna into a murderer in the eyes of the other cities."

"What did you guys find out?" I ask them as Malcolm and I go to sit with Jered on the sofa. I turn to Jered first and ask, "What's happening in Alto?"

"Baal has taken over Emperor Rafael Rossi's body," he tells me. "From what I gather, his wife, Bianca, suspects something is wrong with her husband."

"Why?" I ask. "How is he acting differently?"

"Apparently he's been clamoring to share her bed," Jered says with a small chuckle. "I guess the real Rafael didn't appreciate what a beauty Bianca is while he was still alive, but Baal certainly does. From the information I was able to gather, he's even gone to the extraordinary measure of trying to romance her."

"Baal's romancing a human?" Malcolm asks, sounding certain Jered is talking about someone else. "I didn't think he could love anyone more than he does himself. Are there any ulterior motives on his part besides the obvious?"

"Not that I can tell," Jered says.

"Well at least mine doesn't have a wife to be concerned about," Brutus says. "Mammon has taken over Callum Ellis in Virga."

"I met him a few times at parties Auggie had," I say, fondly remembering the young, handsome prince of Virga. "Why take over the son and not the emperor himself, though?"

"Probably because the emperor is so old," Malcolm reasons. "Mammon's always had a healthy appetite for the ladies. If I were him, I would certainly rather be inside the body of a virile young man in his prime than an old man who could kick the bucket at any minute."

"I'm afraid my news won't make you very happy, Anna," Daniel warns. "Botis found his way to Cirro."

"Who is he now?"

"The emperor."

"But I thought the emperor was on his death bed."

"With Botis in control, the Emperor of Cirro has made a miraculous recovery."

"And how does Empress Zhin feel about that?" I ask.

Daniel clears his throat, as if he really doesn't want to tell me the next part of his report.

"The empress has been taken over by Belphagor."

"Great," I say, massaging my temples because I suddenly feel a painful headache forming. "How am I supposed to kill the emperor *and* the empress of the same cloud city?"

"I don't know yet," Daniel admits. "It does present something of a problem."

"Well, I have some good news and some bad news," Malcolm tells me. "The emperor of Nimbo isn't a prince of Hell."

"Was that the good news or the bad news?" I ask.

"The good news. The bad news is he's still a powerful demon by the name of Agaliarept."

"And what about Stratus?" I ask, knowing Lucifer wouldn't leave it unscathed by his plans. "Who did Lucifer plant there?"

"Abaddon," Brutus says in disgust. "He's another one of Lucifer's high-ranking generals, like Botis and Agaliarept."

"I assume he's taken Lorcan over?" I ask, knowing Brutus wouldn't be so calm if this Abaddon had taken possession of Kyna.

Brutus nods, confirming my assumption.

"Honestly," Malcolm says, "I doubt Abaddon will be any worse of a ruler than Lorcan was. In fact, it seems as though he's treating the down-worlders of Stratus better than Lorcan ever dreamed of doing."

Malcolm's statement brings to mind what Desmond told us the night before, about Lorcan sending supplies to the down-worlders of Stratus. I guess that should have been our first clue that something might be going on with the leaders in the other cities.

"I think he's up to something," Brutus says confidently, not willing to give Abaddon the benefit of the doubt. "He's purposely trying to gain support from the down-worlders and the cloud city citizens. Abaddon has always been a calculating little bastard. He has to be planning something, and is trying to bolster his position before he does it."

"Do you have any idea what that something is?" I ask.

Brutus shakes his head. "No, I have no idea. But you can bet it's something that most people wouldn't ordinarily agree to do, considering how much effort he's put into gaining support."

"Should we just go grab Kyna now and bring her here?" I suggest, knowing if Malcolm were in a similar situation I would do whatever I had to do to ensure his safety.

"I think that's a bad idea," Jered is quick to say. "She could be placed in more danger if we single her out. Abaddon will know we care what happens to her, and he'll make sure to keep her close to protect his own skin."

"Which is exactly why I haven't gone there myself and taken her out of Stratus," Brutus grumbles, obviously not liking the situation but not seeing a better way to protect Kyna.

"We'll think of something," I promise Brutus.

Brutus nods at my words. "I know we will."

Desmond phases into the sitting room.

"How is Catherine?" I immediately ask him.

"As well as can be expected considering what Levi did to her," he says, sounding disgusted by Catherine's condition. "She's going to need a lot of rest and medical care while the lash marks heal. Mentally, I'm not sure she'll ever recover. It's too soon to make a proper diagnosis."

"Gladson and Barlow have arranged to have her taken off-world," I tell them. "I think we should still stick to their plan. Levi knows I care about her now. If she's somewhere he can't find her easily, he won't be able to use her safety against me."

"Agreed," Malcolm says. "We keep to the plan Gladson has worked out and get her off-world as quickly as possible. Maybe a new set of surroundings will even help her forget what happened."

"I had to make a promise on your behalf to the owner of a freight company," I tell Malcolm. "He wanted exclusive rights to transport thorium off of Mars in exchange for helping us with Catherine."

"Vitor?" Malcolm says knowingly, looking slightly amused.

"Yes," I answer hesitantly. "Should I not have made the deal?"

Malcolm shakes his head. "No, it's fine. Vitor has been hounding me to do that for a long time now."

"What kept you from agreeing to do it before?"

"I mostly just wanted to keep the price of thorium low. We can deal with him through a tariff negotiation to yield the same result. It's nothing to concern yourself about. We have bigger issues to deal with at the moment."

"I will arrange for a doctor to accompany Catherine to Mars," Desmond says. "I know of one who has been looking for an excuse to get off-world."

"Barlow said it would take a couple of hours before Captain Vitor would be ready to leave," I tell Desmond.

"Good. That gives me plenty of time to make arrangements. I'll bring the doctor back here so she can do her own examination of Catherine. I'll be back soon."

Desmond phases.

"I can't just sit here and do nothing," Brutus says, looking frustrated by his inability to do something about Kyna's situation. "I'm going to go to Stratus to snoop around and see if I can find out what Abaddon is up to."

"Make sure you're back here by this evening," Malcolm tells him.

Brutus nods and phases away.

"I guess I should make arrangements for Linn to come tonight," Daniel tells us before standing. "She would kill me if she missed it."

"Missed what?" I ask. "What's happening tonight?"

"Our wedding," Malcolm gently reminds me.

"Oh," I say, feeling stupid all of a sudden. "I'm sorry. I didn't realize we were doing it tonight."

"I don't see any reason for us to wait," Malcolm says. "Do you?"

"Absolutely not," I tell him, squeezing his hand. "The sooner the better."

Malcolm smiles at me and returns his attention to Daniel.

"The kids are welcome to come if you want to bring them," Malcolm says.

"I doubt the boys will," Daniel chuckles, "but Bai will want to come."

"I would love for her and Lucas to spend some time together," I tell Daniel, remembering what I once thought about the two of them forming a lasting friendship. It would be nice if Lucas had someone his own age who understood the world of angels and demons, and who would always be a part of his life.

"Then I'll make sure to bring her," Daniel promises. "We'll see you both tonight."

Daniel phases, leaving Malcolm and me alone.

"I guess I should have asked you first," Malcolm says almost apologetically. "I just thought you would want to have the wedding as soon as possible."

The look of uncertainty on Malcolm's face pushes me into action.

I wrap my arms around his neck and kiss him soundly on the lips, deepening it to a point where I leave my future husband breathless. When I finally relent, I pull back and look at him.

"Of course I want to do it as soon as possible," I tell him. "I would do it right this second if I could."

Malcolm smiles and leans in to nuzzle my neck with his lips.

"Good," he says against my throat. "Because I don't think I can wait much longer to have you in my bed."

I giggle and reply, "That goes both ways."

Malcolm lifts his head and looks at me.

"I don't want you to worry about the seals anymore today," he tells me. "It's your wedding day, Anna, and I plan to make it a day and night you won't ever forget."

"I plan to hold you to that promise," I tell him, bringing his head down to mine. "Now kiss me, Malcolm, because it will be the last one we share until God officially makes you mine."

Malcolm kisses me with an intensity that makes me wish we had already exchanged our vows. I simply keep in mind that it won't be too much longer and I send up a silent prayer, asking that nothing happens this time to delay our union.

CHAPTER FIVE

Malcolm doesn't release me from his kiss for a very long time. Not that I was about to complain. If it had been left up to me, I would have taken full advantage of the situation and phased us directly to the honeymoon stage of today's events. The only reason I didn't was because we were so close to Malcolm's goal, and I knew how important it was to him for us to do everything properly. I wasn't going to rush him just to satisfy my own physical needs, even if they were great...and becoming increasingly demanding for some reason.

Malcolm eventually pulls his lips away from mine but gently touches our foreheads together, keeping our physical connection to one another. His eyes remain closed, and his breathing is even and deep. He doesn't say anything, and I don't rush him. He's had a rough day, and I've been the major cause of his worry. I would move all three planes of existence if I thought it would ease his burden.

"Are you all right?" I ask him, taking both of his hands into mine, enjoying the comfort the warmth of his skin has always provided me.

"I will be," Malcolm replies, keeping his eyes closed.

"Is there anything I can do to help you?"

Malcolm's eyelids flutter open and he leans back only a fraction of an inch from me to say, "Stay alive."

"I have no intention of dying," I assure him. "I have too much I want to do, like having your babies."

Malcolm grins, and I see a little bit of his tension ease at the reminder of our son's prophecy.

"Thank God for Lucas' gift," Malcolm says. "Otherwise I might go completely insane with worry."

"Speaking of Lucas' ability to see the future," I say, "he had a vision while you were away."

Malcolm sits back slightly at hearing this news and looks alert. "What did he see?"

"He said he saw a war," I tell him. "He said you, me, and the others were in the middle of a fight, but that we were outnumbered."

"Did he see anything else? Did he see who won?"

I shake my head. "No, he didn't. He didn't even know who it was we were fighting, why we were in a battle with them, or when it would happen."

"Well, I'm sure it will all play out the way it's meant to. There's no reason to worry about something we can't control," Malcolm says in a resigned voice, but I knew I had just added something else to his list of burdens.

"Whatever it is, we'll face it together and win."

"I don't care about winning if it means I might lose you, Anna."

"I thought you said we weren't going to talk about all of that for the rest of the day," I say, gently reminding him about his earlier statement.

"Is there anything you would like to do in particular today before the wedding?"

I smile at the question. "Yes, there is, but I believe we decided that would have to wait until after we said our vows in front of God."

Malcolm chuckles, obviously picking up on my meaning. "Is there anything *else* you would like to do before the wedding?"

"Nothing that would be nearly as much fun," I admit with an exaggerated sigh. "Are we even supposed to be with each other before we get married? Isn't it bad luck for the groom to see the bride before the wedding?"

"Yes it is," a new, yet recognizable, voice chimes in.

I look over by the fireplace to see Lilly standing in front of it. She's wearing a white sleeveless summer dress, looking perfect in her part as an angel on Earth.

Malcolm and I both stand up.

"What on earth are you doing here?" Malcolm asks, taking my hand as we walk over to greet our new guest.

"I heard there was a wedding later on this evening," Lilly says, smiling at us. "And I sort of doubted Anna has had a proper wedding shower considering everything that's been going on down here."

"No, she hasn't," Malcolm says, looking confused by Lilly's suggestion. "What did you have in mind?"

Lilly smiles and holds out one of her hands to me.

"Something special," she says mysteriously, waiting for me to accept her offer.

I release Malcolm's hand and place mine into Lilly's grasp.

"I'll have her back in time for the wedding," Lilly promises Malcolm. "I assume you have things to do until then to keep you occupied?"

"Yes," Malcolm answers. He leans into me and kisses me chastely on the lips in front of our company. "I guess I'll see you later at the altar. Have fun with whatever they have planned."

Before I can reply, Lilly phases us.

I find myself standing in front of a house surrounded by snow-capped mountains. The sun is bright in the sky and a warm breeze blows through my hair, lifting it off my shoulders. The colorful flowers planted in the boxes hanging from the front porch railing permeate the air with their sweet aroma.

As I look at my surroundings, I get an odd sensation that I don't belong where Lilly has brought me. A gentle force seems to be urging me to leave, telling me it's not time for me to be here yet.

"Where are we?" I ask, knowing exactly where we are but having a need to ask the question anyway.

"Heaven," Lilly tells me. "My version of it anyway. Come on. There are some people inside who have desperately wanted to meet you for a very long time."

I follow Lilly up the steps to the front porch. I notice an empty, white painted swing on the right-hand side of the porch swaying gently back and forth in the breeze, making the chains creak. Before Lilly can even reach out a hand to grasp the doorknob, the door is yanked open. Two women stand in the entryway smiling at me for all they're worth. I instantly know who they are because I've seen them in Malcolm's memories, Caylin and Jess.

Caylin walks up to me and takes me into her arms, hugging me lovingly.

"Oh, Anna," she says, tightening her hold even further. "I've waited so long to see you again."

"Stop hogging the bride, kiddo," Jess complains good-naturedly. "I'm her ancestor, too, you know."

Caylin laughs and steps back, giving Jess room to take her place in my arms.

"It's so good to finally meet you, Anna," Jess says before releasing me. "It's been a long time coming."

"It's nice to finally meet the two of you, too," I tell them.

"Where is she?" a woman says loudly from the depths of the home's interior.

Two beautiful black women walk up the hallway from the back of the house. One is dressed in a pair of jeans and a nice dark blue shirt while the other is dressed in an old-fashioned dress with a black and red rose print pattern. I remember seeing the first woman in Malcolm's memory about Lilly's wedding. She was standing on the dais in the place of the maid of honor. The second woman is someone I don't remember ever seeing, but I instantly feel like I know her.

"There's my baby girl," the older of the two women says, taking me into her arms. "Oh Anna, it's been too long."

After the woman lets me go and steps back, I look at her face and can't seem to shake a sense of déjà vu.

"How do I know you?" I ask.

"You and I spent a great deal of time together before you were sent to Earth," the woman says. "My name is Utha Mae, Anna."

"Are you the one Will and I stayed with while I was here?" I ask, remembering Will mention someone very special taking care of me while I was in Heaven.

"Yes, I am," Utha Mae says proudly. She looks at me with a certain amount of pride on her face. If you didn't know any better, you would have thought she was my mother. "I knew you would grow up to be a beautiful woman, inside and out. Malcolm sure is a lucky man. He gets someone with beauty, smarts, and the purest heart of anyone I've ever met."

"Has that man been treating you better?" the young black woman asks. "'Cause if he isn't, I'll find me a way to get back to Earth and kick some sense into him."

"Get in line, Tara," Jess says. "If anyone gets to kick Malcolm's ass, it's me."

"Uh," I say, trying not to laugh at their eagerness to do bodily harm to Malcolm. "He's treating me very well. There isn't any need for a Heavenly intervention."

Jess groans her disappointment. "Man, I was really hoping you would say something different. I've been waiting for a good reason to ask God to send me back to Earth for a visit."

"You're just jealous that we can go back anytime we want," Caylin teases.

"I'm totally jealous!" Jess admits. "But I bet if I have a good enough reason, God won't deny me the chance to go back. At least He'd better not if He wants Heaven to remain peaceful or in one piece."

I look at the women standing before me and can't help but notice someone very important missing from the greeting party.

I look over at Lilly and ask, "Is my mother here?"

I can tell Lilly was waiting for me to ask this particular question, and feel a slight tension enter the merriment of the moment.

"No," Lilly answers, "Amalie isn't here."

"Why?" I ask, feeling my heart drop inside my chest at the possibility that my own mother doesn't want to see me.

Lilly seems at a loss to know how to answer my question.

So Utha Mae tries.

"I'm sure she just needs some time, baby girl," Utha Mae tells me. "Let's be patient. She still has a while yet to show up."

I hold back my tears of disappointment and try to preserve the joy of the moment. But why wouldn't my own mother want to see me? Did she feel like my birth cheated her out of a real life? Did she regret not doing what Lucifer suggested and abort me so they could be together? There really wasn't any way for me to ask these questions of those present. How could they know what my mother was thinking?

"Who's ready to eat?" Tara says in what I can only assume is an attempt to quickly change the subject.

"Leave it to you to bring up food at a time like this," Jess says with a roll of her eyes.

Tara places a hand on a cocked hip. "And what is that supposed to mean, Jess Collier?"

"That you've been eating since you got here, Tara!" Jess answers with a smile.

"And why wouldn't I?" Tara says. "I can eat all I want and not gain a bit of weight. Pretty much sounds like Heaven to me!"

It sounds like a very justifiable reason to me also.

"Come on, baby girl," Utha Mae says, looping an arm around one of mine. "I'll bet you anything you haven't had a meal on Earth like me and Tara made for you today."

"I made dinner for eight people last night," I say proudly. "All by myself."

Everyone stops walking and stares at me as if I just grew a second head.

"You can cook?" Caylin asks, looking sure I must have meant something else.

I nod my head. "Yes. Malcolm taught me."

"Oh, my God," Jess says, her eyes wide in wonder as she looks at me. "You *are* the chosen one."

"Oh, stop teasing her," Lilly tells Jess with a laugh.

"Seriously, Lilly, this is monumental!" Jess professes. "No descendant of yours and Caylin's could boil water much less cook a meal for a dinner party. What exactly *did* you cook, Anna?"

I tell them what I prepared for everyone the night before.

"Yep, miracle child," Jess says, as if my words were confirmation of the fact. "But I guess we all knew that already. This just puts proof in the pudding."

"Quit picking on my baby," Utha Mae says, gently tugging on my arm so we can continue our walk to the back of the house.

When we enter the kitchen, a mixture of aromas that make me feel more at home welcomes me.

"It smells so good in here," I say, breathing in deeply. Just like with Utha Mae, the scent of the food makes me feel a sense of déjà vu. "Did you cook this kind of food when I stayed with you?"

Utha Mae smiles at me. "Well of course I did, child. And I want you to let Malcolm know I taught you how to cook before he did."

I can't help but smile at this new bit of information.

"He thinks he worked a miracle with me," I tell her.

"Well, we can't let him take all the credit now, can we?" Utha Mae says, letting go of my arm. "Otherwise he might get a little too big for his britches."

"That man's ego has always been a little too big for his britches," Tara says. "Though, from what I've heard, you've pretty much got him wrapped around your little finger, Anna."

"I wouldn't say wrapped," I tell her, feeling a little embarrassed by the suggestion. "He just wants to make me happy."

"Wrapped," Jess agrees. "About time, too. I always knew Malcolm was all ooey gooey soft underneath that tough exterior. He just needed the right woman to bring out that side of him."

I look over at Lilly, thinking about Malcolm's memories involving her. Of anyone in the room, she knew the true Malcolm that he kept hidden from most people. Lilly meets my gaze, and in that moment we seem to have a silent understanding with one another. She was once the object of Malcolm's affections, but I can see in her eyes that she knows she was simply a placeholder for me until I was ready to become a part of Malcolm's life.

"He's so lucky to have you, Anna," Lilly tells me. "And I know you'll be good to him and love him unconditionally. It's the way he was always meant to be loved."

"Well, I'm just glad that man is finally settling down," Tara says. "He's been running wild ever since all of us died. It's about time he got married and started a real family."

Tara's statement brings to mind a question.

"Utha Mae," I say as I watch her take a pan of cornbread from the oven, "I was told Malcolm and I will have twins in the future. Have you met them yet?"

It seemed like a logical question to ask. I had apparently spent a great deal of time in Heaven before I was born. Perhaps Utha Mae or one of the others had already met my children.

I don't like the look that comes over Utha Mae's face. She looks troubled by my inquiry.

"No, baby girl, I haven't met them."

No one else says anything. Therefore, I have to assume none of them has met my future children either.

"Is that odd?" I ask, not knowing what the protocol for new souls is in Heaven. Maybe not everyone is able to spend time here before they're born.

Utha Mae hesitates before saying, "The good Lord has always allowed me to spend some time with all the descendants before they're sent to Earth, but maybe the souls of your children just haven't been made yet, baby."

I suspect she's deflecting my question with her suggestion, but I decide not to demand a more thorough answer. For one, I don't think she knows anything more than she's saying, and there would be no point in asking questions she obviously can't answer.

Utha Mae fills a plate for me with a little bit of all the food present. Some of it I recognize and some of it I don't. I must have a perplexed look on my face as she hands me the plate, because she tells me what's on it and points to each item as she does.

"I remembered all of your favorites from when you were here with me," she says. "There's cornbread, collard greens, yams, deep fried pork chop with white gravy, and chicken and dumplings."

"It looks delicious," I tell her. "Thank you."

"You're more than welcome, child."

After we've all taken a seat around the small table in the kitchen, the ladies begin to ask me questions about my life and everything that's happened so far. I don't tell them about going to Hell or learning about what the seals might to do me. I don't want to dampen their spirits with talk about the worst possible outcome of my mission. From Jered's brief history lesson about my family, I learned what each of them did to accomplish their own missions from God. I know they've faced the same sorts of dangers I'm facing now and made it through in one piece. Coming from such a strong line of women, I feel confident I can add my name to the list of descendants who were victorious.

"So," Tara says to me after she's finished her meal, and leans back in her chair. "Tonight's the night, right?"

"Yes," I tell her, putting my fork down on my plate. "We're finally having the wedding tonight."

"Yeah, not really what I was talking about," Tara says with a lifted eyebrow. "Girl, you ever been with a man?"

"Aunt Tara," Caylin says admonishingly, "don't you think that's kind of personal?"

"We're all family here," Tara says in justification of her question. "I just want to make sure she's prepared for what's gonna happen *after* the wedding." Tara looks from Caylin back over at me. "If it's something you haven't done with a man before, I just want to make sure you know what to expect.

Malcolm's...well...to put it bluntly...a lot bigger downstairs than most men. I just don't want you to get scared by that thing."

"Aunt Tara!" Caylin says. "How on earth would you even know something like that?"

Tara just waves a dismissive hand at Caylin. "Never you mind about that. I just know."

I have to admit that I'm a bit curious how Tara knows such a thing as well.

"I'm fully aware of Malcolm's...endowments," I say, earning the stares of everyone at the table.

"Oh," Tara says, caught off guard by my answer. "So have the two of you already..."

She seems reluctant to say the rest of her question. So I finish it for her.

"Made love?" I say. "No, we haven't. Malcolm wanted to wait until after we'd made our vows to one another in front of God before we consummated our relationship in that way."

"He did?" Jess asks, sounding truly astonished. "Well, I'll be damned. I didn't realize Malcolm had that sort of restraint. I mean, look at you, Anna. You're gorgeous! Not many men would be able to hold back like that. And considering how much he loves you I'm doubly impressed."

"I knew Malcolm would be that way with someone he truly loves," Lilly says with a proud smile on her face. "I'm sure he just wants to make things as perfect as he can for you both. He knows this will only happen once in your lives, and he doesn't want to rush something he's been waiting an eternity for."

"Aiden and I waited until after marriage, too," Caylin tells me. "I appreciated the fact he wanted to wait, even if it did drive me completely crazy. It was important for him to prove to himself that he had that much self-control, and I understood and respected that. So I didn't push the matter too much."

"I've pushed," I admit, a little ashamed at some of my prodding of Malcolm. "But I'm glad he's made me wait. It'll just make the experience that much sweeter I think."

"Uh, you *do* realize your first time probably won't be too storybook, right?" Tara says.

I feel at a bit of a loss.

"I'm sorry," I say. "I'm not completely sure I understand what you're trying to tell me."

"I think what my granddaughter is trying to say, in her own subtle way, is that it will most likely hurt your first time, baby girl," Utha Mae says.

"Oh, that," I say, understanding what they're talking about now. "Yes, I understand what will happen. I'm prepared for it."

"I'm sure Malcolm will know how to make it as painless as possible for you," Lilly says confidently.

"It will hurt," Caylin tells me, "but the discomfort will pass, and my mom's right: If anyone knows how to make it a beautiful experience in spite of that pain, it will be Uncle Malcolm. Aiden helped me through it, and I don't see Uncle Malcolm being any less compassionate about it with you."

"I wish I'd waited for Malik," Tara says with a deep sigh of regret. "If I'd waited for someone who truly loved me, I think my first time would have been a lot better and a memory I would actually *want* to remember."

"I truly don't have any worries," I tell them. "Since the moment I saw Malcolm, I've wanted to make love to him. I'm not afraid of the pain. It'll all be worth it in the end."

Without warning, I suddenly feel a sense of melancholy enter the room like a physical entity dampening the happy mood we're all experiencing. It's a strange sensation, and not one I would have expected to feel in Heaven.

I notice Lilly, Caylin, and Jess all sit up a little straighter in their chairs at almost the same instant.

"Thank goodness," Jess says in relief, looking over at me.

"I didn't think she would be able to stay away," Caylin says with a smile.

I lift a hand to my heart because there's an ache there now that wasn't there before.

"Is my mother here?" I ask, piecing together the meaning of what Caylin said and the sense of loss I feel.

"Yes," Lilly tells me. "She's here."

"Is it her sadness I'm feeling?" I ask Lilly.

"Yes."

"Is it because she's separated from Lucifer?"

Lilly nods her head, and I see every woman around the table sympathize with my mother's plight.

"How am I able to feel her pain?" I ask.

"We can all feel it," Jess tells me. "Her soul is the only one in Heaven to retain the sadness she felt on Earth. It's so powerful that anyone who's around Amalie can feel her anguish."

"Does she blame me?" I ask, needing to know the answer to this question before I speak with my mother.

"Oh heaven's no, baby girl," Utha Mae assures me. "If anything, I think she feels guilty for having to leave you when she did. Go to her, child. Let her explain things to you."

Lilly stands from the table and holds out her hand to me.

"I think it's time you met your mom, Anna," she says.

My heart races into my throat, and I feel apprehensive all of a sudden at the prospect of facing my mother. I will my heart to beat at a calmer pace and place my hand in Lilly's. After I stand from my chair we walk out of the kitchen, back towards the front door. Lilly squeezes my hand reassuringly, and I draw courage from her strength as I prepare myself to meet the woman who sacrificed everything just to give me life.

CHAPTER SIX

When Lilly places her hand on the doorknob, I say, "Wait."

Lilly takes her hand away from the knob and looks at me.

"I'm scared," I say, finding it a hard thing to admit. "She gave up so much to have me. What if I haven't lived up to her expectations? What if she tells me I've disappointed her in some way?"

"How could you possibly be a disappointment to her?" Lilly asks, looking mystified at my sudden reluctance to meet my mother.

"Lucifer said she asked him to raise me. He lied to her on her deathbed, Lilly. He told her he would but he lied."

"Do you honestly think she didn't know that at the time?"

I feel confused for a moment, but then remember one trait I've always had: being able to know when someone was telling me the truth or lying to my face. It makes sense that my mother would have had the same ability.

"Still," I say, "I think she was hoping he would change his mind and raise me. What if she was counting on me to develop a relationship with him and force him to change his ways?"

"She's your mother, Anna. All any mother wants is for her child to have a full and happy life. However, you could be right about one thing. She might have hoped Lucifer would learn something about himself by raising you. Nevertheless, maybe all she hoped for was that he would develop an understanding about what it feels like to love someone else more than he does himself. Very few parents place their own needs above those of their children. And those who do usually aren't good parents."

I understand what Lilly is saying. I might not have been Lucas' biological mother, but I did consider him my son. I knew I would walk through the fires of Hell itself if it meant keeping him safe.

"Come on," Lilly says, tugging on my hand slightly. "I know what it cost her to come here today. Don't sadden her even more by hiding away from her."

I hesitate for a moment then nod my head, knowing Lilly is right.

Lilly grabs the doorknob once again, and I don't stop her this time.

The sweet fragrance of the flowers on the porch helps calm my frayed nerves. Their aroma welcomes me as I step out into the light of a Heavenly day. The familiar creak of the chains on the porch swing automatically draws my attention. It's not empty anymore. My mother is sitting on it now, with her right hand wrapped around the chain as she looks off into the distance at the snowcapped mountain range surrounding us.

She's even lovelier in person than any of her pictures or videos. Tiny wisps of her long brown hair flutter in the wind, giving her presence an ethereal quality. Her hair is cut short in the front, falling straight against her forehead to act as a frame around her face.

I notice a slight hesitation in her movements right before she looks over at me. When our eyes finally meet, I feel an instant connection. It's as if I've been missing an important part of myself all my life, only to have it finally returned to me in that moment.

"I'll leave the two of you to talk," Lilly tells me.

I'm aware of Lilly walking back inside the house and closing the door, but my attention is totally consumed by my mother.

Even though I grew up with her picture hanging above my fireplace in Cirrus, being in her actual physical presence leaves me speechless. For one of the few times in my life, I'm not sure what to do next.

My mother stands from her seat on the swing, but doesn't move towards me.

"Hello, Anna," she says, a melancholy smile stretching her lips. She watches me closely, and I assume she's not sure what to do next either.

"Hello," I say, uncertain how I should address her. 'Mother' seemed too formal but 'Mommy' seemed too childish.

My mother folds her hands in front of her.

"I heard that you're marrying Malcolm today," she says, trying to give me a true smile of happiness but not able to reach it because of her own eternal misery.

I nod, unable to think of anything else to say on the subject.

"I never could have imagined Malcolm would end up being your soulmate," she says. "But I couldn't have picked a better man to love you. He's been so lonely for so long. I'm just happy the two of you were able to find one another. I wanted to come here and wish you a happy and long life together."

After that, neither of us says anything for a long time, but as I look at her all my mind and heart can think to say is, "I'm sorry."

My mother cocks her head to the side as she looks at me in confusion.

"What on earth do you have to be sorry about?"

"I'm sorry my birth caused your death. I'm sorry I'm the reason you're so sad. I'm sorry you weren't given the chance to have your happily ever after with Lucifer because of me. Basically, I'm sorry I ruined your life."

"Oh, Anna," my mother sighs, shaking her head at me. "You have absolutely nothing to be sorry about. Why do you feel guilt over something that was never within your power to control? I knew what I was doing when I decided to go through with the pregnancy. I understood what I would be giving up."

"I know Lucifer tried to convince you to abort me," I tell her.

"I never could have done that," she tells me, no hesitation in her statement. "I never could have killed you. You're my baby, Anna. You are the product of my love for Lucifer. How could I have destroyed you when you represent something so beautiful?"

"But you wouldn't be separated from one another now if you had simply let me go."

"But then we would have been separated by *your* death instead of mine. I never would have been able to forgive myself or Lucifer if I had murdered you for such a selfish reason. I don't regret my decision to have you. I never have. My only regret is not being there for you when you needed me. I missed seeing you transform from that beautiful little baby I held in my arms when I died into the gorgeous woman standing in front of me now. I know I shouldn't, but I envy Andre those little moments he was able to share with you while you were growing up. They're moments that will never happen again. Memories I will never get to have with you. It's time I can never get back. I'm the one who should be apologizing to you. I wish I had been stronger and able to survive your birth. I'm sorry I had to leave you."

"It wasn't your fault," I tell her.

"And my death wasn't your fault," she replies.

We're both silent for a moment until I say, "Can I ask you a question?"

"You can ask me anything."

"Why did you want Lucifer to raise me? Why was that so important to you?"

"I knew he needed someone to love after I was gone," my mother tells me. "He has so much love to give, Anna. He just refuses to let many people see that side of him. During the time we were together, he showed me every day just how much he loved me. That's what real love is all about. Grandiose gestures are pleasant enough, but doing the little day-to-day things for someone shows your ability to love on a completely different level. The way they look at you. The way they touch you. The way they respect your thoughts and opinions. All those little things add up over time and give proof to a love that transcends a simple romance."

I understood what she meant because Malcolm was always showing me his love in simple ways. His little nightly notes during our courting period. The way he always holds my hand when we walk beside one another. His eagerness to show me how to build things with him in his workshop. There were a dozen or more small things he would do for me during any given day that showed his love for me with actions and not just words.

"I thought you might be hoping I could change him into someone who would ask for God's forgiveness," I tell her. "If he would just do that, the two of you could be together forever."

"No one can make someone do something they're not ready for," she says. "And I won't say the thought didn't cross my mind, but mostly I just didn't want him to be alone. He needed you after my death. I just wish he could have seen that fact for himself. I still have hope that he will find the strength within himself to ask God for forgiveness, but he's always been extremely hardheaded where his father is concerned. I'm not sure his pride will let him bow down in front of God and admit he's been wrong all these years."

"Do you think God would forgive him if he did?" I ask. "He's done so many bad things during his time on Earth. Even while he was in Heaven, he was sinful. He was the whole reason for the war here."

"Do you believe God wouldn't redeem your father if he asked for it?"

I feel unprepared for the question but answer truthfully.

"I don't know."

"If a person comes to Him truly repentant, God will forgive them. He loves Lucifer as much as He loves you, me, practically anyone you can name. He doesn't pick and choose who is worthy of redemption, Anna. All He does is wait for those who want His forgiveness to come to Him and ask for it with an open heart. As long as you truly mean it and are sorry for the sins you've committed, He can forgive anything."

"Then why doesn't Lucifer do that?" I ask. "I know he wants to be with you as much as you want to be with him. Why is he torturing you both like this?"

"Lucifer's pride has always denied him his greatest happiness," my mother tells me. "It was his pride which stripped him of his place here in Heaven, and it's his pride which keeps him from letting go of his hate and accepting his failures."

"I've been to Hell," I tell my mother.

Her eyes grow wide in alarm. "Why on earth would you ever do that, Anna? Don't you understand how dangerous that place is?"

"Lucifer was keeping information from me. I needed to know what he knew. Did you know he's been hiding there and reliving memories of you since your death?"

My mother's eyes water, and she places a shaky hand over her heart.

"I guess I should have known that," she says, a catch in her voice. "I've been feeling his pain since I left."

"You're still connected to one another?" I ask, finding clarity in how strong the spiritual bond between soulmates actually is. With my limited knowledge of such a connection, I simply assumed the tie would be broken after death.

"If anything, it became stronger after my death," my mother reveals.

She closes her eyes, and I watch as tears course down her cheeks. Her sadness tears at my heart. I walk over to her and wrap my arms around her shoulders, hoping to bring her at least a little bit of comfort.

She doesn't hug me back right away, but when she does I feel her let go of a small portion of her burden as she lays her head on my shoulder and cries.

I wish there was something I could do to take her pain away. However, I know I'm not the person who can do that. Only Lucifer can work such a miracle.

Now that I know the connection between their souls is still present, I can't understand why Lucifer would still let his pride keep them apart. Why does he find it so difficult to simply admit how wrong he's been and ask God to forgive him? Or is Hell itself preventing such a thing from happening? Is that another reason it's been showing Lucifer memories of my mother? Does it want to keep him trapped within its bowels because it knows it will never find someone as powerful as him to feed its insatiable need for power fueled by hate?

I don't try to rush my mother. I simply let her cry on my shoulder and do my best to help her through her sorrow.

Suddenly, I feel her wince like someone physically hit her in the gut. She pulls back from me.

"I'm sorry," she says, new tears forming in her eyes. "I need to leave."

"Why?" I ask. "What's wrong?"

She shakes her head at me, tears streaming down her face once again.

"I can't…I can't take the pain he's going through right now," she tells me. "I don't know what Hell's showing him but…I'm sorry. I need to leave."

She leans in and kisses me on the cheek. "I love you, Anna. Please don't forget that."

My mother phases away, leaving me on the porch alone.

I instantly know exactly where I need to go.

When I phase to Hell, I find Lucifer sitting on the bench in the replica of Malcolm's courtyard. His eyes look glazed over, and he doesn't seem to notice my sudden appearance. He seems locked inside his own little world, a place where his memories of my mother have him trapped.

I look behind me to see what scene Hell is making him watch. I see Lucifer pacing back and forth inside a little chapel. He's dressed in a nicely tailored black tuxedo and looks agitated for some reason. Malcolm stands in the back of the little church with his arms crossed over his chest. His mien is grave as he observes Lucifer's behavior.

"Nervous?" Malcolm asks him in a mocking tone.

Lucifer stops pacing and looks over at Malcolm. It's obvious from the expression on his face that he thought he was alone.

Lucifer turns to face Malcolm.

"I'm wondering why I agreed to do this," Lucifer confesses.

"So am I," Malcolm admits. "I didn't think you loved her this much, if you want to know the truth."

"I love her more than a mangy little mongrel like you could ever understand, Malcolm. Why are you here anyway? Amalie knows we hate each other. I don't think she expects you to be here to show your approval."

"I don't approve," Malcolm says with a shrug. "But that doesn't really seem to matter to her. I'm here in case you chicken out, and I need to help her pick up the pieces when you abandon her."

"I won't abandon her," Lucifer says stridently. "I wouldn't do that to her. She means everything to me."

"So you say," Malcolm says, sounding unconvinced, "but when it comes down to it I know you'll end up disappointing her. If not today, some other day. It's only a matter of time, Lucifer. And when it happens I'll help her through it."

"Why? Are you in love with her, too?"

"No, but I do love her," Malcolm says. "She's my friend, and I'm always loyal to my friends even when I think they're making a monumental mistake. I doubt that's something you can understand. You're too selfish and self-centered to sacrifice a little bit of yourself for someone you love."

"Don't stand there and pontificate to me, Malcolm. You have no idea what I would give for Amalie. But, then again, our father hasn't seen fit to provide you with a soulmate yet, has he? Oh wait…you thought it was Lilly at one time. You were wrong about that, and you're wrong about Amalie and me. I think you're just jealous that you haven't been able to experience a love like ours. Is that the real reason you're against us doing this today? Is your jealousy eating you alive?"

"Don't transfer your own feelings onto me, Lucifer. You and I are nothing alike."

"We're probably more alike than either one of us would want to admit," Lucifer says. "We're both stubborn to a fault when we think we're right."

"I don't think I'm right," Malcolm says. "I know I am. I'll make a promise to you, though, even if you don't deserve it. When you break her heart, and I know you will, I'll help her through it as much as I can."

"It won't happen," Lucifer says, but his voice lacks conviction. It's almost like he knows what Malcolm has said will happen one day, and he won't be able to prevent it.

"When it does," Malcolm says, no hate in his voice, just resignation, "I will be there for her."

The doors to the little chapel open and my mother walks in, dressed in a simple white dress.

Malcolm phases as if he doesn't want her to know he was there at all.

I'm not sure she would have noticed him if he had stayed. All of her attention is on Lucifer. Her face lights up with joy when she sees him, and her unadulterated happiness fills the little chapel to bursting. She walks up the short aisle to stand with the man she loves.

"Are you ready?" she asks, taking his hands into her own.

"Do we have to do it like this?" Lucifer asks, and I can tell it's not the first time he's asked this particular question.

"It's what I've always wanted," my mother says. "I won't feel like it's real unless we do it this way."

Lucifer sighs heavily. "Only for you would I agree to do this."

My mother smiles because she knows she's won. I see her close her eyes. A few seconds later, God appears next to them.

God looks from my mother to Lucifer.

"It's been a long time, My son," God says to him.

"Yes," Lucifer says, reluctantly acknowledging his father's presence. "A long time."

"Thank you for coming," my mother tells God.

"I will come whenever you ask, Amalie," God replies, smiling at her. "Are you ready to get married?"

My mother nods her head and looks back at Lucifer. "I've been ready since the moment I saw him."

Lucifer can't prevent himself from smiling back at my mother in her moment of joy.

"Then let's begin," God says.

The scene freezes like someone pressed pause. I look back at Lucifer, and see him staring at his memory like he's frozen in time, too.

"Tragic, isn't it?" a woman with a throaty voice says.

I look past Lucifer and see a slender woman in her mid-twenties standing in the shadows, a fully-grown hellhound standing close to her side. Her wavy, long blond hair is parted to the right, and she's wearing a red-sequined, spaghetti-strapped dress. She stares at me with eyes the same pale blue color as Lucifer's. I feel my heart grow cold simply by her presence. Her perfectly shaped scarlet lips stretch into an awkward smile to show whiter than white teeth. She looks picture-perfect in every way, which instantly tells me she isn't real. No one can look as flawless as she does.

"Who are you?" I ask.

"I am no one," she answers, slowly walking forward with the hellhound matching each of her measured steps.

"Then, what are you?"

"Ahh," she says with a tilt of her head, exposing the lily-white flesh of her neck. "Now that's a smarter question to ask, Anna."

"Do you plan to answer it?" I ask as she comes to stand directly behind Lucifer.

The woman looks down at him in revulsion.

"Look at him," she says in disgust. "How the mighty have fallen. He was once one of the most powerful creatures in all of existence. But now his power has been weakened to the point where he's almost useless to me now, and all because of a woman."

Her gaze turns to me, devouring me with her eyes in an almost lustful manner.

"But, you, my dear," she croons, slinking around the bench towards me. "You are a creature worthy of my attention."

"Are you Hell?" I ask her, having no other conclusion to draw from her words and actions.

She walks around me, looking me up and down in such an appraising way that I'm not sure if she wants to eat me or kiss me.

"Yes," she answers, coming to a stop barely a foot away from me. "I thought it might be easier for me to speak with you in this form."

"What do you hope to gain from this conversation?"

Lucifer

"Nothing," she says with a shrug. "I simply wanted to meet you, Anna. I suspect you and I will be spending quite a lot of time with one another in the future."

"Why would you think that?"

The physical manifestation of Hell smiles at me.

"Oh, don't you feel it, dear one? The power of the seals has already taken root inside your soul. It's only a matter of time before it consumes you all together. When it does, I'll be waiting for you with open arms. Just think of all the chaos we can cause if we pool our resources. We could bring down both Earth and Heaven in one fell swoop."

"I have no intention of helping you do anything," I tell her.

"Oh, but you won't have much say in the matter after you collect all the seals. The person you are now won't exist anymore. Pity that," she says, looking me up and down again. "I do like you the way you are now. But I can't have it both ways, can I? Plus, the creature you will become will be the closest thing to a god I've ever had the pleasure of serving."

"That won't happen to me," I tell her, though my statement doesn't sound very convincing even to myself.

The woman laughs. "Oh, Anna, you are quite amusing in your naiveté. You actually seem to think you'll have a choice in the matter. You won't in the end, you know. There will be so little of you left by that time that this righteous conscience you possess now won't even exist anymore. And when that time comes I'll be waiting here for you."

"You'll have a long wait," I tell her.

The manifestation of Hell smiles at me.

"Since we will soon be so close, you can call me Helena, Anna. It might be easier for you to accept me if I have a human name. And if you ever have need of me, simply say my name, and I will come to you."

"You can leave this place?"

She shakes her head. "No, that I can't do. But when you come back here, I can be by your side at a moment's notice."

"How do you know I'll come back?"

"Oh, you won't have much choice. You'll feel the draw to me like a child to its mother. In time you won't want leave the warmth of my bosom, Anna. I will never judge you or tell you that you have to be something you aren't. You can be as terrible as you want to be here and receive my undying loyalty. The more powerful you become the more turmoil you'll cause. All of it will make me stronger."

Helena looks over at Lucifer again.

"He has given me all he can, but you," she says, looking back at me with a wicked possessiveness, "you, my dear, are untapped power. In a very short while you will become master of this domain, master of me. Don't you want that?"

Helena reaches out with one of her pale white hands like she's about to touch me, but I back away before she can. My soul is sending out a blaring warning, that if I allow her to touch me I will be lost forever.

Helena smiles and drops her hand back to her side.

"Until we meet again, Anna. I have to confess I'm very much looking forward to it."

Helena lays her hand on the hellhound at her side and vanishes in a wisp of black smoke.

"Anna?"

I look at Lucifer and see that he's no longer frozen.

"What are you doing here?"

"I came to see you," I tell him. "I needed to know you were all right."

Lucifer looks confused by my concern. "Why? What made you think I wasn't?"

"My mother said you were in a great deal of pain. I came to see if I could help you."

"You saw Amalie?" Lucifer says in a whisper.

"Yes, I just came from her." I walk over to Lucifer and kneel down on one knee in front of him. "Lucifer, you have to know that the connection between your souls is still there."

"Of course I know that," Lucifer says. "I just thought she wouldn't be able to feel me while I was in Hell."

"She can feel it wherever you are," I tell him. "Wouldn't you rather be with her again instead of simply reliving these old memories?"

"I would give anything to be with her again."

"Then you know what you have to do."

"You make it sound so simple, Anna. But in order to receive true forgiveness you have to mean it. You can't exactly fool God."

"Why is asking for forgiveness so hard for you to do? Why do you continue to hold a grudge against God?"

"Because I still think humans are just little monkeys He loves more than his angels. Even if I told Him otherwise, He would know it was a lie."

"After all this time, you still hate humanity?"

"Yes."

"God doesn't love humans more than angels," I tell him. "He loves us all equally. Why can't you see that?"

"Because it's not true. Why can't *you* see *that*?" Lucifer counters.

"You're smart, but completely blind," I tell him. "Why do you think He sent my mother to you?"

"So I would have to live the rest of my days in this torture."

"And why do you think He sent me here?"

"To rub salt in an already open wound and make me pay for the things that I've done."

"You're so wrong on so many levels," I say. "Can't you see that everything He's done has been to bring you back to Him? My mother was meant to show you the beauty in humanity. You can't sit there and tell me she didn't mean the world to you. Would you call her a monkey? Does she deserve to be called an animal? Do you think of me as a monkey, too?"

"You're different," he defends. "You're my daughter and a descendant of Michael. You're not completely human, Anna. Neither was your mother."

"If that's the way you want to justify your feelings for us I guess there's really nothing else I can say that will change your mind, but I'm more human than you might want to believe. I have human frailties and insecurities. I might be more powerful than most because of who my ancestors are, but my humanity is what gives me the strength to carry on. It's what makes me special."

I stand up.

"I'm marrying Malcolm today," I tell him. "I would like for you to come to the wedding."

Lucifer's head jerks up as he looks at me in surprise. "Why would you want me there? You know I don't approve of you marrying that mongrel."

"Because you're my father," I tell him, calling him by his true position in my life. "And you should be there on the most important day of my life to wish me luck, despite your misguided opinion."

"And what if I just come to try to talk some sense into you?"

"There's nothing you could say that would change my mind about marrying Malcolm. It's what we are meant to do. It's the one thing in the mess that my life has become that makes sense."

Lucifer stands up. "And what if I can prove to you that this wedding shouldn't happen?"

"There's nothing you can say or do that will stop it."

"Nothing *I* can say…" Lucifer says, mulling my words over in his mind. "Fine. Then I'll just have to figure out a way to make you see reason."

Lucifer phases, and I see his phase trail leads directly to the palace in Cirrus.

His choice of destination worries me. Why would he go there? What proof does he hope to find that will make me call off the wedding?

CHAPTER SEVEN

I phase back to Heaven, hoping no one noticed that I left.

Of course, someone did...

Jess is leaned up against the porch railing, her head bowed slightly as if she's deep in thought. When I appear, she looks up at me and slowly begins to shake her head in disappointment.

"Why would you go there, Anna?" she asks, clearly thinking I won't give her a good enough explanation for my trip to Hell.

"How do you know where I went?" I ask.

"There's only one phase trail that looks completely black. Now answer my question."

"I needed to see Lucifer," I tell her, suddenly feeling guilty for my little trip given Jess' obvious disapproval. "He was remembering the day he married my mother, and it was causing them both a lot of pain. I wanted to try to talk some sense into him."

"Lucifer is as stubborn as Heaven is infinite," Jess tells me with a heavy sigh. "I think one of the only reasons Amalie was able to make him admit his feelings for her was because she was even more stubborn than he was."

"Jess, Malcolm told me that you tried to help Lucifer ask for forgiveness once. Why do you think he didn't? What stopped him?"

"Lucifer doesn't like to admit his faults; no one does really, but him least of all. He thinks that if he admits he's been wrong all this time, everything he's done, everything he's given up will have been for nothing. His legacy would mark him as a failure, and I think he would rather die than do that."

"You were the only true human he ever felt connected to. Do you think it was just because you were Michael's vessel?"

"I've always believed that it was *me* he cared for," Jess says. "Having Michael's spirit inside me might have drawn him to me in the beginning, but it was *Jess* he always came to talk to. I think I was the only human he ever tried to get to know. After we got close, I think he began to doubt what he's always believed about humans. Realizing that you are wrong is hard for anybody. But for Lucifer, I think it made him begin to doubt himself in a way that he never had before."

"He just tried to justify what he feels for me and my mother by saying we aren't completely human."

"He'll do and say anything to make sure he doesn't have to admit he was wrong. My best advice to you is...don't push him. He has to go to God of his own free will or it means nothing."

"That's pretty much what he told me," I say. "But how can I make him want to do that willingly?"

"You can't," Jess says sympathetically. "I know how much you want to help your parents, Anna, but all you can do is be there for Lucifer if he decides to go to his father. He's the only one who can change his fate."

"Not if Helena has anything to say about it," I grumble.

"Helena?" Jess asks. "Oh my god... has Hell given itself a name?"

"And a body," I tell her. "A beautiful one, but still really creepy."

"Hell, Helena, whatever the bitch wants to call herself, I don't care. You stay away from it. You need to stop thinking these little trips to Hell are like going down to the store or something. It's not. That place wants to consume you, Anna. It's hungry for power, and you *are* becoming extremely powerful. We all feel it."

"You feel it?" I ask, puzzled by this revelation. "What do you feel?"

"There's an energy surrounding you that none of us have experienced before," Jess tells me, looking me up and down. "And your aura is becoming...darker. We used to be able to see you on Earth because your light was so bright. We still can to an extent but ... it's like you're pulling away from us somehow. It's kind of hard for me to explain."

"I think I sort of understand," I say. "I think it's one reason Will had such a hard time reviving me the last time I died."

"It could be," Jess agrees. "Normally, the soul of the descendant comes to Heaven for a short period of time when they die on Earth."

"Really?" I ask. "I guess that makes sense. I just never thought about it before. So the last time I died, my soul didn't make it up here?"

Jess shakes her head. "No, it didn't."

"Where did I go?"

"I don't know, sweetie," Jess says, sounding completely baffled. "Will wasn't even sure. He said it was like you were being hidden from him. That's why it took so long for him to finally pull you back."

"That's kind of scary, actually," I say, my heart racing after learning this new information.

"Well, then, why don't you just try to stay alive down there, ok?"

I nod. "Yes, ma'am; I will do my best."

Jess smiles and walks up to me to place one of her arms across my shoulders.

"Now, let's go back inside and get to the gift-giving portion of this shindig."

"Gifts?" I ask in surprise. "Does Heaven have stores?"

"Hmm, not exactly," Jess says mysteriously. "But we put some things together that we thought might help you out back on Earth."

Jess and I walk back into the house and find the others sitting in the living room. Lilly is the first to see me.

"Everything ok?" she asks, looking between Jess and me from her chair by the fireplace.

"She made it back from her impromptu trip to Hell in one piece, if that's what you're asking," Jess says. "I would say that's a small miracle. Oh, and apparently Hell has given itself a drop-dead gorgeous body and a name, Helena."

"Not exactly original," Caylin retorts. "But easy enough to remember, I suppose."

"Well, I for one would much rather talk about happier things right now," Utha Mae says. "I want to give my baby the gift Tara and I made for her."

Utha Mae waves me over to the empty spot between her and Tara on the couch.

After I sit down, Utha Mae hands me a medium-size glittery green box tied with a silky white ribbon. I pull on the ribbon and the box and ribbon disappear in a wisp of white smoke, leaving only the gift inside it sitting on my lap. It's a beautifully bound brown leather book with 'Family Recipes' stitched in gold thread on the front in a fancy script.

"We thought you might like some of the recipes that have been handed down from one generation to the next," Utha Mae tells me with pride.

"This is perfect!" I say, becoming excited that I might be able to surprise Malcolm by cooking something he wouldn't expect me to know how to cook. "Thank you so much."

"It's not just any cookbook either," Tara says, reaching over to flip the cover open to reveal the first recipe.

Each page has two recipes written in long hand on note cards bordered with gold cording.

"Touch one," Tara says excitedly.

I touch one of the notecards and instantly hear Utha Mae begin to speak about the ingredients I will need to prepare an apple pie. I touch the card again, and it instantly stops the oration.

"It's well enough to have a written recipe," Utha Mae says, "but sometimes you just can't tell everything by reading one. Good cooking is an art form, Anna. After all the time you spent with me in the kitchen, I kinda thought you might be able to cook, even if *some* people thought I was just wasting my time making this for you."

"I didn't say it was a waste…exactly," Tara says. "I just figured it would end up collectin' dust, is all. Didn't I help you make it in spite of that fact?"

"Reluctantly, yes," Utha Mae replies.

"Well, I had no doubt in my mind you would be able to use my gift," Caylin says, handing me a small, white, rectangular, glittery box tied with red silky ribbon.

I sit the box on top of the book and pull the ribbon. The white box and ribbon disappear, leaving only a silver-handled paintbrush with off-white bristles.

"If you're ever in need of something," Caylin tells me, "just close your eyes, visualize what you want in your mind, and paint it in the air. When you're done painting it, it will materialize."

"Anything I want? Can it make people appear?" I ask, thinking this might be a way to get my papa back.

"No," Caylin says regretfully. "It can't transport people, only inanimate objects. Also, the object can only stay solid for about two hours. It's not permanent."

I feel a little let down by this fact but try not to show it.

"Here, kid," Jess says, tossing me a small purple glittery box tied with black ribbon.

The box lands on top of the recipe book. I pull the ribbon and find myself in possession of a black leather bracelet that has a silver angel wing charm on it.

"Tell Malcolm I had Caylin swipe that out of his vault for me," Jess says. "I think it might come in handy one day."

"What does it do?" I ask, assuming it has some sort of magical properties.

"When you wear it," Jess begins to explain, "you can ask it to let you know how someone is feeling. But be prepared to feel what they are, because their emotions will come at you totally unfiltered. So be careful. Don't ask if you don't want to know."

I slip the bracelet onto my right wrist as Lilly walks over and hands me a box with a baby blue bottom and pink top, tied with a ribbon which has a swirl pattern of the two colors mixed together.

"I know you'll need this," Lilly says confidently.

I untie the ribbon and find myself in possession of a silver dumbbell-shaped baby rattle. I pick it up and hear the crystal-clear chime it makes.

"Guaranteed to make any baby stop crying almost instantly," Lilly tells me with a smile.

"Girl, that thing right there is priceless!" Tara exclaims. "Don't you dare lose it if you want to keep your sanity with twins around the house."

"I wish I'd had one when I had my twins," Lilly says in all seriousness. "It would have saved Brand and me some sleepless nights."

"Thank you all so much for my gifts," I say. "I love them all."

"Well," Lilly says, standing from her chair, "although I would love to keep you here longer, I don't think Malcolm would appreciate me making you late to your own wedding."

"Is it time already?" I ask, thinking I'd only been in Heaven for a couple of hours at most.

"Time in Heaven moves differently than on Earth," Lilly tells me. "You should still have plenty of time to prepare yourself for the ceremony."

We all stand up, and the ladies take turns giving me a hug goodbye.

"You take care of yourself down there, baby girl," Utha Mae says, looking nervous about what the future holds for me.

"Don't worry," I tell her, even though it's something I can't seem to make myself do either. "I won't let you down."

"Oh, child," Utha Mae says, leaning in to kiss me on the cheek. "That possibility never even crossed my mind. Just take care of yourself. That's all I ask."

After the goodbyes are said, Lilly phases me back to my bedroom in Malcolm's house.

"Oh!" Millie says, jumping slightly as she walks out of my bathroom just as Lilly and I phase in. "Gracious, you two almost made my old heart stop on the spot."

"Sorry, Millie," I tell her, guiltily finding her reaction a little amusing. I place my gifts down on the nightstand by my bed.

"No worries, my sweet. I'm just glad to see you back. The ceremony is only a couple of hours away. We should probably get started on getting you ready for it."

My eyes are drawn to something lying on my bed. It's an exact duplicate of the wedding dress Levi destroyed when I went to Cirrus to retrieve it.

"Oh, Millie," I say, reaching out to touch the silky fabric. "I can't believe you made me another one so quickly!"

"Where there's a will, there's a way," Millie says proudly.

"It's absolutely gorgeous," Lilly says, looking at the dress. "Malcolm won't know what hit him when he sees you in it."

"Can you stay for the wedding?" I ask her.

"No," she says with a shake of her head and a wistful smile. "Caylin and I thought that we should stay in Heaven for this event. This is your special time with Malcolm. We wouldn't want our presence to take anything away from that experience. Just know that we love you both and wish you a happy and long life together."

"If you won't stay," I tell her, "will you at least promise to come back one day?"

Lilly smiles, looking pleased by my request.

"Of course I will. I'm sure I'll want to see the newest additions to our family. Something tells me they'll be very special."

Lilly leans in and gives me a hug.

"Enjoy tonight," she says to me as she pulls back. "It will be one of the best of your life."

Lilly phases and I look back at the wedding dress, feeling flushed with excitement as I realize tonight is the night I finally make Malcolm mine forever.

"Let me go make a bath to help you relax a bit before we get started," Millie says, making an about-face and heading back into the bathroom.

I'm just pulling my sweater over my head when I hear someone yell, "Wait!"

I pull the sweater back down and look towards the door to the room.

Lucifer is standing there with one hand covering his eyes, shielding them from the sight of me almost half-clothed.

"What are you doing here?" I ask apprehensively, knowing Lucifer phased to Cirrus earlier to help him find a reason to keep me from marrying Malcolm.

"Are you decent?" Lucifer asks, stoutly refusing to take his hand away from his eyes until I answer.

"Yes," I tell him, smoothing out the edge of my sweater against my hips.

Lucifer lowers his hand away from his eyes slowly, as if he's afraid he might see something again that he doesn't want to.

"Are you going to tell me why you're here, or are you going to make me guess?"

Lucifer takes something out of his pants pocket.

"I'm hoping I brought you something that will change your mind about this wedding."

"You're totally wasting your time," I tell him with absolute conviction. "There's nothing you can say that will stop me from marrying Malcolm tonight."

"So you said before," Lucifer says, sounding unconvinced. "Which is why I went to find something that will hopefully knock some sense into you."

"Who are you talking to, my sweet?" Millie says, walking out of the bathroom.

Her eyes immediately find Lucifer in the room.

"Hello, Lucifer," Millie says, looking confused by Lucifer's presence but not exactly surprised. "Did you come to give your daughter away at her wedding?"

"Absolutely not, Millie," Lucifer says rather indignantly. "I've come to see if I can stop this travesty from happening at all!"

Millie looks even more confused. "Why on earth would you want to stop the wedding? Don't you want to see Anna happy?"

"Of course I do," Lucifer says, as if Millie's question is completely absurd. "But Malcolm isn't the man to do that. I know him. He'll eventually get tired of Anna and toss her to the side like he does all his women. I'm not even sure the word monogamy is in that man's vocabulary."

Millie doesn't look confused anymore. She looks mad.

"That's the most ridiculous thing I've ever heard you say! Master Malcolm is one of the most honorable men I know. When he makes his vows to Anna, I have no doubt he will keep them!" Millie says in defense of Malcolm, like an overprotective mama bear.

"When have you known Malcolm to care about a woman for more than a few months, Millie?"

Millie defiantly raises her chin a notch. "That's always been your problem, Lucifer. You never understood Master Malcolm's true nature. How do you think he has been able to withstand your offers to remove the curse for all these years?

Even *you* can't say he doesn't have a strong sense of morals. And if you honestly think he would ever betray Anna in such a way, you're more of a fool than I thought you were!"

As I listen to Millie defend Malcolm's honor, I wonder why Lucifer is allowing her to speak to him as an equal. I knew he and Millie had some sort of relationship while my mother was alive, but this interaction between them makes me believe she and he had a slightly deeper connection than I was previously led to believe.

"We'll see about that," Lucifer quips back. "I just hope I've brought some sanity into the situation."

Lucifer walks up to me and holds his hand out, palm up.

I look down and see that he's holding one of the crystal devices used to display real-time holographic images.

"What do I need that for?" I ask, looking up from his outstretched hand to meet his gaze.

"Turn it on," Lucifer tells me, "and see for yourself."

Tentatively, I take the crystal and swipe my other hand over its controls to activate it.

I feel my eyes begin to burn with tears as I look at the figure standing in front of me. I faintly hear Millie gasp in surprise over the roar of the blood rushing to my head, making me feel a bit faint.

"Papa," I sob.

CHAPTER EIGHT

I reach out a shaky hand to my papa, knowing it's a futile attempt to touch him, but neither of us seems to care because he does the same thing. Our hands meet and fade into one another. We may not be able to physically touch, but the mutual attempt at least makes me feel closer to him.

"Where are you?" I immediately ask, wiping at the tears on my face with the back of the hand that still holds the crystal. "Are you in Cirrus somewhere? Just tell me and I'll come and get you, Papa. I can phase now."

My papa smiles at me sadly and shakes his head.

"I'm sorry, my little cherub. I promised Lucifer I wouldn't tell you where I am. But don't worry about me. I'm in a good place, and no, I'm not in Cirrus. Levi hasn't harmed me in any way. You have no reason to fear for my safety."

"Did Lucifer bring you here to talk me out of marrying Malcolm?" I ask.

I see immediate confusion and alarm appear on my papa's face.

"Marrying Malcolm?" he asks, as though the two words shouldn't even be joined in the same sentence. "Why on earth would you be doing that?"

"Exactly!" Lucifer says triumphantly.

I look over my papa's right shoulder and see Lucifer standing behind him, a self-satisfied smirk on his face.

"I guess I'll let the two of you talk privately for a little while," Lucifer tells us, sounding pleased with himself because he obviously thinks he's won this particular battle. "I think you have a lot of catching up to do."

Lucifer phases.

"Oh, Lord Andre," Millie says happily, "it's so good to see you again and to know you're safe. We've all been worried sick about you."

"Thanks, Millie," my papa says, chancing a glance at her but quickly returning his attention to me. "I'm perfectly fine. There's no need to worry."

"That's so wonderful to hear," Millie says, looking between the two of us. "I'll just go finish preparing some things so the two of you can discuss matters."

Millie turns around and heads back into the bathroom, making what looks to me like a hasty retreat.

I stare at my papa for a moment, almost feeling like a kid who has done something wrong. Yet I've done nothing wrong except find the man I'm supposed to marry and build a family with. Surely he'll understand that.

"Tell me, Anna," my papa says, still looking worried "Why are you marrying Malcolm?"

"He's my soulmate, Papa," I tell him, hoping that it's reason enough for him.

"Malcolm?" Papa says in utter disbelief. "You're absolutely sure about that?"

I nod. "Yes. Why do you sound so surprised? Honestly, I thought you of all people would be happy for us. You're his best friend, aren't you?"

"Yes," Papa says, "which is probably why this news makes it feel so strange to me. I know him better than anyone except for Jered, maybe. The three of us have been through a lot together over the years." My papa takes a deep breath and lets it out slowly. "Give me a moment to think about this. You've kind of thrown me for a loop, Anna."

I remain silent while my papa seems to have a silent conversation with himself, as if he's weighing the pros and cons of Malcolm and me being soulmates. He shakes his head, and then nods. Then he shakes it again and still looks mystified by the news.

"I love him," I finally say, hoping this will erase any doubt he has that I'm making a mistake marrying Malcolm.

"It's just…" he says, shaking his head. "You're my *daughter*, Anna. I realize you've figured out that I'm not your biological father, but I'm still the man who raised you. I love you as my own flesh and blood and nothing will ever change my feelings for you."

"I love you, too, Papa."

"But," he says, raising one hand to his forehead to rub his temples and propping his free hand onto his hip as he continues to come to grips with the news. "I have to say the possibility of you marrying Malcolm never even crossed my mind. I'm having a little trouble imagining it."

"Why?"

"Because you're both family to me!" he says, raising both of his hands in the air to emphasize his point. "Basically, I feel like my daughter is marrying my brother! I need some time to wrap my mind around the situation."

"I think Lucifer was hoping you would try to talk me out of it," I tell him. "You're not going to try to do that, are you? If so, I'll tell you the same thing I told

Lucifer. It won't work. Even if you disapprove, Papa, I'm marrying Malcolm tonight one way or the other."

I'm not sure if it was my words or the way I made my proclamation, but my papa let out a deep sigh of resignation and looked at me in surprise.

"I think this is the first time you've never wanted to know my thoughts on a subject," he says, looking proud and sad at the same time. I'm no longer the little girl who relied on him to make the important decision for me. I suppose realizing your child has grown beyond the need for your guidance is a hard thing for any parent to come to terms with.

"It's not that I won't listen to what you're thinking," I tell him. "I would never disrespect you in such a way, Papa. I know me, Papa; my life would never feel complete without Malcolm as my husband. I need him as much as I need the heart beating inside my chest. Without either I would be dead inside. As long as I have Malcolm, I feel like I can make it through the rest of the mission God has given me. I know I can succeed if we're together, and the vows we make to one another tonight will make our bond even stronger."

It takes a few seconds, but my papa finally smiles at me.

"I guess you really are a woman now," he says with pride. "I'm glad I raised you to listen to your heart and allow it to tell you what's right and what's wrong. I can't say the whole situation isn't still odd for me, but I trust your judgment. If getting married is what you both want, then I have no reservations about it whatsoever. I'm not going to lie and say it's something I ever expected to happen, but all I've ever wanted was for you to be happy, Anna. As long as Malcolm makes you happy, you have my blessing."

"I don't suppose you could explain that sort of logic to Lucifer?" I ask in jest. "He seems hell-bent on stopping me from marrying Malcolm."

My papa sighs heavily. "The two of them have had a very difficult relationship over the years, Anna. I'm not sure if there's anything that can fix the animosity that's built up between them. However they both love you, and therefore they do have *some* common ground. I'm just not sure it will be enough to keep them from trying to rip each other's throats out. Maybe in time they can come to a mutual understanding where you're concerned."

"I hope so," I tell him. "Papa, why don't you tell me where you are? I can come and get you and this whole mess can be over. You don't owe Lucifer anything. You don't have to keep your promise to him."

"Anna," my father says, in that disappointed voice that I always hated to hear as a child, "you of all people should know me well enough to understand that I can't just break my word once I've given it. If a man doesn't keep his word, he isn't a man worth knowing, in my opinion. I won't break it just to save my own skin. I'm sorry my being trapped like this has been so difficult for you, but I'm perfectly fine where I am. I *am* disappointed that I won't be able to walk you down the aisle, though. It was always something I wanted to do if you were ever allowed to have a real wedding."

"I'm sorry you won't be here for that, too," I say, unable to stop the tears of my disappointment.

"Oh, cherub, don't cry," my papa says to me. "We'll have plenty of time later to make other memories. We'll find a way to be together again."

"So," Lucifer says. I look over my papa's shoulder and see that he's returned. "Have you been able to talk some sense into her yet? Have you explained what a fiasco her life will become if she marries Malcolm? You know him well enough to explain what a cad he can be, Andre, especially where women are concerned."

Papa turns around to face Lucifer. "I've given her my blessing, Lucifer. You should know better than anyone that, when two soulmates meet, nothing can keep them from wanting to be with one another. Even though you don't want to admit it, Malcolm is an excellent choice for her. He'll take care of Anna better than any other man in this world."

Lucifer rolls his eyes, like he expected this to happen.

"Did you at least talk her out of retrieving any more of the seals?"

"Why would I do that?" Papa asks, sounding confused.

Lucifer looks at me. "I thought you would have talked about that, too."

"No," I tell him. "We didn't."

Lucifer looks back at my father and says, "The seals are changing her. Their combined power is evolving her into something darker. She needs to stop collecting them!"

My papa looks at me in alarm. "Levi mentioned you were gathering the seals, but he didn't say they were causing you to change. Why didn't you say anything?"

"It's nothing to worry about," I tell him. "I can handle it."

"No, she can't!" Lucifer says in exasperation. "She's only collected two seals so far, and that guardian angel of hers came close to losing her the last time she died."

"The *last* time she died?" Papa exclaims. "How many times have you died since I've been gone?"

I hesitate, but know I have to answer. "Twice."

"Anna!" Papa says, in surprise and worry. "Tell me everything."

I go on to give my father a truncated version of the events that took place after his incarceration by Levi. I omitted my recent conversation with Helena, however. I didn't want Lucifer to know Hell was preparing to make me its master instead of him. He seemed to have enough problems to deal with. Plus it would have just been another hit to his pride, which I didn't feel he could suffer through right now.

Papa listens to my tale closely, allowing me to get through the retelling of recent events before asking any questions.

"And are you feeling any different?" he asks me.

I look between my papa and Lucifer, debating whether I should admit it or not. However, I think my hesitation has already given them the answer they want.

"Yes," I say. "I feel more powerful."

"In what way?"

I look around the room and see the chair Millie has been laying my daily clothes out on.. I lift it with my new telekinetic power, rotate it while it's in the air, and set it back down in the exact same spot it was before.

"Her powers will only increase," Lucifer says emphatically.

"I can handle them," I try to say with conviction, but there is a small part of me that doubts I'll be able to. "With Malcolm with me, I'll be able to finish this mission and take the seals back to Heaven. I'm stronger when he's with me. I can do this."

Papa doesn't say anything. He just looks worried.

"What does my father say about it?" he finally asks me. "Does He think you can handle what the seals will do to you?"

"Yes," I tell him. "He wouldn't have sent me here to take them if he didn't."

My papa takes a deep breath and slowly lets it out.

"I've always trusted His judgment about matters like this, and I don't see any reason to doubt Him now. Do what you need to do, Anna. You have my full support."

Lucifer lets out a feral growl. Before I know it he's charging towards me, walking through the holographic image of my papa, and grabbing the crystal out of my hand. He squeezes it with enough force that I hear it crack, and the projection of my father disappears.

"Why did you do that?" I scream at him.

"Because Andre was completely useless!" Lucifer yells back. "I had hoped he would be reasonable and tell you to stop this travesty of a marriage and to stop collecting the seals for your own good!"

"He trusts my judgment. It's something you should learn to do."

"You're twenty-one years old! You haven't lived long enough to understand the powers you're playing with." Lucifer grabs my arms and shakes me a little bit. "You will end up killing yourself, Anna! Stop before it's too late!"

The worry in Lucifer's eyes tells me that he's only doing this because he truly cares for me.

"Then help me through it," I plead. "Instead of trying to stop me, help me. With your knowledge about things like this I'm sure I can succeed. I'm going to try…with or without your help."

Lucifer lets me go with an aggravated growl and pushes me away from him, making me lose my balance and sit on the bed behind me.

"You're just like your mother. Completely stubborn," he says, looking down at me.

"And if she hadn't been so stubborn," I tell him. "She might have listened to other people and stayed away from you."

"Maybe she should have. We might have all been better off!"

"You don't mean that," I tell him, seeing through his attempt to belittle what he had with my mother. "She made you a better man. Look at you now. You're trying to save my life. Do you honestly think you would have even cared if it hadn't been for the love my mother brought out in you? I think you want to be more than you are, Lucifer. You just have to admit that fact to yourself."

Lucifer is silent. He just looks at me, but I can tell my words have hit a spot of truth.

"Perhaps your husband-to-be will be able to talk some sense into you when he learns what the seals are actually doing," Lucifer says. "I assume you haven't told him everything yet?"

"I will," I say in my own defense. "I just haven't had the time."

"Ri-ight," Lucifer says. "I think you're afraid he'll tell you to stop."

"He won't."

"I wouldn't bet on it," Lucifer says knowingly. "If Malcolm actually does love you, he will. You can bet on it."

Lucifer begins to phase but I reach out and grab him, forcing him to stop.

"Come to my wedding," I beg him. "Share in the happiest moment of my life."

Lucifer looks at me and shakes his head. "I can't be a witness to the beginning of the end of you, Anna. I'm not strong enough for that."

I let go of Lucifer and he phases away, back to Hell.

I wonder what memory Helena will make him relive while he's there. A red-hot hatred builds up inside me, and I have a sudden urge to go down there and knock her senseless. It's an absurd thought because she isn't real, just a manifestation that Hell devised to communicate with me.

"Are they gone?" Millie asks, peeking out of the bathroom.

"Yes," I tell her, standing up because I realize I'm sitting on my wedding dress. The last thing I need to do is wrinkle it. "They're gone."

Millie walks over to me. "It was so good to see your father again."

110

"Which one?" I ask.

"Both I suppose," Millie admits. "But Lord Andre more so than Lucifer, if I'm being honest."

"Millie, the way you talked to Lucifer made it seem like the two of you knew each other quite well. I seriously doubt he would let just anyone speak to him the way you did."

Millie looks uncomfortable with my observation.

"Oh, that..." she says, wringing her hands together, obviously not liking the turn of the conversation.

I cross my arms. "What aren't you telling me, Millie?"

Millie looks at me with an almost guilty expression.

"I promised Lucifer I would never mention it...to anyone."

"Does it have something to do with me?" I ask, becoming even more intrigued with the secret relationship Millie seems to have with Lucifer. "If it does, you have to tell me, Millie. I need to know everything I can about Lucifer if I'm ever going to understand him."

"I'm not someone who breaks her word easily," Millie says, still looking uncomfortable about the subject. "But considering how things are between the two of you, I feel like you should know. Perhaps if you know more about him, you can better understand his feelings for you."

"Tell me, Millie. Please," I implore. "I need to know."

Millie sighs before she tells me her secret.

"On the night of your first birthday, I was putting you in your cradle when I felt like someone was behind me. I turned to see if it was Lord Andre sneaking in for one last kiss from you, but I saw no one. Still, I didn't like the feeling that someone had been there. So I acted as if I left the room and waited for a couple of minutes, listening in at the door. When I heard a male voice in your room, I barged in, ready to fight whoever it was."

"Was it Lucifer?"

Millie nods. "Yes; he confessed to me that he'd just wanted to see how much you had grown in the past year. I didn't see any harm in it. I even told him about all your little milestones like your first step, your first word..."

"What was my first word?"

"Papa, of course," Millie chuckles. "Oh, you've loved Lord Andre from the moment you saw him, I think. Anyway, every year on your birthday until you were ten years old, Lucifer would come during the night to see you. I would wait for him and let him know anything notable that happened to you during the year. We formed an odd acquaintance during those times."

"Did you ever tell Papa about Lucifer's visits?"

"No," Millie says, looking guilty. "I promised Lucifer it would be between me and him. I didn't sense that you were in any danger. So I didn't see the harm in keeping the secret from your father."

"You said he came up until I turned ten. Do you know why he stopped?"

Millie shakes her head. "No, I don't. You would have to ask him that."

Millie's confession just adds to my certainty that Lucifer cares for me more deeply than he might want to admit. I am almost certain now that he loves me, even if he doesn't want to say the words to me.

"Why don't we see if we can put a smile on that beautiful face of yours instead of a frown?" Millie suggests. "I suspect Master Malcolm would rather see you happy when you go walking down that aisle towards him."

I follow Millie to the bathroom, where she already has the tub filled with water and bubbles. After I strip off my clothing and submerge my body in the water, I feel a sense of calm wash over me as soon as I imagine Malcolm's happy face watching me walk down the aisle towards him.

I smile and close my eyes, letting the bad events of the day drift away, only keeping the good in the forefront of my mind.

CHAPTER NINE

For the wedding, Millie styles my hair into long loose curls and pulls small sections of it away from my face. She pins them into place on the backside of my head with a diamond and pearl hairclip shaped into a design that reminds me of a vine of flowers. The pearls act as flower buds and the oval diamonds leaves.

"That's pretty," I say, watching her reflection in the vanity mirror as she clips it into place to hold my hair back. "Where did it come from?"

"Oh, the other Watchers brought you some jewelry as a wedding gift," she tells me. "Now, let me see if I can remember correctly. I believe the hairclip was from Desmond."

"What else did I get?" I ask, excited to see what other treasures I was given.

Millie walks over to my bedside table and picks up a medium-sized black box. She brings it over and hands it to me. I lift the lid, and, inside, beautifully displayed on a piece of black velvet, is a necklace and a pair of earrings in the same design as the hairclip.

"I was asked to tell you that the necklace is from Brutus and the earrings are from Daniel," Millie says. "And Jered said your gift from him will be arriving tomorrow morning."

"Do you know what his gift is?" I ask, intrigued to know what Jered would give me.

"I have no idea, my sweet," Millie says with a shrug. "But he seemed quite pleased with himself for thinking of it, whatever *it* is."

There is a soft scratching at the door.

"Anna?" Vala says from the other side.

Millie goes to the door and opens it for my four-legged friend. I not only get Vala but also Luna. The little hellhound runs in and jumps up onto my lap. Her little tongue is hanging out as if she just ran a marathon, and her bright blue eyes practically glow with happiness. Vala leisurely walks into the room, shaking her head at the pup's antics.

"It's almost like she knows what's going on," Vala tells me, sounding amused. "She's been excited ever since the others began preparing the chapel."

"Chapel?" I ask Vala, while rubbing the little hellhound between the ears in an attempt to calm her down.

"Yes," Vala says, coming to sit down beside my chair. "There's one at the end of the east wing of the house."

"Oh," I say, wondering if it's the same chapel my mother used for her own wedding.

It makes sense that it would be. Where else would she have gone?

"I think it's time to get dressed," Millie tells me. "You don't want to keep your man waiting at the altar any longer than you have to."

"I couldn't agree with you more, Millie," I say, placing Luna down on the floor and slipping off my robe as I walk over to the bed. "I think Malcolm and I have both waited long enough, and it feels like it's been forever instead of only a few hours since I last saw him."

"Love has a way of changing the pace of time in your mind," Millie agrees.

"Have you ever been in love, Millie?"

Millie smiles sadly as she holds out my dress for me to step into it.

"Hasn't everyone been in love at least once in their lives, my sweet?"

"Who was he?" I ask, slipping my arms through the one-shoulder dress.

Millie steps around me and pulls the fabric together in the back to zip it up.

"A young man who used to work for Master Malcolm back in the day," Millie tells me.

"What happened? Where is he now?"

"He went off-world to make his fortune, and never came back," Millie says.

"Why?"

"Apparently he found someone else he liked better," she replies, not sounding like she wants to discuss her lost love any further, and I certainly wasn't going to push the matter.

"Well, his loss was my gain," I tell her. "You've been like a mother to me, Millie. I know my life wouldn't have felt complete without you in it."

I can see Millie tear up at my heartfelt declaration. She sniffs and smooths out the front of the skirt for me.

"Pretty as a picture," she declares, taking a couple of steps back to see me fully. "I knew you would make a much prettier bride in this dress than your last one. You're wearing the dress this time, not the other way around."

I giggle because I remember quite well how ridiculous I looked in the monstrosity of a gown they forced me to wear to my coronation.

"Oh, Anna," Vala says, coming to stand beside Millie, "you look absolutely gorgeous!"

"Thank you," I tell them both. "Do you think it's time yet?"

"Very close," Millie says. "Jered told me to keep you in here until he came for you. Are you nervous?"

"Not one bit," I tell her truthfully. "I'm just excited. I feel like I've been waiting for this moment my whole life, Millie. It seems like it's taken forever to finally happen."

"Well, I'm just happy I'm here to see it. I do wish your father could have stayed for the ceremony."

"Me, too."

"Oh!" Millie says, obviously remembering something. "I completely forgot to tell you that Mr. Gray and Mr. Stokes will be attending the wedding. After they took Catherine and her doctor to the freighter, they came back to watch you get married."

"So Catherine's safe now?"

Millie nods. "She is on her way to Mars as we speak, from what I was told at least."

It brings me a sense of relief to know that Auggie's mother is well taken care of. I just hope she's able to recover from the torture Levi made her endure. His complete disregard and sadistic behavior towards her simply adds another reason to my growing list of them for me to kill him as soon as possible.

Millie helps me put on the jewelry the other Watchers gave me. I decide to slip off Jess' bracelet, since it doesn't really go with my wedding outfit, and safely tuck it into the drawer in my nightstand with my other Heavenly gifts.

Not long afterwards, someone knocks on my door.

"Anna, are you ready?"

I instantly recognize the voice as Jered's.

Before Millie can even move, I phase over to the door and open it.

I gasp in shock at the sight of Jered. I just stand there and stare dumbfounded at his face, trying to decide if it's actually Jered standing in front of me or some tortured imposter. Under any other circumstances, I knew Jered would look quite handsome in his tailored black tuxedo. He's holding a small bouquet made up of lavender and off-white roses tied together with a silky lavender ribbon, which I assume is meant for me. However, his appearance throws me completely off-kilter.

His entire face is a mass of black and blue bruises. One eye is completely swollen shut, and his lower lip is busted open straight down the middle. Yet Jered doesn't give the appearance of someone in excruciating pain. He stands before me smiling cheerfully, looking happier than I've ever seen him.

"Jered, what happened to you?" I ask in alarm, wondering if there was trouble here on Earth while I was visiting Heaven.

Jered's smile goes a little lopsided. "Oh, it's nothing."

"How can you say that?" I exclaim. "Your whole face looks like it was used as a punching bag!"

"It'll heal in a little while," he says, brushing it off as if it's not enough damage to worry about.

"But what happened?"

"The boys and I just had a little competition."

"A competition?" I ask, not finding this any better an answer. "What were you fighting over?"

"We all wanted to walk you down the aisle since Andre can't be here. Since we couldn't come to an agreement, we decided to make it a contest."

"Why would you fight over something like that?"

"Mostly just for fun, really," he says, a bit embarrassed that they used my wedding as an excuse to have an all-out wrestling match with one another. "I know. It's juvenile and we're old enough to know better, but sometimes it's just fun to have a good fight. Plus we couldn't come to an agreement. So, we decided a brawl would be the fairest way to decide."

I stare at Jered's swollen face for a moment before I lose myself to laughter.

"I'm sorry," I tell him. "But you make quite a picture standing there in your tuxedo with that face."

"Wait until you see the losers," Jered says with an awkward wink of his good eye, which does nothing but make me laugh harder.

"The next time you guys decide to fight each other, let me know," I tell him. "I would love to see how you all fight one another."

Jered bends at the waist. "As you wish, my lady."

I hope Jered remembers my request because seeing a group of angels fight has to be a sight not many people get to witness.

"So, Empress Anna Greco, are you ready to make Malcolm the happiest man on Earth?" Jered asks, holding out his arm for me to take.

"Absolutely," I tell him, accepting his escort to the chapel.

Once we reach the polished wood paneled doors that lead to the interior of the little chapel in Malcolm's home, Millie kisses me on the cheek.

"I'm so proud of you, Anna. You finally found the man you are meant to be with. There aren't many people who can say they did that in their lives, you know."

"Thanks, Mille."

"Now don't be nervous," Vala says to me, using her nose to push Luna through the crack between the double doors leading into the chapel.

"I'm not nervous," I tell her. "I'm more ready for this than anything in my life, Vala."

And it's true. I'm not sure if it's because my soul has been prepared for this union since it was created, or if it's because I knew Malcolm was meant to be mine the moment I saw him. The reason really doesn't matter. Either way, the love Malcolm and I share is an always and forever kind of love which not even death can sever.

Vala nods, letting me know she understands how I feel before she follows Luna into the sanctuary. Millie follows in after her and closes the doors.

As I wait for the doors to open, I simply try to concentrate on my breathing. What I told Vala was the truth. I'm not nervous, but my heart feels like it's about to race out of my chest from excitement.

The dulcet tones of the wedding march begin to play inside the chapel on a finely tuned piano. Brutus and Desmond, both dressed in nice tuxedos, soon swing the doors in front of me inward. They both manage to smile at me, even though their faces look about as swollen and bruised as Jered's does. I don't have much time to ponder the state of their physical well-being because my attention becomes wholly riveted by the man standing before God, waiting to make me his wife.

My lips stretch into a smile so wide my cheeks begin to hurt, but in a good way. It's not only because I'm overjoyed to see the man I love again. It's also because he kept his promise to me about wearing his formal Watcher outfit one day. He simply chose our wedding day to keep his word. The black feather cloak hangs from his shoulders like a ceremonial robe made for a king. His chest is bare, and his black leather pants are tightly-fitting, all the way down to his matching boots.

Malcolm's hands are resting on the shoulders of our son, who is standing in front of him dressed handsomely in a black tuxedo. Lucas' little face beams with joy when he sees me, and I faintly wonder why he's there with his father. I notice that he's holding a single white rose with both his little hands around its stem.

When I look back at Malcolm, I know the perfect brilliance of his smile has to be a match to my own. My heart skips a beat not only from the happiness I see on his face, but also because of the love I see in his eyes. It's a love that's only for me, and I silently promise to cherish the gift of him for the rest of my life.

Jered slowly begins to walk me down the aisle. His stride is even and steady, as it should be for such a momentous processional. Unfortunately, it's just not fast enough for me. I pick up my pace, which makes him have to pick his up too or be left behind. There are a few chuckles from the few family and friends we have present, but I don't care. All I can think about is getting to Malcolm as quickly as possible, and walking slowly is just wasting time better spent.

Malcolm's smile grows broader as he watches me race down the aisle towards him. Once I'm standing in front of him, he winks at me and whispers, "What took you so long?"

I giggle and roll my eyes at him. Our son soon captures my attention as he lifts the single white rose to me. I kneel down on one knee before Lucas and accept his gift, tucking it into the middle of my bouquet.

"Lucas would like to say something to you before we begin," Malcolm tells me, looking down at our little boy.

"What would you like to say to me, sweetie?" I ask.

Without saying anything, Lucas instantly wraps his little arms around my neck and hugs me tight. I wrap my free arm around him and close my eyes because I've never felt so much love in one place before. It's not only the love of my son and Malcolm that brings tears to my eyes, but also the love of our family and friends in attendance that makes me feel a happiness not many people get to experience in their lives.

Lucas pulls back from me and takes a deep breath before speaking.

"I know my dad is gonna promise you a bunch of stuff in a minute," he tells me. "And I wanted to make a promise to you too. I promise to be a son you can be proud of. I promise I'll always eat my vegetables, keep my room clean, take a bath every night, and never argue with you about anything. I promise I'll always protect you and the babies, and I promise I'll never give you a reason to regret becoming my mommy."

I pull my little man back into my arms and hug him so tightly he doesn't have any doubts about my feelings for him.

"I love you, Lucas," I tell him.

"I love you, too, Mommy," he says back, hugging me as tightly as he can before letting me go.

Malcolm ruffles Lucas' hair. "Ok, my turn. Why don't you go take your seat?"

Lucas holds his hands out.

"I can hold those for you," he says, looking at my bouquet.

I hand him my flowers, and he walks over to take his seat on the front pew by Millie.

Malcolm holds his hands out to me, and I place mine into his as we stand before God and all our family and friends.

"Today is a special day in the lives of Anna and Malcolm," God says as I keep my gaze solely fixed on Malcolm. "Who gives this woman to this man so that they may be wed before Me?"

"We all do," I hear everyone in attendance say, which makes me smile. I love knowing that those closest to us recognize that Malcolm and I are meant to be together.

"The meeting of two souls," God says, "and the sharing of one heart between two people is a sacred event. It is not something that should be entered into with any reservations. The commitment you make to one another tonight is a holy and eternal one. Do the two of you come to Me this evening with open hearts and a firm desire to be united as husband and wife?"

"Yes," Malcolm and I say in unison, neither of us doubting that we are meant to be of one mind, heart, and soul.

"Malcolm, please make your sacred vows to Anna and know that what you say is an everlasting promise to her."

Malcolm looks into my eyes with a seriousness that he doesn't display very often, and I know he is choosing his words to me carefully.

"Anna," he begins, squeezing my hands ever so gently, "you are my one true love. I gave up on ever finding happiness like this a long time ago. I never could have dreamt that I would be given the chance to experience a love like ours with a woman like you. I'm sorry for the way I treated you in the beginning, and find it a miracle that you still accepted my love even after everything I did to push you away. I didn't deserve your forgiveness for being such a dolt."

I hear someone cough, "Amen."

I know who it was without even looking. It was Jered. He witnessed first-hand Malcolm's efforts to push me away when we first met. It's something Jered will probably never let Malcolm forget.

Malcolm chooses to ignore Jered's agreement and continues his vows to me.

"I've been thankful every day afterwards that you love me enough to accept me even with all my flaws. During our life together I'm sure there will be days when I do things you disagree with, but I hope you'll always know that I only do them because my love for you is all- consuming. I will do everything within my power to protect you and our family from forces we can and cannot see. I promise to give all of myself to you and to our children so that you will always know and never doubt how much you're loved by me. I will stay true to you physically and emotionally so that you never second-guess my commitment. You are my one and only love, Anna. I will strive to be the man you need in your life from this day forward on Earth and in Heaven. Death will never separate us, because no matter where we are our souls will always find one another. I hide nothing of myself from you, and I hope you will continue to accept me as I am. I'm not a perfect man, simply one who loves you with every fiber of his being and will always stand by your side no matter what life throws at us. I will support you in any endeavor you attempt to undertake and help you succeed in all the goals you set for yourself and our family. I am yours, Anna, forever and always. Will you accept me, flaws and all, to be your husband?"

I nod my head. "Yes. With all my heart, Malcolm, yes."

"Anna," God says, "would you like to make your own vows to Malcolm as a declaration of your love for him?"

I nod my head again. "Yes, I would."

I look deeply into Malcolm's eyes and squeeze his hands even more firmly than he squeezed mine.

"Malcolm, you know from the first moment I saw you that I loved you. I think that was the first night I truly knew what it meant to be alive. Just being near you gives me strength to want to make a better future, not only for our family but also for the world we live in. There is nothing in my life that I would want to do without you by my side. You're not the only one in this relationship who has flaws. I'm stubborn and strong-willed. I'm certain that we'll end up having fights about things, but I want you to know that I promise to always listen to your side of the argument. I won't dismiss your words of wisdom out of thoughtlessness or pride. I will always respect your opinions and take to heart your concerns. The life I see for us is a bright one, filled with endless possibilities and at least a dozen children."

There are a few chuckles from our attentive audience at my promise.

"When I lived in Cirrus, I knew there would come a time in my life when I met the man who was made just for me to love. I have absolutely no doubts that you are that man. I'm so grateful that we found one another, but I don't believe our destinies would have allowed us to stay apart. We are meant to change the world for the better, Malcolm. I believe that with everything that I am. You are the caretaker of both my heart and my soul. Until I met you I never realized half of me was missing, and now I can't imagine my life without you in it. I vow to you that I will never take your love for granted. I will cherish it in this life and in the next. Malcolm, will you accept me as your wife and love me for who I am?"

I expect a simple yes, but Malcolm pulls me against him instead and kisses me soundly on the lips in front of God and all our friends.

God clear His throat to regain our attention, but Malcolm doesn't let me go. If anything, he deepens the kiss.

"Well," God says, sounding amused. "I suppose that's Malcolm's answer, everyone. Anna and Malcolm, may you stay strong in the love you have for one another during the times to come, and always find refuge in each other's arms when those times seem impossible. It is My great pleasure to now pronounce you husband and wife."

Our friends and family begin to clap their congratulations, but it's a distant sound inside my mind because my husband has captured my full attention.

As well he should...

CHAPTER TEN

As Malcolm continues to kiss me, I know I'm experiencing the happiest moment of my life. At least up until this point in our wedded bliss. I plan to experience many happy moments with my husband during our life together, and I promise to do my best to make each one happier than the last. But right now I'm simply enjoying this one perfect moment in time and basking in the love of my husband.

Malcolm eventually pulls his lips away from mine to look into my eyes.

"I love you," he whispers for only my ears.

I throw my arms around his neck and whisper back, "And I will always love you, Malcolm."

He wraps his arms around me and hugs me close. I've always felt that Malcolm was meant for me, but in that moment I feel he is truly mine and mine alone. Nothing will ever tear us apart, and I will keep true to the vows I made to him forever.

When we finally do pull away from each other, we face God together, hand in hand.

"Thank You for coming here to do this for us," I tell Him. "It wouldn't have felt real without You marrying us."

"It was my pleasure," He tells me, smiling proudly at us.

God's eyes narrow on me slightly. Just from that one look, I can tell He knows what happened in Hell. He knows about Helena, and He knows what she wants from me. Not that it comes as any great surprise that He would know. God is omnipotent, after all.

"Always be truthful with one another," He says, but His words sound more like a warning meant for me to hear. "Never keep secrets because they will always be found out in the end."

I nod, letting Him know I understand what He's really saying.

"No secrets," I promise.

"Am I missing half of the conversation here?" Malcolm asks, looking between his father and me.

I look over at Malcolm and smile reassuringly. "I'll tell you everything later. I promise. It's nothing to worry about right now."

"All right," Malcolm says, not sounding like he wants to wait that long for an explanation, but he recognizes now isn't the time for a serious talk.

"If you need Me," God says to us both, but seems to be giving me a meaningful look, "just pray for Me to come and I will. Right now, I believe your family and friends would like to celebrate your union with you. Enjoy this night together because it will only happen once in your lifetimes. I love you both. Please remember that."

God phases away.

I soon learn that Malcolm and the others spent the day not only decorating the chapel for the wedding, but also preparing a wedding feast for us to enjoy afterwards.

I almost feel guilty for not wanting to partake of the festivities they worked so diligently to provide for us that evening. All I really want to do is get my husband alone in either my bedroom or his. It doesn't matter to me which room it is as long as there's a bed. And to make matters worse, Malcolm is extremely attentive with his touches and casual kisses all through the meal as we sit and eat with our friends and family. To take my mind off the hand he has resting possessively on my thigh, I decide to talk to Gladson and Barlow about our little project of rebellion within the cloud cities.

"How is the video coming along?" I ask them, trying to ignore the way Malcolm's hand is gliding up and down my thigh underneath the table.

"It's almost ready to broadcast," Gladson tells me. "Barlow's brother was able to hack the satellites we needed to get the footage you wanted us to gather. Plus, he can use them to transmit the video when the time is right."

"So," Jered says, "this footage is of the conditions in which the down-worlders work and live, correct?"

"Yes," I tell him. "It's just as we discussed after that attempted ambush by Levi's men when we left Celeste's house. Gladson used his contacts to make sure we knew what needed to be shown from each cloud city's down-world. Hopefully, it'll wake some people up and make them force their leaders to change things."

"Don't get your hopes up too high," Barlow says to me, looking dubious about the plan. "People in the cloud cities might not care as much as you think they will. When you're not made to see the conditions those less fortunate than you live in every day, you forget about them. It's the 'out of sight, out of mind' syndrome. Not everyone has a sense of morality like you do, either, Anna. A lot of them will continue to think that as long as the poverty they see doesn't affect them personally, why should they care? It's the way the world has been for a very long time. I'm not sure a video is going to make those people change their nature."

"I understand that," I tell Barlow. "But at least it will get them talking. People like us will have to force change to happen. You at least need to make people aware of things first. This is only a first step, not a solution. It's going to take a lot of patience and time to alter the way things are done. I'm willing to dedicate my life to this endeavor. Are you?"

Barlow grins at me. "You know I would follow you anywhere, Anna. I believe in you, and I believe in what you're trying to do, for not only our down-world but all of the down-worlds. As long as you don't give up, neither will my people or I. We will do whatever it is you ask of us."

"And so will my faction," Gladson tells me. "The number of people joining our little rebellion continues to grow every day. People in some of the other cloud cities who want to become a part of the movement have even contacted me. Moreover, I agree with Anna. A revolution won't occur overnight. There are many complacent people in the world. But change has to begin somewhere, and I think we're making a good start."

"Ok, enough talk about politics," Malcolm says, standing from his chair beside me and walking to the back of mine to pull it out so I can stand, too. "This is my wedding night, and I would like to dance with my wife now, if you gentlemen don't mind."

Malcolm takes one of my hands and leads me out of the room. Everyone follows behind us and I know they're all there, but it's my husband I can't seem to keep my eyes off of.

"Have I said how much I like that outfit?" I ask him, eyeing him up and down appreciatively.

"Just as I thought," Malcolm says in feigned resignation, looking at me out of the corners of his eyes, "you only married me for my body."

"Not only," I tease, "but I'm certainly not going to complain about the package your heart and soul came in."

"Did you know we Watchers got to pick out our own bodies before we came to Earth?" Malcolm says.

"Job well done, then," I praise. "I don't think I could have picked a better one for you."

Malcolm stops in the hallway, in front of a pair of doors that lead to a room I haven't been inside yet.

"I want you to know," Malcolm tells me, "that everyone pitched in to decorate. Millie and Giles made the cake, though. Are you ready to see it?"

"See what exactly?"

Malcolm turns the knobs on the double doors and swings them inward.

I almost start to cry because of what's revealed to me. The ballroom is decorated with myriad twinkling white lights strewn across the ceiling. They provide the only illumination in the room, which has a hardwood floor and one long mirrored wall. The other long wall is made of glass, and faces the inner courtyard. Glass pedestals stand in intervals around the room with large white and lavender rose arrangements. A large, round, four- layer cake stands in the middle of the room on top of a white clothed table with lavender rose petals spiraling out from it.

I turn around to my friends and say, "It's beautiful. Thank you for making this night so special for us."

"It was our pleasure, my sweet," Millie says, dabbing at the tears threatening to escape from the corners of her eyes. "We're just happy to finally see this day come."

"Come on," Malcolm says, smiling as he retakes one of my hands, "dance with me."

When we walk into the room, I see a white grand piano in the far left corner. As Malcolm escorts me onto the dance floor, I see Daniel's wife, Linn, walk over to it and sit down. It's then I know who played the wedding march for the ceremony. Linn begins to play a slow song and Malcolm pulls me up against his torso. We begin to dance around the floor as a complete complement to one another.

"Have I ever told you how beautiful you are?" Malcolm says to me.

"Yes," I say, smiling, "but if you say it every day for the rest of our lives, I don't think I'll hear it enough."

Malcolm stares at me, and I see a shadow of disbelief enter his eyes.

"I still can't believe you're real and that you're mine," he tells me. "I feel like I'm in a dream meant for someone else. Everything about my life right now feels surreal; it's just too perfect. I never thought I would be given an opportunity at happiness like this, and I pray to my father that I don't screw it up. I know what I have, and I refuse to lose it for any reason, Anna. I'll never take your love for me for granted."

"Malcolm," I say, tightening my hold on his hand and shoulder, "I'm not sure I can wait much longer."

I can tell by the fire my words ignite in his eyes that I don't have to elaborate on what I'm referring to. I haven't exactly been shy about letting Malcolm know how much I want us to make love. The only reason I haven't phased us directly to his bedroom already is because of the people surrounding us. I wouldn't disrespect them in such a blatant way. I love them too much to be that self-absorbed. However, I do want my husband to know what is paramount in my mind in that moment, and that we shouldn't tarry here any longer than is absolutely necessary.

I want Malcolm. I want him finally free of the trappings of clothing and completely naked underneath my hands. I want to feel the full length of his warm flesh pressed against me. I desperately need him to make love to me physically just as much as I need him to love me with his whole heart.

"I'm not sure I can wait much longer either," Malcolm murmurs as his gaze lowers from my eyes to the rest of me, making my knees weaken from the heat of his own want.

"How long?" I ask, not needing to say more.

"Let's give them an hour," he says, pulling me in closer to his body. "Then you're all mine."

"I've been yours since the moment we met," I tell him, even though I know what he's really saying. "But I want you to make me yours in every way possible tonight, Malcolm. I don't want you to leave even an inch of me untouched by you."

"Don't worry," Malcolm assures me, wearing a rakish grin, "nothing will be."

After our dance is over, it seems like every man in attendance wants to dance with me at least once. At some point Linn is relieved of her piano duty, and Desmond and Daniel provide the music. Desmond plays a guitar while Daniel plays his violin.

While I'm dancing with Gladson, I notice Lucas and Bai playing chase in a corner of the room. It warms my heart to see my little man laughing with someone his own age. Once we've dealt with the threat of the princes, I hope he and Bai will have more opportunities to see one another and develop a lasting friendship. I smile at their play up until the moment Lucas catches Bai by gently grabbing one of her arms. I watch as Lucas suddenly stands completely still, and his eyes get a far-off look to them, just like the time he had a vision about the war to come.

"Excuse me," I tell Gladson, immediately leaving him to go to my son.

Bai sees me coming.

"What's wrong with him?" she asks, sounding worried about her friend.

Just as I kneel down beside Lucas, he seems to come out of his trance-like state. He lets go of Bai's arm and looks over at me.

"Are you all right?" I ask him, praying he didn't see something horrific this time.

He nods his head and looks back at Bai.

"I'm sorry," he tells her. "Did I hurt you?"

Bai shakes her head. "No. I'm fine."

"Lucas," I say, drawing his attention back to me. "What did you see?"

Lucas looks over at Bai, like he's not sure he wants her to hear what he has to say. Apparently he decides he doesn't, because he leans over to whisper in my ear.

"I saw my future," he says to me.

"What did you see?" I whisper back.

"I saw me marrying Bai."

I feel surprised by this news for a moment but then realize it makes perfect sense. If I'm successful in having the two of them spend more time together as they grow up, it stands to reason that they might fall in love with one another.

"We should probably keep that to ourselves for now," I tell him.

Lucas leans back and nods his head in agreement. He looks over at a confused Bai and holds out his hand to her.

"Would you like some cake, Bai?" he asks her.

"Sure," Bai says, grabbing Lucas' hand and dragging him towards the cake.

I think Lucas' offer of cake meant more to him than Bai understood. I can't stop myself from smiling as the two of them make their way towards the wedding cake in the middle of the room.

"I suppose it's time to cut the cake," Malcolm says, coming to stand beside me.

"It looks that way," I say, but something catches my eyes through the windows that face out towards the courtyard.

Lucifer is standing in front of the bench, watching me. Snow is falling outside, and I faintly wonder if he's brought his own personal Hell with him to my wedding, but know it's simply wintertime in the down-world.

"I need to go out there for a moment," I tell Malcolm, keeping my eyes on Lucifer to make sure he doesn't phase away before I have a chance to speak with him. "Could you ask the guys to play another song for me?"

"Take this," Malcolm says.

I chance a glance at my husband, and see him take his feather cloak off and place it over my shoulders.

"It'll at least keep you warm," Malcolm tells me. I can tell by the tone of his voice that he doesn't want me going out to talk to Lucifer. Nevertheless, he doesn't make an attempt to stop me from going.

"I'll be right back," I tell Malcolm, leaning in to kiss him on the lips just before I phase outside to speak to my guest.

"You missed the ceremony," I tell Lucifer as I stand in front of him.

"Like I said earlier," Lucifer says, "I wasn't strong enough to watch you ruin your life."

"Malcolm will not ruin my life. He is my life."

"I have no faith in him," Lucifer replies, not bothering to mince his words. "I hope for your sake that I'm wrong, Anna."

"You are," I tell him without any doubt.

I hear the music I requested begin to play inside the house.

"I believe it's customary for the father to dance with his daughter on her wedding day," I say to Lucifer. "Will you dance with me?"

Lucifer looks surprised by my request.

"I haven't been much of a father to you, Anna. I don't deserve the honor. Andre should be the one you dance with."

"He isn't here," I say. "And even if he were I would want a dance with both of you. You haven't been in my life for very long, but I've come to care about you, and I think you care about me, too. Millie told me about your yearly visits to me on my birthdays when I was younger."

"She shouldn't have told you that," Lucifer grumbles, looking uncomfortable that I know this information.

"Why did you stop?" I ask, needing to know what happened to make him end his yearly visits.

Lucifer shakes his head. "I couldn't stand to look at you anymore."

His words cut like a knife against the inner chambers of my heart, but from the look on his face I can tell the words hurt him just as much to say.

"Why?" I whisper, scared to hear the answer but needing to know.

Lucifer looks at me, and a silence filled with sadness on both our parts lingers between us.

Finally, he says, "You began to look too much like Amalie. It started to hurt to look at you because all I could think about were all the happy times she and I should have had with you."

I hold my hand out to Lucifer. "Then don't miss any more. It's not too late. You can still be a part of my life if you want. You can still be a father to me.

Dance with your daughter on her wedding day, and let's make a memory we can both cherish."

Lucifer looks down at my hand, and I fear he won't take it. I begin to wonder if this is how Jess felt when she offered him his crown and a chance for his father's forgiveness. I wasn't exactly offering him redemption for his soul, but I was offering him a chance to make right one of the things he did wrong in his life. I was offering him a chance to be a part of my family, to be a father to me. But would he take it, or would he walk away from me again?

I wait for what seems like forever. I keep my hand outstretched to Lucifer, praying that he takes it and accepts his place in my life.

Slowly, I see him raise his right hand. I realize I'm holding my breath, waiting to see if he changes his mind at the last minute.

He doesn't.

I firmly grab hold of his hand and move in closer to him. We begin to sway to the music still playing inside the ballroom.

"I haven't danced in years," Lucifer warns me, even though his movements are sure-footed.

"You're doing fine," I tell him, letting him lead the dance.

"Don't take this as my approval of your marriage." Lucifer is quick to say, as if making sure I understand that fact.

"I wouldn't dare think you were that wishy-washy in your opinions," I assure him.

Lucifer grins and lets out a half-laugh. "Good. I don't want you to think I'm someone who changes his mind easily."

"I would never associate you with someone who was indecisive. However, I do hope in time you come to understand Malcolm better. I would like for the children I have with him to have a relationship with their grandfather."

"Grandchildren." Lucifer says the word like it never even occurred to him that I would one day have children with Malcolm. "I hope you're not planning to have them anytime soon."

"As soon as possible," I tell him truthfully. "After the seals are safely back in Heaven, I don't see any point in waiting."

Lucifer doesn't say anything, but I see his jaw muscles tighten like he's holding back some words of advice I probably wouldn't appreciate.

The music inside the house comes to an end. Lucifer lets go of me and takes a step back.

"You should probably return to your friends," he tells me. "I do wish you the best, Anna. I just have a hard time believing Malcolm can be the man you deserve."

"He's the man I love," I tell him. "And I want you to know that you are welcome in our home anytime you want."

Lucifer looks surprised by my offer. "I don't think Malcolm will appreciate that."

"He understands how important you're becoming to me."

"Why?"

It's my turn to look surprised by a question. "Why? Because you're my father. I would like to get to know you better."

"Not many people would want that."

"No one else is your child."

Lucifer doesn't seem to have a comeback for my response.

"I hope you enjoy the rest of your party," he tells me. "And... I'll see you soon."

Lucifer phases away, and Malcolm phases in as if he was simply waiting for Lucifer to leave.

"How did it go?" Malcolm asks.

"He still hates you, but at least he danced with me." I sigh. "That was a step in the right direction, I think."

"I wish you didn't feel a need for me and Lucifer to form an amicable relationship with one another, Anna," Malcolm says gently. "It's never going to happen. Too much has passed between us for either of us to simply forget we hate each other."

"I know. I understand that. But I want a relationship with him, Malcolm. You won't do anything to try to prevent me from having one, will you?"

"No," Malcolm says. "I might not think it's the healthiest thing in the world, but I can see how much it means to you. I would never try to stop you from doing something your heart needs. The only reason I would is if he started taking advantage of you or hurt you in some way. I won't stand by and hold my tongue if I think he's damaging you emotionally, Anna."

"He won't," I say confidently. "I think he wants to know me better, too."

Malcolm holds his hands out to me, and I place mine into his.

"Can we stop talking about Lucifer and go back inside to eat some cake?" Malcolm says, drawing me in closer to him. "And after all of that is done, maybe we can go up to our room so I can have my real dessert. I'm sure your skin will taste much sweeter than any confection."

"Well, if you would just take me to bed already, you could find out just how sweet I taste," I tease.

"Never fear, my love," Malcolm says, lowering his head to mine. "I intend to take my time and explore every lovely part of you until you beg me to stop."

"I don't beg," I tell him as his lips hover over mine.

"Is that a challenge?" Malcolm says, his eyes lighting up with excitement.

"If you want it to be," I say. "All I know is that I want us to finally break down that wall between us. Our bodies are the only things that we haven't shared with one another completely. Now that we're married, there's nothing preventing us from enjoying each other in the most intimate way two people can."

"Then let's go eat some cake and make our goodnights," Malcolm says, pulling back from me. "I would like for you to get at least a couple of hours of sleep tonight."

"It's not that late," I tell him with a smile. "How long does making love usually take?"

Malcolm's serious face reappears. "This will be your first time, Anna. I plan to take things slowly and make it as enjoyable as I can for you. But there will be some discomfort I won't be able to prevent. All I can do is make it as easy for you as I can by bringing you more pleasure than pain. There are ways to make it less uncomfortable, but in the end you will end up feeling it. I just want to make sure the experience is worth the agony."

"I can take pain," I tell him. "And Malcolm," this time it's my turn to be completely serious, "don't you dare hold anything back from me tonight because you're worried you'll hurt me. Holding yourself back from me would hurt me even more."

"I won't hold back," he promises me. "I'll give you all of me tonight, Anna. Everything."

"Then let's go back inside and do what needs to be done so we can start this long love- making session you have planned."

"Your wish is my command," Malcolm says with a grin as he phases us back inside the ballroom.

I silently pray I can make it through the next few minutes, and will my hormones to stay under control for just a little while longer.

CHAPTER ELEVEN

Unfortunately, we have to delay the cutting of the cake because everyone seems to want to give a toast to wish us well and congratulate us on our marriage. I try my best to be gracious. I really do. But sometimes when you want something done you have to take matters into your own hands, literally.

When we actually do get around to cutting the cake and begin to feed it to one another, *somehow* the laws of gravity intervene. The large piece I attempt to feed Malcolm slips over the tips of my fingers. It tumbles down his chest, makes a mess of his leather pants and lands, icing side down, on top of his right boot.

"Oh, I'm so sorry," I say, not meaning a word of it. Malcolm grins, which tells me he's on to my hastily implemented scheme. "We should probably clean that up before it ruins your outfit."

I turn to our guests and see the mark of amusement on most everyone's face. I instantly know my attempt at subterfuge isn't fooling anyone.

"Yes, you really should, my sweet," Millie agrees with a conspiratorial wink. "Or the leather will be ruined forever."

"Oh yes," Linn agrees, smiling at me. Although, I am quite positive she's holding back a laugh. "You need to get those clothes off right away. You know... before they get stained."

"Those were my exact thoughts, too, ladies. I'm so happy to hear you agree with me." I look at the rest of our guests. "Malcolm and I would like to thank you all for making our wedding and the rest of this evening one we will always remember. Now, if you'll excuse us, I believe I have some wifely duties that I need to attend to."

I place the palm of my right hand over Malcolm's heart and phase us directly to the bathroom attached to his bedroom.

"I don't think they suspected a thing," Malcolm teases as he chuckles about my non-subtle ruse to finally get him alone.

"At this moment, I really don't care," I say, throwing my arms around Malcolm's neck and kissing him thoroughly to finally assuage at least a small portion of my pent-up desires for him.

Malcolm wraps his arms fully around my waist and holds me close. Yet he doesn't make a move to help me remove my clothing. I release his lips from mine and look at him in total bewilderment.

"Is something wrong?" I ask, breathless from the impact of our kiss.

"No, my love, nothing's wrong," he says, smiling down at me with such tenderness it makes my heart melt inside my chest.

"Then why am I still wearing this dress?"

Malcolm chuckles again as his lips stretch into a pleased smile at my blatant eagerness to start our evening together as soon as possible.

"Like I told you earlier," he says, kissing my lips ever so lightly, "I want to take things slow tonight."

I take a deep breath and gradually let it out, trying my best to rein in my almost uncontrollable passion for the man holding me.

I bring my arms down from around his neck and take a step back from him.

"Then tell me what you want me to do next," I say. "I get the impression you have everything about tonight all planned out."

"I *have* been thinking about it for quite some time," Malcolm admits with a devilish grin. He raises his right hand and gently cups the left side of my face. "I laid out something for you to wear. It's on my bed. Why don't you go put it on while I clean the cake off my clothes?"

"Sorry about dirtying you up a bit," I say sheepishly, looking at the trail of white icing Malcolm is wearing. "I just couldn't think of a better way to conjure up a believable excuse for us to leave our own party."

"Don't be sorry," Malcolm murmurs. "If you hadn't done something when you did, I would have."

I smile at his statement, because it completely erases the guilt I feel about my ploy to get us away from our party sooner rather than later. I reach out a hand to touch his chest again because I can't seem to control my need to be physically connected to him. I run my index finger through the streak of icing on his chest and bring it to my lips to taste the sweet confection.

Malcolm watches me as I suck the icing off my finger, and I see his Adam's apple bob up and down as he swallows hard. I begin to wonder what his reaction would be to me eating the rest of the icing directly off his chest. I take a step closer to Malcolm, forcing him to drop his hand away from my face as I begin to lower my mouth to the streak of white marring his otherwise perfect skin. I glance up into his eyes before I begin, and see that he's watching me closely as he remains perfectly still. I take that as my cue to follow through with my desires. I know then that whatever I want, whatever I need to happen that night, will be given to me by Malcolm.

As I begin to lick off the rest of the icing, Malcolm's breathing becomes more labored. I lightly stroke my tongue against him, tasting the saltiness of his skin underneath the sweetness of the icing. I decide to be very thorough, and take my time cleaning every single grain of sugar off because I can't seem to get enough of Malcolm and all I know is that I want more. I want everything.

Once I've completed the task to my satisfaction, I look back up into my husband's face and see his own pent-up desires for me fully exposed in the heat of his gaze. Malcolm grabs hold of me and brings me fully up against him, ravishing my mouth with his lips and tongue in such a way that I'm left with no doubt that he wants me just as much as I want him. When he finally does pull himself away from me, neither of us is breathing steadily, and I'm certain if he let me go at that moment I would fall to my knees.

"I've never wanted anyone like I want you right now, Anna," Malcolm tells me, his voice raw with desire. I can feel his arms tremble as he controls his need to have me.

"Then take me, Malcolm," I almost beg because my longing to have him is just as great, if not more so. I feel like I've waited my whole life for this moment. It's not just the sharing of our bodies that excites me, but the ability to finally show in actions and not just in words how much I love the man I've pledged my heart, body, and soul to. I want him to know just how much he's loved and that everything in his life up to this point, good and bad, was meant to happen. If one thing had been changed, it wasn't outside the realm of possibility that we might not have ever met.

Malcolm leans forward and kisses me on the forehead lovingly, making me sigh in disappointment. It's a sure sign that he isn't going to throw caution to the wind and simply throw me down on the bathroom floor to have his way with me. He intends to keep to his original plan of making my first experience as gentle and pleasurable as he can make it.

"Why don't you go put on what I left for you on my bed?" Malcolm suggests. "I'll clean up and be out shortly."

I sigh but don't say anything, just phase to the bedroom as he requested.

Lying on the thick red velvet comforter is a white negligee with thin spaghetti straps and a low-cut V-neckline with a lacy edge. The material looks extremely thin, and I can't imagine that it will leave much to the imagination.

I quickly shed my wedding dress, being careful to lay it out on a nearby chair. I wouldn't disrespect Millie's gift to me by simply letting it lie on the floor in a crumpled heap. I slip on the nightgown and find that it only reaches down to just above my knees. I take out the pin in my hair and let the heavy mass of curls fall freely past my shoulders. I also unhook the earrings and lay them on the nightstand beside the bed.

Malcolm comes out of the bathroom shortly after, dressed in his dark green bathrobe. He walks over to the fireplace and stands in front of it. The red-orange glow from the flames accentuates the angles of his face as light fights shadow. The beauty of my husband completely takes my breath away, and I almost feel unworthy to have a man like him love me. Almost.

His eyes find mine easily in the near-dark of the room, and he makes one simple, softly-spoken request.

"Come to me, Anna."

I hesitate.

I don't hesitate because I don't want to go to Malcolm, that's not it at all. I hesitate because I suddenly feel the flutter of nervous butterflies inside my stomach. This is it. This is the moment I've been waiting so long for. It's the first time since we met that I feel any trepidation in making love with Malcolm. It's only then that I realize his decision to make our first time together an unhurried experience for me was extremely wise. He probably knew I would eventually feel this uncertainty, and wanted to walk me through it gradually, not rush me along just to satiate his own burning desires. I knew I would be relying on his skills that night.

For a fleeting moment I imagine the rest of our lives together, and see a multitude of moments such as this one. Each flash of our imagined future together only confirms for me that we were always meant to be. Neither of our lives would have been made whole without the other one.

I pluck up my courage and walk over to Malcolm, feeling my body become flushed with excitement and nervous anticipation. As I stand in front of him, I feel uncertain about what to do next and simply put my faith and trust in him to guide me through with a gentle hand.

Malcolm doesn't touch me right away. Instead he walks around to the back of me, gingerly pulling my hair off my shoulders, better exposing my neck.

I feel him undo the latch of my necklace and remove it from around my throat, only to replace it with another necklace.

I reach up a hand and feel the braided silk choker that has a star-encrusted with gems dangling from the middle.

"I know we haven't exactly talked about it," Malcolm says. "But I thought it would be prudent to delay having children until your mission is complete."

"I agree," I tell him. "There's no way of knowing what the seals would do to them."

"This necklace was made by JoJo. She's also the one who made your outfit. As long as you wear it, you won't get pregnant."

"She sounds like she was a very resourceful person to have around."

"She was," Malcolm says, letting his fingers linger around my neck after latching the necklace's catch. "I'll tell you more about her sometime, but not right now."

The instant I feel Malcolm's warm lips press against the side of my throat, my eyes close of their own accord. The unhurried movement of his lips and tongue produce a pleasurable torment, heightening my need to have him. Malcolm gently sucks the sensitive flesh where my neck and shoulder meet, making every inch of my body come alive and crave more. As he slowly works his mouth up the side of my neck, I sigh my contentment and simply wonder what will happen next.

"Anna," Malcolm whispers in my ear, tugging at my earlobe with his teeth, "open your eyes, my love."

"Why?" I ask, instantly abiding by his request. I'm only curious about his answer. I would never second-guess Malcolm's motives.

"Because I want you to watch everything I do to your body," he whispers. "I want you to see how much pleasure it gives me to make you feel how much I love you, how much I want you."

Malcolm splays his fingers against the small of my back, spanning its width. He slowly glides his hands over the thin veil of fabric, reaching around to the front of me until they come to rest on my abdomen. Malcolm angles his hands upward until each breast is cupped within the warmth of his palms. He gently teases my nipples with the tips of his fingers, sending tiny sparks of electricity throughout my body with each new twist and tug.

Malcolm brings his body firmly up against mine from behind as he continues to tease my breasts with his hands. I gasp slightly when I feel the proof of his desire push itself into my lower back. I feel a moment of unease as I sense the fullness of him, realizing just how well-endowed Malcolm is compared to how small I am.

"Are you all right?" Malcolm asks, returning his lips to the side of my neck. "Your heart's racing."

"How can my heart not race when you make love to me?" I ask, leaning even further back against him and allowing his loving manipulation of my body to wipe away any nervousness I might feel.

"If you need me to stop at any time," he breathes against my neck, "I will, Anna. You just have to tell me."

"Don't you dare stop," I say, feeling my heart ache with just the thought of Malcolm not making love to me that night. "I've waited for this moment for far too long. I trust you with my heart and my body, Malcolm."

One of Malcolm's hands leaves the breast it holds to slide down past the flat plane of my stomach. I feel his fingers work to gather the material of my nightgown until his hand is able to go beyond the hem and caress a part of me that no one, besides myself, has ever touched. A gasp parts my lips as Malcolm slides his fingers into the folds and gently coaxes the core of me into a frenzy of sensations.

"Malcolm," I moan repeatedly as the sensations his hands produce threaten to overtake me. I turn my head to the side, needing to taste the sweetness of his mouth with mine as he slowly brings my body to its boiling point. I begin to ache from the pleasure of it all and my legs tremble uncontrollably, threatening to lose their strength.

Malcolm must sense the brink to which his careful ministrations have brought me because he steps back from me, pulling his hands away from my body. I feel him run one hand down my left arm until our fingers intertwine.

He looks at me and a small smile appears on his face. In a way, he almost looks like this is his first time, too, and perhaps it is in a way. Our emotional connection to one another is overpowering by itself. What will happen when we're able to finally connect physically?

I eagerly follow him over to the bed, knowing he'll finish what he started by the fireplace and not leave me with this burning need deep inside. Once we're standing beside the bed, he lets go of my hand to pull down the comforter and top sheet. He turns to me and hooks his index fingers underneath the straps of my nightgown. He pulls them to the side, past my shoulders, and lets the gown float to the floor, leaving me completely naked to his gaze.

"Do you know how gorgeous you are?" Malcolm asks, his eyes not just looking at my body with lust but also with reverence.

"I know I'm pretty," I admit, not wanting to sound conceited about my physical attributes, but not wanting to act unnecessarily naïve about them either.

Malcolm shakes his head. "No. You're not just pretty, Anna." He raises his gaze to mine as if to make sure I hear his next words clearly. "And it's not just your physical beauty that makes you gorgeous to me. I love your body, but it's your spirit that completely floors me every time I look at you. I've never met anyone like you, and I doubt I ever will again in my lifetime. There isn't one thing about you that I don't love completely. And I intend to show you just how great my love for you is tonight."

Malcolm moves his hands to the tie of his robe, but I place a hand on top of them to stop their movements.

"Let me do it," I say, feeling a need to be a participant in tonight's events and not allow Malcolm to do all of the work.

Malcolm drops his hands and simply watches me.

I tug at the knot of his robe tie and loosen it easily with my fingers. The robe hangs open in the front, providing me an excellent view of his naked, muscular form, but my full attention becomes riveted by the center of him, and I can't help but openly stare. I'm curious to know more about that part of his body. I reach out a tentative hand but stop just short of caressing him.

"Touch me, Anna," Malcolm urges. "I want you to know all of me."

I hesitate for a moment but my intense desire to learn everything there is to know about Malcolm wins out. I wrap my fingers around the length of him, marveling at how silky his skin feels, yet how rock-hard the blood-engorged organ is in my hand. I glide my fingers up and down his shaft, feeling him grow impossibly fuller. Malcolm gently stops my movements by placing one of his hands over mine.

"I'm sorry," he says in a husky voice. "I need you to stop doing that or this evening might not last as long as I would like."

I immediately unwrap my fingers from around him.

"I definitely don't want it to end just yet," I say with certainty.

Malcolm grins. "Neither do I, my love."

Malcolm pulls his robe completely off and lets it fall to the floor behind him. In one swift movement, he picks me up and lays me down in the middle of the bed. He lies down beside me sliding one of his legs in between mine and leaning over to continue plundering my mouth with gentle caresses of his lips and tongue. He glides one of his hands from my chest to my hips in one leisurely motion, igniting the flesh he touches along the way.

Without removing his lips from mine, Malcolm slides into a new position until his legs are straddling my hips. He holds his torso up with his arms on either side of me, and I feel the warmth of him rest between my thighs. Malcolm's lips say a gentle goodbye to mine as they begin their leisurely adventure over territory they have not yet had the opportunity to lay claim to. I try to contain the growing need I feel between my legs and simply enjoy the slow, pleasurable torture Malcolm's warm mouth is putting my body through. After his lips make a wet path from the base of my throat to my chest, I watch him as he gently squeezes each of my breasts with his large hands. He slides his mouth over one ample mound to lavish its nipple with his undivided attention, using his tongue and teeth expertly for a long while before giving its twin the same amount of adoration.

Malcolm slides his hands along the sides of my body as he scoots himself further down the bed. His mouth makes a trail from my breasts to across my abdomen. When his mouth reaches the junction of my thighs, I take in a sharp breath of anticipation and continue to watch him even as his head dips below my line of sight.

The first flick of his tongue against me makes me squirm, and Malcolm gently takes hold of my hips to help keep me centered. As his lips and tongue weave their magic spell over me, I feel the pleasure of Malcolm's efforts build a fire that isn't meant to be contained. I call out his name when the sensation becomes too much to bear, and feel a warm glow of pleasure wash over me like a tidal wave crashing against a rocky shore. Malcolm's mouth lingers where it is, slowly bringing me back down to Earth. He kisses the soft flesh on the inside of my thighs before unhurriedly kissing his way back up to my lips. His fingers soon take the place of where his mouth had been, and he slides one inside me as if testing to see if I'm ready for him. To me, it simply feels like a tease of what's to come.

I pull my lips away from his to speak.

"Malcolm," I say, his name sounding more like a plea than me simply saying his name, "I want you."

I don't have to tell him what it is I want. He already knows what has to be done to satisfy what I most desire to have from him. From the almost drugged look in his eyes, I can tell he has his own desires that need to be met. I feel excited by the thought of him finding his own pleasure inside me and finally ending the torture we've both been living through.

Malcolm straddles my hips once again. With his initial entry into my body, I can feel an impossible stretching take place. He holds back from pushing his entire length in, only introducing the tip of himself to me. He leans down to kiss my mouth once again as he slides his fingers over my already sensitive core, and slowly builds my need for him even more. I feel him slowly push into me a little further, but he stops himself once again, allowing my form precious time to stretch and accept him. I can only imagine the restraint he's using to slowly introduce himself to my body, allowing it time to adjust to him.

I feel a slight ache when Malcolm pushes into me even further. He breaks the contact of our lips, lifting his head slightly until our eyes meet.

The worry on his face tells me the next push will cause me pain and that he would much rather take the sting of what's about to happen onto himself, if such a thing were possible.

I simply bring his mouth back down to mine and wrap my legs around his waist, telling him with actions and not words that I'm ready to accept him. I know any discomfort I might feel in the beginning will be well worth it in the end.

Malcolm moans against my mouth as his kisses become more aggressive. My willingness to accept what will come next seems to excite him to a fever pitch as his fingers feverishly work their magic against me. Just as a wave of pleasure from his delicate strumming of my body washes over me, I feel Malcolm push past the barrier marking my sexual purity, causing an intense agony. I close my eyes as the throbbing ache overwhelms me. Tears born solely from this pain fall unhindered from the corners of my eyes.

Malcolm lightly kisses each of my cheeks before kissing away my trail of tears.

"Anna..." he whispers, sounding upset that he's caused a pain we both knew would have to happen.

I force myself to open my eyes because I don't want the man I love to feel any guilt about what he just did. There is no one else in the world who I would have wanted to share this experience with, and I feel lucky to have someone so gentle and caring to walk me through it.

I silently reassure him that I'm all right by lifting a hand and wrapping my fingers around the back of his neck, pulling his lips back down to mine. I wrap my legs even tighter around his waist, knowing he'll realize what it is I want to happen next.

Malcolm understands my silent request and begins to move his hips rhythmically against mine. His movements are slow at first but soon pick up in speed and intensity. With each hard thrust, I feel him excite something within me that I never even knew existed until that moment. As Malcolm continues to rub himself against this sensitive bundle of nerves, I feel an impossible eruption of sensations. There comes a point when I have to pull my mouth away from his just to draw in enough air to survive the pleasure.

Malcolm's breathing becomes ragged as his movements increase in their intensity. With each thrust he makes a warm wave of pleasure washes over my body, making the center of my being feel hot and raw with need. Just when I think it isn't possible to experience more bliss, I feel something inside me shatter, causing an explosion of ecstasy so great I feel as if the world itself has just come apart around us. I faintly hear Malcolm growl out my name as he reaches his own powerful release.

My body welcomes the warmth of him inside me with open arms, as if it's been patiently waiting all this time just for him. I close my eyes, accepting the gift from his body as my own slowly floats back down to Earth, like a feather on a warm summer breeze. I instantly feel a completeness that I've never experienced before. It's almost like I was unknowingly missing a part of myself that has finally found its way home.

Malcolm withdraws from my body and lies down beside me, lovingly pulling me into the warmth of his arms. I wrap my own arms around his neck and begin to cry again, but this time the tears are simply evidence of a happiness so pure words simply aren't enough.

CHAPTER TWELVE

"How do you feel?" Malcolm asks as I lay in his arms, luxuriating in the afterglow of our lovemaking.

"Complete," I sigh, snuggling the side of my face against his chest and tightening my hold around his torso.

"Well, I'm glad I could complete you," Malcolm teases, and I feel the rumble of his own amusement inside his chest.

Malcolm places an index finger underneath my chin, gently prodding me to lift my head and look at him. When I do, I can't prevent myself from sliding up and kissing his lips. Malcolm plunges his hands into my hair, cradling my head and rolling me over onto my back with his hips strategically positioned between my thighs.

I pull my lips away from his in surprise.

"I thought it would take you more time to recover," I say, feeling the hard proof of his arousal pushing against me.

"Obviously not," he says, with a rakish grin.

"I'm not complaining," I quickly tell him. "I just didn't expect you to be ready again so soon."

Malcolm leans down and kisses me lightly on the lips.

"First things first," he says rising off me and standing up from the bed. "Stay in bed for a moment. I'll be right back."

I watch him as he walks toward the bathroom and sigh in great disappointment when he enters it, ending my own private display of a naked Malcolm. I pull the top sheet up over me and curl up in its soft comfort with a contented smile on my face. Making love with Malcolm was everything I could have hoped for and more. His gentle nature with me was simply further proof of how much he loved me.

I could hear the flow of water in the bathroom, making me wonder why Malcolm would be taking a bath at a time like this. He soon returns to the bedroom, providing me with another generous opportunity to blatantly admire his physique. His natural beauty would be a feast for any woman's eyes, but as his wife I feel proud to be able to think of him as belonging only to me.

When he reaches the side of the bed, he holds out a hand for me to take.

"Come with me, my love," he says. "Let's take a bath together."

He doesn't have to suggest such a thing to me twice. I eagerly throw off the sheet and scoot over to the side of the bed. I take his offered hand and stand up. After I'm on my feet, I wince from a slight ache which I can only attribute to our lovemaking.

Malcolm lifts me easily in his arms, and I don't protest because my legs do feel a little wobbly. When we reach the bathroom, Malcolm gently lowers me into the tub full of warm water. I expect him to immediately join me, but he doesn't. Instead, he dries his arms off with a nearby towel.

"Where are you going?" I ask, wondering about his curious behavior.

"I need to change the sheets on the bed," he tells me.

"The sheets?" I ask.

"There's a little blood on them," he replies, tossing the towel in his hands onto a nearby chair. He leans down and kisses me on the lips. "I won't be long."

I watch him walk out of the room to take care of the proof of my lost virginity and marvel at his thoughtfulness. Not only did he want to make the bed comfortable for the rest of our night together, but I think he also knew a warm soak would ease the ache I feel between my legs. I toss my hair over the end of the tub so it doesn't get wet as I lay back and let my body delight in the soothing heat of the water.

Malcolm is true to his word, and returns to me a few short minutes later. I watch him walk over to the sink and pull out a drawer in the vanity. He picks something up out of it and shuts the drawer before walking behind me. Malcolm gathers my hair in one hand, and I feel him tie it back with something, then lift it through what must be a ponytail holder to loop it and make a small bun.

"Scoot up a bit, my love," Malcolm tells me.

I do as asked and he steps into the tub behind me. He sits down and gathers me into his arms until my back is resting against his chest. I hear him sigh in contentment and can't help but smile happily at the sound.

"Is the water helping the pain?" he asks me, sliding both his hands across my stomach, underneath the water to hold me close.

"It doesn't really hurt that much," I tell him. "It just aches a bit."

"We don't have to do anything else tonight if you're in pain," he says understandingly. "I'm perfectly fine with just holding you, as long as you're naked, of course."

I rest my hands on top of Malcolm's in the water. I push one down between my legs and lift the other one up to cup a breast.

"I'm not fine with just holding," I tell him, in no uncertain terms.

Malcolm's fingers begin to move in the strategic positions I've placed them, soon making my body ache in a very different way.

"I need more," I moan to him. "Please, Malcolm."

"Sit up for a moment," he instructs, removing his hands from me.

I do as asked and Malcolm phases to the other side of the tub to position himself in front of me.

"Lie back," he tells me as he leans forward to partially rest on top of me. He places one hand on the side of the tub to prop himself up with and the other travels underneath my bottom to keep me from sliding as he enters me easily, unobstructed this time.

As Malcolm makes love to me for only the second time in our married life, I hold onto his shoulders as he pleasures my body with his, and brings us both past the point of no return. Afterwards, I hold onto him and feel my body tremble against his.

"Are you all right?" Malcolm asks worried.

I nod my head against his shoulder.

"Yes. I'm just trying to believe this is real and not a dream."

"If it is a dream, I hope I never wake up from it," Malcolm says fervently, kissing my shoulder.

I pull back and hold Malcolm's face between my hands, kissing his lips tenderly.

"I want you to do something for me," I murmur against his mouth.

"Anything," he replies.

"Let's get out of this tub and go back to bed first."

I don't have to make my request twice. Malcolm rises from the tub, looking like a god rising from the depths of an ocean as the water clings to his skin, making it glisten. He helps me out of the water and uses the towel he dried off with earlier to soak up the water from my body.

He quickly dries himself off and then takes one of my hands into his as we walk back to the bedroom together.

"What is it that you want me to do?" Malcolm asks, sounding intrigued by my vague request.

"Lie down on the bed," I tell him, lifting my hands to the makeshift bun my hair is in to make sure it's still secure.

Malcolm does as I ask, watching me closely and with open curiosity.

I crawl onto the fresh linens and sit beside him.

"You've been doing far too much of the work this evening. I may be new to all this, but I want to learn how to pleasure you, too," I tell him, running one hand over his thigh. "And I want you to tell me what you like and if I do something that you don't like."

"I'm not sure there's much you could do that I wouldn't like," Malcolm says hoarsely as he watches me.

I smile and move to kneel between Malcolm's legs. When I take hold of him, I hear him groan in pleasure just from that simple act.

"Just let me know if I do something you *don't* like then," I tell him. "I'm sure your responses to my touch will reassure me if I'm doing it right."

As I begin my own private lessons on how to pleasure my husband, I realize I may not have known exactly what I was doing, but I don't hear any complaints from Malcolm while I learn from him for the rest of the night.

When I wake up the next morning, I'm a little disoriented by my surroundings until I feel Malcolm's warm, steady breath tickle the back of my neck. One of his arms is underneath my head and the other is wrapped around my waist. I smile, feeling on the verge of happy tears.

The night before was everything I could have ever wanted and more. We did things to each other's bodies that I didn't even know were possible, but Malcolm was a patient and tender lover who didn't ask anything of me that he didn't reciprocate ten-fold. His desire to pleasure me seemed like the most important thing to him. I had no doubt that it would always be like that with

Malcolm. He would always make sure my needs were met first, and quite often, before ever gratifying his own desires.

I rest one arm and hand over the one he has around my waist, basking in the joy of having such a man to have and to hold for the rest of my life. I feel Malcolm's arm tighten slightly around me as his lips plant tiny kisses across my exposed shoulder.

"Good morning, my love," he whispers, sounding drowsy from sleep.

"Did I wake you?" I ask, wondering if my movement woke him before he was ready.

"I'm a light sleeper," he explains. "Why didn't you join me in my dreams last night? Didn't you sleep?"

I lay there for a moment realizing Malcolm is right. I didn't join in his dream world when we fell asleep. I feel a knot form in the pit of my stomach as I realize why my connection to him in that way has been affected.

"Yes, I slept," I tell him, rolling over to face his confused expression.

"The seals?" he asks knowingly, not really needing me to confirm his own assumption.

"They must be affecting my ability to do that, too," I say, feeling a deep disappointment that I can't share that time with Malcolm any more.

"Hey, don't look so sad," Malcolm tells me. "We'll be able to do it again after you take the seals back to Heaven. It won't last forever."

I feel tears threaten to show my worry over this new development, but Malcolm's reassurance helps me fight them off.

"Anyway," Malcolm says, smiling at me. "What we can do in real life is so much better than just dreaming about it."

I can't help but smile back and agree. "That is very true."

I feel the proof of Malcolm's arousal stir against my legs.

"So early in the morning?" I ask, amazed at Malcolm's eagerness to continue where we left off the night before.

"It's the best way to start off the day," Malcolm assures me, leaning in for a kiss and showing me just how great a day we were going to have with one another.

By the time Malcolm and I decide to roll out of bed, it's midday. The only reason I relent in allowing him to talk me into leaving the room is because my stomach is protesting against not being fed since the night before. We decide to walk down to the kitchen instead of phasing. Mostly because I know when we get there we'll run into people, and I'm not quite ready to lose these private moments with Malcolm just yet. It becomes obvious that my husband isn't ready either. More than a few times, he stops and either pulls me to him for his sweet kisses or pushes me up against whatever wall we're nearby for an impromptu make-out session. I have absolutely no complaints about his manhandling of me, because I can give as good as I get.

We do eventually make it to the kitchen and find Millie, Jered, Giles, Lucas, Vala, and Luna present. The humans in the room are sitting at the table eating lunch together, while Vala keeps a watchful eye on Luna.

"Well," Jered says, looking up from his bowl of soup as we enter the room. "We didn't expect to see the two of you so soon."

"My wife was hungry for food," Malcolm says. "I couldn't have her wasting away on me."

Lucas smiles at us. "So when are the babies going to come?"

Giles coughs loudly, like his soup went down the wrong pipe after hearing Lucas' innocent question.

"I guess we'll just have to wait and see," I tell my son. I see no reason to tell him that we've decided to hold off on having children for the time being. He doesn't need to know the details. "It may take some time before they're ready to come into this world."

"I hope they come soon," Lucas says longingly. "I really want to play with them."

"We'll do our best to provide you with a brother and sister as soon as possible," Malcolm promises. "I'll make it my own personal mission to get the job done."

This seems to satisfy Lucas, because his smile grows wider. I just look at Malcolm and roll my eyes.

"Then I know it'll happen," Lucas says to his father. "You always do what you say, Daddy."

"And I always will," Malcolm reassures him.

"Would the two of you like some soup?" Millie asks, even though she's already stood from her chair and is heading to the pot on the stove before we even have a chance to give her our answer.

Malcolm and I sit on either side of Lucas as we settle to eat. My son leans over and hugs me around the waist.

"You were the prettiest bride I ever saw, Mommy," Lucas says with pride.

"I think I'm probably the only bride you've ever seen," I tell him good-naturedly, hugging him back.

"Yeah, but you were so pretty yesterday."

"She's pretty every day," Malcolm chimes in.

"Ok, both of you stop it," I say. "You're going to make me blush if you don't."

While we eat, Giles speaks with Malcolm about some business in the city, and Jered tells me about something of interest happening in Stratus.

"Brutus and Desmond are spending the day there," Jered says. "Apparently, Lorcan is supposed to make some grand declaration this afternoon."

"Does anyone know what he intends to say?"

"No," Jered says. "Only he seems to know what he plans to announce. I'll wager it isn't anything good, considering it's really Abaddon who's in charge. Though Lorcan wouldn't have been any better. Like Malcolm said before, Abaddon might even be a slight improvement to the real Lorcan Halloran."

"How is he treating the people in Stratus' down-world? The last time Desmond spoke about Lorcan, he was sending them aid. Of course, that was before we knew it was really Abaddon in charge."

"He's still sending supplies," Jered confirms. "Which makes us all very curious about his announcement. He's gained the down-worlders' support and seems to have the aristocrats of Stratus backing him completely now."

"He's already emperor," I say. "I don't see what else he could possibly want."

Jered shrugs. "I'm not sure. We'll just have to wait and see, I guess. Whatever it is, it will probably be something the people of Stratus wouldn't otherwise agree to."

"War?" I ask. "Do you think he means to try to stage a coup of one of the other cloud cities?"

Jered shakes his head. "No. I don't think that's it since Lucifer has people in positions of power in the other cities already. Honestly, I don't have a clue what's going to happen. We'll just have to wait and see like everyone else."

"Mommy," Lucas says, tugging on the sleeve of my shirt, "what are we going to do today?"

The question catches me off guard. I had fully intended to take Malcolm back to our bedroom after we ate and have my way with him for the rest of the day and night, but our son seems to want us all to spend some quality time together.

"Lucas," Millie says kindly, "it's usually customary for the bride and groom to spend some time alone with one another after they wed. I would imagine your mommy and daddy would like to do that today."

Lucas' face falls in disappointment. I'm about to tell him that rules are meant to be broken when there's a good enough reason, but Jered speaks up before I get a chance to.

"Besides," Jered says to Lucas, "I thought you might like to come with me to Travis' place. He needs to do a check-up on Vala today to make sure she's functioning properly. Would you like to do that instead?"

And just like that Lucas' frown disappears and he's happy again.

"Cool!" Lucas says. "I like it there. Do you think Travis could teach me some stuff, too? Like how to fix things?"

Jered winks at Lucas. "I'm sure he will. But before we leave, I would really like to give your mother her wedding gift from me."

"What *did* you get me?" I ask, curious to find out why I had to wait to see Jered's gift. All of the other Watchers gave me jewelry to wear at the wedding. Only Jered's gift was kept a secret.

"Why don't we take a walk and I'll show you?" Jered suggests, standing from his seat at the table.

"I'll join you in a moment," Malcolm says to me. "I just have a little business to attend to."

"Oh, I would like to see what it is, too," Vala says. "May I come?"

"Yes, of course," Jered says. "But we might want to leave the hellhound behind. I wouldn't want to frighten her."

"Frighten her?" I ask, becoming even more intrigued by my surprise gift.

Jered smiles. "You'll see."

Millie takes charge of Luna while the rest of us walk out of the kitchen. Lucas holds my hand as we make our way out, and Vala walks beside me. Jered and Giles lead the way, and I soon discover that we're heading towards the stables. When we draw near, Giles picks up his pace to get inside before us. Just as we all walk in, Giles is leading a horse out of one of the stalls. It's a beautiful dapple-grey mare with finely chiseled bone structure, an arched neck, and a high tail carriage. I instantly recognize the breed.

"An Arabian?" I ask Jered. "I thought the breed died out years ago."

"Modern technology has allowed for a comeback," Jered tells me. "While I was in Alto doing my reconnaissance, I learned that a group of scientists had genetically engineered the breed back into existence. Now you have a horse just your size, my lady."

I giggle and let go of Lucas' hand to give Jered a hug.

"Thank you," I tell him. "She's beautiful."

"You're welcome," Jered says, hugging me back.

"We should take her out for a ride to stretch her legs," Malcolm says after he finally phases in to join us.

Our separation may have only lasted a quarter of an hour, but it felt like forever to me.

"I know the perfect place," I tell him.

We arrange for Giles to saddle our horses for us while Jered takes Lucas and Vala to Travis Stokes' workshop. Malcolm attempts to delay our departure by tempting me with his hands, but I stoutly refuse to have my plans for us that afternoon delayed. I tell Malcolm to dress in his overlord outfit, to which he just raises an eyebrow at me but doesn't protest. I dress in my white leather outfit and strap on my baldric and sword. I also grab one of my wedding gifts from Heaven, Caylin's paintbrush.

By the time we re-enter the stables, Giles has our horses saddled and ready for our departure.

"So where are we going?" Malcolm asks, mounting his mammoth steed while I take my seat on Jered's more appropriately proportioned gift to me.

I hold out my hand to Malcolm.

"You'll see," I tell him.

Malcolm doesn't ask any more questions. He simply slips his hand into mine, and I phase us to our next destination.

CHAPTER THIRTEEN

The sun shines brightly in the sky overhead and the squawk of seagulls fills the air around us. Waves crash against the shore, spraying cold, foamy sea water up against the horses' legs, but they don't seem to scare easily even with the sudden change in their surroundings. I've phased us a good distance away from the little beach house. In fact, it's the spot where we came to shore the night of my wedding in Cirrus. It was right after Malcolm and the others rescued me from Levi and his ridiculous scheme to impregnate me.

"Which way is the beach house from here?" I ask Malcolm.

Malcolm turns his steed towards the north. "About a mile up that way."

"Wanna race?" I challenge, eager to see if the reputation of Arabian horses' speed and agility are true. Up until now, I've only seen videos of them in action.

"My horse wasn't built for speed like yours," Malcolm tells me, looking dubious about such a contest.

"Fine. I'll give you a ten-second head start. Will that even the odds?"

"Make it twenty and maybe," Malcolm chuckles, still not sounding too confident. "What does the winner get?"

"Oh, there won't necessarily be a winner," I tell him with a smile. "I feel confident we'll both come out victorious at the end of *this* race."

"Then start counting," Malcolm tells me, urging his horse into a run up the shoreline.

I count to twenty as I watch Malcolm's mount make long strides across the wet sand, kicking it up in large clumps behind him.

My horse moves anxiously beneath me, and I have to hold her back to prevent her from just running to join in the fun. Once I reach the count in my head, I let her do what comes naturally. In no time at all, we catch up to Malcolm and his behemoth mount. As we pass them, I can't help but giggle and wave. Malcolm just shakes his head and laughs at me.

As expected, I reach the beach house first. I'm tying the reins of my horse to a post on the elevated back porch when Malcolm finally makes it over.

"Slow poke," I tease, walking around my horse to walk up the rickety wooden steps to the porch.

"Could be," Malcolm says suggestively, with a cheesy grin on his face as he looks up at me from underneath his hood.

I just laugh and roll my eyes at his provocative phrasing as I make my way into the house. I unzip my jacket once I'm standing inside the familiar living room, but I don't stay in it for very long. I find one of the other rooms, which looks like it used to be a bedroom once upon a time. I take my baldric off and prop my sword up alongside the wall behind me. I then pull the paintbrush Caylin gave me out of the waistband of my pants and try to remember what she told me to do to make it work.

I mentally picture the object of my desire and begin to paint its picture in the air. Malcolm walks into the room and stands silently beside me while I wield the magic of the paintbrush. Once I'm through, the image I painted materializes into a real piece of furniture in the middle of the room, while the picture itself fades away.

"How the hell did you do that?" Malcolm says in amazement.

I hold up the silver-handled paintbrush in front of him.

"My wedding gift from Caylin," I tell him. "All I have to do is paint what I want and it magically appears. The only catch is that it only lasts for a couple of hours."

Malcolm looks back over at the circular bed I conjured. It's seven feet in diameter and covered in pale blue silk sheets with two matching pillows.

"Then I guess we'd better not waste any time," he says, pulling me roughly up against him.

I smile sweetly at him before I push hard against his chest, causing him to stumble back a few feet into the nearest wall. I hear the crack of wood as he hits the wall and a small plume of dust billows out around him. I walk over to Malcolm with purpose and hold his arms down by his sides. He doesn't struggle against me, but it wouldn't have mattered if he did. I know I'm stronger than he is and so does he.

Malcolm watches me closely, looking amused, but doesn't say anything as I keep him pinned to the wall.

"I loved your nice and gentle love-making last night. It was exactly what I needed for my first time, and I'll want it again this evening. But right now, in this place, I want you to let go, Malcolm. Let down your guard and show me what it is you really want to do to me. I'm not breakable. You don't always have to be so gentle."

I let go of Malcolm's arms and quickly find myself the one trapped up against the wall. Malcolm crushes his mouth down onto mine and presses his hips against me, proving that he's very ready and willing to satisfy all of my demands. But letting him have all the fun really wasn't what I had in mind. I grab the front of Malcolm's open overlord coat and push him back until he's lying flat on the floor in front of me.

He props his torso up on his elbows and watches me as I walk over to him, shedding my jacket and t-shirt along the way, revealing that I'm not wearing anything else underneath.

"Are you just as naked beneath those pants?" Malcolm asks, his voice hoarse as he looks me up and down.

When I reach him, I place one booted foot on his stomach.

"Only one way to find out," I tell him.

Without needing further instructions, Malcolm pulls down the zipper of the boot and slips it off my foot. We do the same for the other boot until both are off and tossed haphazardly onto the floor. Malcolm rises up onto his knees in front of me and releases the snap holding my waistband together. He yanks the tightly-fitting leather pants down until they're around my ankles, and helps me step out of them so I can stand completely naked in front of him.

"How strong do your legs feel, my love?" Malcolm asks, massaging the tops of my thighs in a slow circular motion with his hands, looking up at me.

"Very strong," I tell him. "What do you have in mind?"

Malcolm grins before lowering his head between my legs.

"Just try to remain standing," he tells me.

After that, I completely lose track of time. I feel lucky I remember my own name an hour later when we lie together on the bed, cuddling against the chill in the room. The wintry temperature didn't bother me while we were otherwise engaged in more vigorous activities. In fact, I even managed to work up a sweat at one point during our lovemaking.

"Get your sword," Malcolm tells me, slapping me playfully on my bottom before rising from the bed. "There should still be a pile of firewood out in the other room from when we were here last."

I get up and grab my sword, lighting its flames. Malcolm places the pieces of dry wood in the fireplace in the bedroom, and I ignite it with my blade. We soon have a roaring fire that slowly brings warmth into the room. After we climb back into bed together, I watch the flames flicker while Malcolm holds me alongside him, gently caressing my body lovingly with one hand while he props his head up with the other one.

"I don't want to lose this," I tell him, not intending to feel the weight of the world on my shoulders in that moment, but unable to push my mission to the back of my mind any longer.

Malcolm is the love of my life. If I can't confide my worries to him, who else is there?

"We'll never lose this," he reassures me, knowing what's running through my mind without me having to spell it out for him. "We'll never lose each other. As long as we're together, Anna, my love will always protect you."

I turn onto my back and look up at him as his hand continues to glide up and down my body. The way he looks down at me with so much love makes me believe everything will be all right. I won't lose myself to the seals as long as the bond holding my soul to his is stronger than the ones tethering it to their power.

"I need to tell you something," I say, realizing it's time for me to let him know about Helena. If he's truly going to help me hold myself together in the days to come, he needs to know exactly what we're up against. I also need to tell him about Lucifer bringing my papa to see me before the wedding and his motive for doing such a thing.

After I finish my recount of the previous day's events, Malcolm brings me into his arms and just holds me. I don't sense that he's mad at me for not telling him sooner. I think he's just glad I didn't try to hold anything back and attempt to conceal the information I had from him so he wouldn't worry.

"I'm not sure if I'm more concerned about Hell taking on a human persona," he says, pulling back from me, "or Andre knowing I've had my way with his little girl."

I look at Malcolm and see true concern on his face. I begin to laugh at the absurdity of him worrying over my father's reaction to us having sex just as much as Hell trying to make me its new master.

"It's not funny," Malcolm says, though I hear a tinge of amusement in his voice, like he's just now comparing the two. "I'm completely serious, Anna."

I wipe at the tears produced from my laughter and just smile up at him.

"Papa's fine with us being together. You don't have to worry about his reaction when you see him again. He knows you're my soulmate and that nothing could ever separate us."

"I'm glad *you* know that, too," Malcolm says, leaning down to give me a light kiss on the lips. "Nothing, not even the power of the seals, will ever tear us apart, Anna. I will never let Hell, or Helena, whatever it wants to call itself, take you away from me. Especially after I went through all the trouble of teaching you how to pleasure me. I doubt I could find someone else who is such a quick study."

I roll Malcolm onto his back and hold his wrists above his head, pinning him into place while I lie on top of him.

"Do you honestly think I would ever let another woman touch you like I do?" I ask him.

"Do you honestly think I would ever want another woman to touch me the way you do?" he retorts.

"You'd better not," I warn. "I have a feeling I could be a very jealous woman, and you wouldn't like the consequences."

"Oh?" Malcolm says with a raised eyebrow. "Would you end up removing a very important part of my anatomy for such a transgression?"

"Your assumption is very astute," I tell him. "I have an extremely large sword, and I know how to wield it with precision."

"The possibility of me being unfaithful should never even cross your mind, my love," Malcolm tells me in all seriousness. "It would never cross mine. I can assure you of that."

"Lucifer tried to warn me otherwise," I say, remembering his attempt to throw doubt on Malcolm's ability to remain faithful.

Malcolm sighs heavily. "He would have said anything to prevent you from marrying me. I'm just glad you didn't listen to him."

"Of course I wouldn't listen to something so ludicrous. I know you, Malcolm. You're loyal to a fault, and I know you would never risk losing me just to bed another woman."

"I've had other women," Malcolm admits. "But I've never had a connection like ours with any of them, not even my first wife. You are everything to me, Anna. You are the sun my life revolves around now. Without you, I would live in total darkness."

As I look at Malcolm, I know I will do whatever it takes to make sure he doesn't lose me. Whatever pain I have to physically endure…whatever torment my soul has to suffer through, I will find a way to survive it all for the man looking at me as if he is completely exposing his heart and handing it to me to cherish for the rest of our lives.

"We have a little less than an hour left before this bed disappears," I tell Malcolm.

"Was that your subtle way of asking me to make love to you again?" Malcolm replies, moving his hands down to cup my bottom.

"Who was asking?" I say.

Malcolm grins as I bring my head down to his and meet his smiling lips with my own.

When we return home, we stable our horses and make our way into the house only to be welcomed by strident shouts of anger.

"What on earth..." Malcolm says as we walk into the sitting room hand in hand.

We find Jered, Desmond, and Brutus standing in the room, speaking to one another. I say speaking. Brutus' face is so red it looks like his head might explode from anger at any moment.

I immediately know Malcolm and I will have to continue our honeymoon later. It's obvious our friend is in desperate need of our help.

"What's going on?" Malcolm asks as we come to stand with the others.

"That son of a bitch wants to marry his own sister!" Brutus yells with so much hatred that it contorts his face into a mask of rage, making Brutus' normally handsome visage almost unrecognizable.

"Lorcan is trying to marry Kyna?" I ask, hoping I misunderstood what Brutus just said.

"Yes!" Brutus yells, but seems to be unable to say anything else because anger is blinding him.

"Well we won't let that happen," I say, with so much certainty it seems to calm Brutus down a bit. "Has anyone spoken up against this arrangement? Surely it can't be acceptable to the people of Stratus to allow such an incestuous union to take place."

"The people there seemed to be genuinely stunned by the proposal when he made it," Desmond says, "but no one spoke up against it. I think the down-worlders don't care what he needs to do to stay happy as long as he still provides them with the extra supplies they need. And the up-worlders simply don't want to piss him off. They like this new Lorcan and don't want to see the return of the sadistic one any time soon."

"Was Kyna with him when he made this announcement?" Malcolm asks.

"No," Brutus tells us. "From what we could gather, Lorcan has her locked up in the palace until the wedding takes place."

"And when is this wedding supposed to happen?" I ask.

"Tomorrow."

I look at Malcolm. "That doesn't give us much time."

"No it doesn't, which is probably what he was counting on."

I look back at the others. "I assume there will be a wedding celebration this evening? Every royal wedding has one the night before."

"Yes," Jered says. "In fact, it's supposed to start in a couple of hours but only the aristocrats from Stratus were invited to attend."

"Then I suggest we all get ready to crash a party, gentlemen." I look at Brutus and place a comforting hand on his arm. "We won't let this happen, Brutus. Even if she wasn't your soulmate, I would still speak up and not allow Kyna to be married off to her own brother against her will. I'll find a way to bring her home with us even if I end up having to kill the emperor of Stratus myself."

"Abaddon has always been a sadistic bastard," Brutus says in disgust. "I'm not surprised at all that he's doing this while he's disguised as Lorcan. I can't say I blame him for wanting Kyna, but even he should know this world doesn't look kindly on brothers marrying their own sisters."

"Did he give people a reason why he thought this was a good thing to do?" Jered asks.

"He tried," Desmond responds with a shake of his head. "He spouted off some garbage about keeping the Halloran bloodline pure to increase the amount of royal blood in the next heir, and that doing such a thing would ensure that Stratus would remain peaceful under the rule of a true Halloran. It was complete rubbish and everyone knew it. They were just too chicken to call him out on it."

"The sooner we get Kyna away from Lorcan... Abaddon... whatever name you want to give him," I say, "the better. Let's get over there quickly before he decides to escalate his plans. I think it's time he was put in his place and understands I won't sit idly by and watch something like this happen. It might be a good lesson for all of Lucifer's people to learn."

186

"Are you really going to kill him?" Jered asks me, concerned over such a possibility.

"I will if I have to in order to save Kyna. Hopefully Lorcan is smarter than that and will simply hand her over to me."

"You can bet he won't make it that easy," Malcolm tells me.

"Then I guess we might have a fight on our hands," I reply, "because Kyna Halloran is coming home with us, one way or another."

CHAPTER FOURTEEN

The fashion of Stratus was a modern take on medieval era attire. I didn't exactly have anything to wear that fit that description in my own wardrobe. Therefore, I decide to wear the red gown I wore to the dinner party Malcolm and I gave, which also happened to be the night Malcolm proposed.

If it hadn't been for Millie being in the room helping me get ready, I'm not sure the dress would have ever made it onto my body, considering the way Malcolm kept chancing glances in my direction. Whenever our eyes met, I could tell he was thinking about one thing--taking the dress off and throwing me onto his bed. Not that I would have made any sort of protest if he had, but I'm pretty sure Millie would have run out of the room in complete mortification.

Malcolm donned the same suit he wore to my own wedding celebration in Cirrus, sans the lily-shaped pin. Honestly, I wouldn't have minded him wearing the pin, but I think not wearing it meant something to him. There wasn't a shred of doubt in my mind that Malcolm now loved me with his whole heart. Even if he had worn the pin, I would have just taken it as a sign of respect for a friend that he still held dear. Now that I knew Lilly, I felt a special connection to her also. She was the first in a long line of women who were chosen by God to help protect our world. I felt honor-bound to make sure I didn't bring disgrace to such a noble lineage. If anything, I hoped to make my own mark in our family chronicles.

After Millie puts the finishing touches on the thick braid into which she styled my hair, Malcolm and I talk about what should be done to retrieve Kyna.

We come up with a plan that seems to amuse my husband to no end.

Malcolm chuckles. "I have to admit I'm looking forward to you making him squirm."

"So you don't think he'll give me any trouble?" I ask, slipping on a pair of elbow-length black satin gloves.

"Not a bit. He won't present much of a challenge for you," Malcolm says confidently. "If I thought you might get hurt, I would try to talk you out of it. As it is, I'm just looking forward to watching him show his true colors. The only thing you have to worry about is his weapon."

"It's not a whip like Levi's, is it?"

"No. It's a sword he calls Phantom."

"Why is it called that?"

"It gives him the ability to make it appear as though he's in one place when he's actually in a completely different one. If you try to use your eyes to keep track of his movements, it will distract you from the real fight."

"So should I just keep my eyes closed?"

"Let me worry about that part," Malcolm says with a smile.

"Why? What do you have planned?"

"Something I had hoped to try out in private first, but I guess that won't be possible now."

"Which is?"

Malcolm walks into his closet and comes back out with a black silk tie in his hands.

"Turn around," he tells me.

I do as instructed and Malcolm ties the silk over my eyes, blocking my sight.

"I've never fought without being able to see," I tell him.

I feel a little disoriented at first but quickly discover that my hearing has become more sensitive. I hear Malcolm moving around the room and know exactly where he is. Suddenly, I sense an object approaching my head and duck out of the way, only to hear it shatter against the wall behind me.

"Was that really necessary?" I ask Malcolm, feeling a little exasperated by the act.

"I wanted to make sure you could sense an inanimate object coming at you quickly," he says in his own defense. "Now I'm going to phase around the room. Point in the direction you think I am. If you guess wrong, I'll let you know."

Malcolm must phase within the room twenty times with me pointing to where I think he is before he finally phases right in front of me.

"Very good," Malcolm says, placing his hands on my waist.

I feel him lower his head towards mine, but he doesn't kiss me. His warm breath caresses my mouth, making it water in anticipation.

"What are you waiting for?" I ask him breathlessly.

"I think if I start kissing you now we'll never make it to Stratus tonight," Malcolm admits hoarsely, letting his hands glide up the front of my dress and slide over my breasts before travelling back down to my hips.

"Millie would kill you if you ruined my hair," I say jokingly.

Malcolm reaches around to the back of my head and loosens the knot there to take off my blindfold.

"Well, we can't invoke the wrath of Millie," Malcolm says in all seriousness. "She only looks like a docile house servant until you cross her."

"I wouldn't know," I say, trying to imagine a livid Millie. "I've never given her a reason to be mad at me."

"Smart woman," Malcolm says with a smile, holding his arm out to me. "Shall we go and rescue Brutus' damsel in distress?"

By the time we make it back downstairs, Jered, Desmond, and Brutus have also changed into proper attire for the royal function. Brutus looks a bit nervous as he tries to adjust the cuffs of his sleeves beneath his jacket. He then fidgets with the slim black tie he's wearing. I walk up to him and act as though I am setting it straight, even though it's already perfectly in place.

"You look quite dashing," I tell him. I know exactly what's going through Brutus' mind. This will be the first time he and Kyna will come face to face. She will finally see him, and the connection between them will finally be realized. "She won't be able to resist you."

"I suppose we'll see," Brutus says, sounding uncertain about his first formal introduction to Kyna.

I find it a curious thing for him to say but don't have time to delve into it any further.

Malcolm informs everyone about our plans before we prepare to leave.

"This I can't wait to see," Desmond says with a smile.

"Abaddon's vanity should work well to your advantage," Jered tells me. "We should probably go ahead and phase over there. Who knows what Lorcan's reaction will be to our unexpected arrival? He might even try to kick us out."

"Perhaps we shouldn't all go at once," I suggest. "Why don't you and Desmond phase there first and get lost in the crowd that's probably already present? Malcolm, Brutus, and I will make an official appearance and draw Lorcan's attention. If they try to kick us out, at least the two of you will still be nearby to help Kyna."

With our plan set, Desmond and Jered phase first, presumably letting themselves get lost in the crowd of Stratus aristocrats present in the palace to celebrate in their emperor's upcoming unholy nuptials.

"Have you ever been to Stratus?" I ask Malcolm.

"Once, a long time ago," he says. "Have you?"

"No; I wasn't allowed to leave Cirrus, remember?"

"I can phase us into the palace where the party is being held," Brutus says. "I was there recently."

"Did you go there hoping to catch a glimpse of Kyna?" I ask him, finding Brutus' concern over Kyna's welfare endearing.

"I just wanted to make sure she was all right," he admits with a small shrug of his rather large shoulders.

I place my hand on one of Brutus' arms and hold out my other hand for Malcolm to take.

"Then let's not waste any more time, Brutus. Let's go rescue your woman."

Brutus smiles and phases us directly to the palace.

The music of a full orchestra welcomes us as we phase into the seat of power of Stratus. The home of the Hallorans is a mish-mash of various European palaces throughout history, which were destroyed either by time or by the Great War. From my childhood history lessons, I know the room we're standing in is an oversized replica of the Hall of Mirrors from the Palace of Versailles.

The room is a little over three-hundred-feet long and forty-feet wide with a sixty-foot high mural-painted ceiling. Seventeen mirror-clad arches are in complete alignment with seventeen arched windows on the wall opposite them, which are situated between rectangular white marble pillars. The Halloran castle is built slightly above the regular dwellings of Stratus. The smaller homes of the aristocrats in the city can be glimpsed through the windows in the room.

It seems like every person of note within Stratus society has shown up for the spectacle of the Halloran wedding celebration. I'm sure it isn't every day that you get to witness the marriage of a brother to his sister. Among polite society, it was taboo to marry within your own family, even if it was a long-lost cousin. I can only imagine the gossip that's spreading among the citizens of Stratus about what the true relationship between Lorcan and Kyna has been all these years. Sometimes people thrive when given the opportunity to feed off others' misfortunes, making them feel falsely superior. I can see in the way people are whispering to each other that those in attendance are feeling quite pompous.

Locating Kyna is far simpler than I originally thought it would be. Apparently, Lorcan wanted to make sure everyone in the room could clearly view his bride to be and understand that he is in complete control of her.

Hanging from the ceiling on the opposite end of the room from where we stand is a gilded golden cage, like one you would use to trap a songbird. It is large enough for Kyna to stand in and watch the proceedings below. She looks hopping mad, and I can't say I blame her one bit considering how jovial the crowd beneath her is acting about her forthcoming marriage.

Lorcan even dressed her up to look the part of a captive bird. Kyna is wearing a high-collared coat composed of bird feathers, which have been painted gold. The slim-fitting coat reaches down to the full skirt of a mermaid-style dress she's obviously wearing underneath it. The skirt itself is white with an intricately embroidered design around the bottom edge in gold thread. She's wearing a gold gem-encrusted crown on her head, marking her rank as the princess of Stratus, but there is a gold and pearl mesh attached to the base of the crown, which acts to cover her face and obscure its features. I can see her lips moving like she's trying to say something to the people below her, but no one seems to realize she's speaking. I assume the mesh also acts to silence her voice, probably a force-field of some sort, to block her speech so people can't hear her shouts of strident protests at the situation.

"I'm getting her the hell out of that thing," Brutus says with such fierce intent I'm surprised he even bothered to tell us what his plans were.

He tries to phase to do just what he said, but I grab one of his arms and pull him back.

"Don't," I warn him. "We don't need to cause a scene. Let me handle Lorcan first."

"I can't allow him to keep her caged like an animal," Brutus says passionately.

"If you try to take her away from here now," Malcolm says, "the two of you will be on the run until we can get things under control. Let's stick to our plan and use yours as a last resort, Brutus."

I can tell by the look on Brutus' face that he doesn't like just standing idly by while the woman he loves is being treated so poorly. But he also knows my plan to get Kyna back is the best course of action.

Brutus nods his head, silently agreeing to abide by the strategy we have in place, at least for now.

"Ahh, Empress Anna," I hear a friendly familiar voice say behind me.

I turn around to find Empress Olivia Ravensdale of Nacreous walking up to us. She's wearing a plain black dress, signifying that she's still in mourning for her husband, Horatio. I feel a sense of guilt when I see her. I promised her I would make Botis pay for killing her husband and taking his body. And I don't like leaving promises unfulfilled…

"I see you've come to investigate the barbaric goings-on here in Stratus as well," she says knowingly.

"I've come to stop it," I tell her with complete confidence.

Olivia smiles and I see a look of approval enter her eyes. "Then I wholeheartedly support your efforts. If there is anything I can do to help, please let me know."

"If you could lend me your support when I make my demand to Lorcan," I tell her, "I would appreciate it."

"You have my full sponsorship," Olivia says, her eyes leaving my face to look at the cage Kyna is imprisoned in. "The sooner we get her out of that thing the better."

"Agreed," I say.

Suddenly the music being played comes to an abrupt halt, and the people in the room stop dancing. Complete silence reigns as I turn back around to see what those around me are staring at on the other end of the room.

I see Lorcan Halloran standing in front of an enormous black obsidian throne. He's wearing a dark grey wool suit, with the lower half of the sleeves and pants made of black leather. The jacket collar is double layered with the same black leather as a separate underlying collar.

"Greetings," Lorcan says as his eyes narrow on me. His face is a lesson in complete control.

With this one word uttered by their emperor, the people of Stratus act as though it were a command for them to gather against the sides of each wall. Their parting clears an unobstructed path between my small group and Lorcan.

"I must say," Lorcan continues, "I don't remember extending an invitation to our little soiree to such....*esteemed* guests, two empresses and an overlord no less. How generous of you all to grace us with your presence and come to personally wish Kyna and me well in our upcoming nuptials. Don't you think it was thoughtful of them, my dear?"

Lorcan looks up at Kyna in her gilded cage with a cocky smirk. If Kyna's voice were audible, I'm sure we would have all heard some choice words from the princess in answer to her brother's question.

I begin to make my way down the room towards Lorcan, which immediately draws his attention back to me. Malcolm and Brutus walk slightly behind and on either side of me. Olivia trails behind us, giving me the lead in our little processional.

I don't say anything as I walk towards Lorcan, and my continued silence has the desired effect. The closer I get, the less sure of himself he looks. If I had respected his rule as Emperor of Stratus, the code of conduct all rulers abide by would have dictated that I speak to him by now. However, my continued silence shows to those present that I do not respect his status or his rule. In some circumstances it could ignite a war, but in this instance I'm only looking for a battle.

Once I stand in front of him, I stare Lorcan in the eyes until he backs down and glances away. His action tells me exactly what I need to know. Deep down inside his shallow exterior is a coward of the worst sort. It's a trait I plan to exploit to the fullest.

"It's been a long time since I saw you last, Lorcan," I finally say. "I had a hard time believing you actually intended to marry your own sister. So I came to verify your ridiculous intentions for myself."

"Our union will yield a pure-blooded Halloran to carry on the family line," Lorcan says, sounding self-righteous about such a fact. "Perhaps we'll start a new trend among the royal families. They should be more careful in protecting their own bloodlines in such a way. It might prevent people of," Lorcan looks me up and down scathingly, "lesser ancestries from polluting the strength of future leaders."

"And what does your sister think about such an arrangement?" I ask, hearing Kyna rattle the bars of her cage, letting everyone in the room know exactly what she thinks about her brother's malevolent plans for her future. "Well, I guess that answers my question."

"Kyna simply doesn't see the brilliance in my plan yet," Lorcan answers. "But after our wedding night, I'm sure she won't have any complaints."

Some of the people in attendance snicker at Lorcan's crude comment, making me wish I could turn on them and slap some reason into them. I don't understand why they desire to see Kyna suffer at the hands of her brother.

"When I was a child," I say, slowly tugging at the tips of the glove on my right hand with my left one. "Empress Catherine made sure I understood the laws within each cloud city. There is one here in Stratus, even though it is a bit on the archaic side, that I remember quite distinctly. It's a little something called 'wager of battle'."

I completely pull off my glove and throw it down in front of Lorcan's booted feet.

The look on Lorcan's face tells me he has no idea what the significance of the glove at his feet holds.

"I'm afraid I'm not very familiar with that law," Lorcan admits, looking up from the glove back into my eyes.

"The law states that anyone can challenge a peer of equal rank to a duel to settle a dispute," I say.

"I wasn't aware Stratus had a dispute with Cirrus," Lorcan says snidely.

"*I* have a dispute with *you*," I tell him, not trying to hide the disgust I feel for him from my voice. "I accuse you of forcing your sister into an unholy matrimony that most people with any self-respect," I say looking at some of the party's attendees, "would speak up against. But since the people of Stratus seem to be willing to overlook your transgression against Kyna, I feel it's my duty to speak on her behalf and act as her champion."

199

"I don't believe Kyna asked you for such a thing," Lorcan says, fully understanding what it is I'm asking for now.

I look up at Kyna in her gilded cage to make sure she's looking down at me.

"Princess Kyna Halloran," I call up to her, "do you agree to have me act as your champion in this matter?"

Kyna looks hesitant and worried by my request. It's obvious she doesn't understand why I would want to wager her freedom on an act of physical combat against her brother. To ease her worry, I wink at her. I see her shoulders sag a bit, letting me know that some of her worry has been put aside for the moment. Slowly, she begins to nod her head in acquiescence to my request.

I look back at Lorcan.

"Since the princess accepts me as her champion, you need to pick between one of two options, Lorcan. Either you can pick up the glove I've lain at your feet and accept my challenge to resolve this issue by combat, or you can graciously accept defeat and allow me to take Kyna away from this place. The choice is yours. Personally, I hope you pick up the glove. I haven't had a good fight in a while."

Lorcan's face turns blood red. I can't determine if it's from embarrassment or anger. Though it might simply be a result of both emotions playing across his face.

Lorcan slowly crouches to the floor and gingerly picks up my glove.

"I accept your challenge, Empress Anna," he says, rising back to his full height.

"Since I'm the one who gave the challenge," I say, "you are allowed to choose which weapons we use."

"Swords," Lorcan says without hesitation.

It was what we expected. Abaddon would think his weapon gave him an advantage over me.

"Swords it is then," I say. "And as the impartial referee in our duel I suggest we use Empress Olivia, since she is the only other person of our rank in attendance."

"Whatever," Lorcan says indifferently. "Will this be a fight to the death?"

I hear a combined gasp issue from the crowd around us at such a suggestion.

"If you wish," I tell him, "though, if you find that you would rather live than die, you can use the code word from the old days to declare you have been vanquished by your opponent and still keep your head."

"And what word would that be?" Lorcan asks cockily, like he has no doubt he will win the fight and have no need of its use.

"'Craven'," I tell him. "If Empress Olivia hears either of us say it, she will call an end to the fight."

"And when shall we have this fight?" he asks.

"I see no reason to delay," I tell him. "How about now?"

"As you wish," Lorcan says, a touch of madness in his voice as he stares down at me.

I sense Malcolm phase away from my side, but he returns less than five seconds later with my sword in hand.

I turn towards Malcolm and take my sword from him. Malcolm pulls me up against him and kisses me for all of Stratus to see. I hear some gasps of surprise but could not care less what these people think of me. I have absolutely no respect for any of them. They were willing to allow Lorcan to enter into an incestuous union with his sister. If they think I'm morally corrupt because Malcolm is simply my lover in their eyes, so be it.

When Malcolm pulls his lips away from mine, he lowers his head next to my ear.

"Remember to use all your senses," Malcolm tells me. "He can't defeat you unless you lose focus."

I nod my head, letting him know I understand what he said.

"Tear this dress off of me, husband, so I can get to work."

Malcolm raises his head and smiles down at me.

"As you command, my love."

Malcolm kisses me again. Then he lets me go and kneels down in front of me on one knee. He begins to rip the lower half of my gown away from the waist down. I hear a surprised murmur come from the crowd around us, but feel their disappointment when they learn I'm wearing my white leather pants and boots beneath the skirt. Once Malcolm is finished, he stands back up with the lower half of my dress in his hands.

I turn to face Lorcan again.

"Are you ready to begin?" I ask him.

Lorcan turns his back to the crowd and me. When he turns back around, he's holding his phantom sword. The blade is composed of three curved black blades twisted around each other like a triple helix. The hilt is gold and reminds me of the wings of a bird. Wispy white smoke flows within the center of the blades, making the sword appear rather ominous.

"Ready when you are," he replies with a tight-lipped smile.

I walk down to the middle of the room, setting my own sword aflame. I catch a glimpse of myself in the mirrors in the room and wonder how this fight will look to those in attendance. I just hope they have the good sense to stay out of my way.

As I'm about to look away from my reflection, I notice a man watching me. Everyone in the room is watching me, but his stare is more piercing than the rest. He's tall with short brown hair and dark brown eyes. His demeanor speaks of someone who is used to being obeyed, possibly someone men would follow into battle without question. There's something oddly familiar about him, but I can't quite place where I know him from or if I actually know him at all. Unfortunately, I don't have much time to ruminate on who he is. I have a fight to win first.

Once I'm in the center of the room, I turn back around to face Lorcan.

Malcolm rips off a strip of fabric from the remnants of my skirt and walks behind me.

"This will help," he tells me, covering my eyes with the fabric.

After he blindfolds me, I feel him rest his hands on my shoulder and lean in to whisper in my ear.

"Now go kick his ass, wife," Malcolm tells me, kissing me on the side of my neck.

I smile. "That's exactly what I intend to do."

CHAPTER FIFTEEN

I stand completely still and wait for Lorcan to make the first move. Although there are other people in the room, I can easily distinguish his presence from theirs. A particularly bad aura surrounds him and helps separate Lorcan from everyone else. It's almost like I can sense his smarmy attitude without having to actually see the smirk on his face. His sword does nothing to help hide his position either. There's a faint sulfuric scent wafting from its blades that lets me know exactly where it is. If I didn't have the blindfold on, I'm not sure I would have even noticed it. However, without my sight, my hearing and sense of smell are greatly enhanced.

I hear the sound of Lorcan's sword sing through the air behind me and know that he phased there to try to catch me off guard. I quickly turn and meet his oddly bladed sword with my own. I wonder what the people watching this fight will see. Does Lorcan's phantom sword make it appear like he's still standing in front of me or does direct contact with it vanquish the illusion that it's supposed to help him perpetuate? I have no idea, since I'm blinded and can't actually watch the fight as it progresses. All I hear is the clash of our blades as they reverberate through the silence in the room.

Lorcan tries to use brute force to push me back. Apparently, he didn't get the memo from his fallen brothers that I'm stronger than any of them. He might not be a prince of Hell, but his physical strength is just as great. As he attempts to back me up, I show him, in no uncertain terms, that he's no match for me in that area.

He changes tactics and uses the power of his sword to try to find an opening by catching me unawares. His attempts do nothing to gain him an advantage over me. I know exactly where he is as soon as he phases in. At one point I hear him growl in frustration, which only brings a smile to my face. My only regret is that I can't watch the fight that's taking place. The reflection of our duel in the mirrors in the room must be a remarkable sight as my flaming swords clashes against Lorcan's phantom one.

I patiently wait for my opening to take Lorcan down. I'm aware of time and know that our fight has gone on for a good half hour. Finally, I find my opening as he lowers his guard, and I 'see' my chance to end this fight. I bend down and sweep Lorcan's feet out from under him by slicing him mid-calf. He screams out in pain and falls to the floor. I tear off my blindfold just as I stick the point of my sword near his throat. By this point, we're both breathing hard from the exertion of the fight.

"Do you yield?" I demand.

Lorcan smiles, sending a shiver down my spine.

"You really shouldn't have done that," he says to me.

"Done what?" I ask. "Beaten you?"

He shakes his head, continuing to smile madly.

"No. Taken your blindfold off."

I hear Malcolm shout out my name and am able to dodge Lorcan's true-self's blade just enough to only receive a cut across my right arm, causing me to lose my grip on my sword. The Lorcan I had on the ground disappears into a wisp of white smoke, and I turn in time to see the real Lorcan raise his sword like he's about to stab me in the chest with it.

I instantly feel the sting of an all-consuming hatred enter my heart. Using my newest gift from the seals, I mentally pick Lorcan up and throw him up against one of the mirrors on the wall behind him. The force of the impact causes the mirror to shatter inward, and Lorcan loses hold of his sword. Before he can recover enough to pick it back up, I phase over to him. My hands ignite with blue flames, causing the ordinary citizens of Stratus to gasp in surprise at my ability.

I grab Lorcan by the throat and squeeze the tender flesh there.

"Yield," I whisper to him. "Or I *will* kill you."

"And if I yield, what do I get in return?"

"A chance to live."

"What's to stop you from just coming back and killing me later?"

"Nothing. But if you release Kyna and promise to leave her alone, I'll let you live. You have my word. You're not a prince and have nothing that I need right now. I can afford to let you live for the time being, as long as you continue to treat the people of Stratus with generosity. If you do anything to harm them or Kyna, I won't give you this opportunity to save your own skin again. I'll simply kill you. Is that understood?"

"Yes."

"Then say the word that will end this fight, or I will end it my way."

Lorcan stares at me for a moment, and I know I've just made an enemy for life.

"Craven!" Lorcan shouts out, casting the shadow of a coward on his reputation from that moment on.

"Emperor Lorcan has asked for mercy," I hear Olivia Ravensdale say to the room. "Do you accept his surrender, Empress Anna?"

I squeeze Lorcan's throat tightly, making sure he feels the power I have and understands my words to him were not empty ones. I can back them up with action.

"Yes," I say. "I accept the emperor's surrender."

I continue to stare at Lorcan, feeling the power I have over him and finding it completely intoxicating. I could easily extinguish his life and be done with a possible future threat. Wouldn't it be smarter to just kill him now before he can cause more trouble later? What's the point of keeping him alive if he's simply going to make me kill him at a later date? In a way, it might be more of a kindness to slay him. Wouldn't it be crueler to give him hope that I'll continue to let him live as long as he acts the way I want him to?

I tighten my hold on his throat and see fear enter his eyes. I'm not sure if Abaddon has ever felt true fear before this moment, but I know without a shadow of a doubt that he feels it now.

"Anna…" I hear Malcolm say beside me. "You've won and shown these people the coward that he is. It's time to let him go."

S.J. West

"But I could end it so easily," I say.

"Not this way," Malcolm says. "You're not a murderer, my love."

I hear the truth in Malcolm's words, but I also know the line between leaving Lorcan alive and killing him is almost transparent.

"Anna…" Malcolm says, entreating me to do the honorable thing.

I release my hold on Lorcan's throat and watch him fall to the floor onto his hands and knees, gasping for air. Two Stratus guards quickly come over to help lift their emperor to his feet.

"Free Kyna," I order.

Lorcan looks at me scathingly.

"As you wish," he says.

I watch as he brings up a set of holographic controls over the palm of his left hand and presses in a code. I hear Kyna scream as the cage she is in suddenly vanishes. She begins a swift freefall to the floor beneath her. Before I can react, I see Brutus phase in and catch her before she hits the floor.

I breathe a sigh of relief as Brutus sets her on her feet. Gently he lifts the mesh veil covering her face, giving back her voice. I watch to see what her reaction will be as the two of them come face to face for the very first time in their lives.

Kyna looks at Brutus and smiles, but it's simply a polite one as she says thank you. I guess I expected her expression to mirror the fact that her world suddenly felt like it shattered and was made whole again just by meeting her

209

soulmate. Yet she doesn't look like that at all. There's interest in her eyes as she continues to study Brutus, but not total recognition of who the man standing before her truly is.

"I don't understand," I say to Malcolm as I continue to watch the interaction between Brutus and Kyna.

Malcolm looks over at them and seems to figure out what it is I'm confused about.

"I'll explain it to you later," he tells me, walking over to where I dropped my sword and retrieving it for me before returning to my side. "Right now, we need to attend to your wound."

I look back at Lorcan, making sure he listens to what I have to tell him before I leave.

"We'll be watching your every move," I warn him. "If we see anything we don't like, you know what I'll do to you."

"You have nothing to fear from me," Lorcan says, and I wish I could know for sure whether he's lying. Simply by using my own judgment of his character, I assume he's lying.

I notice Olivia watching our exchange and walk over to her.

"Thank you for your support in this matter," I tell her. "And I want you to know that I haven't forgotten the promise I made to you. I do intend to keep it."

Olivia smiles wanly. "I know you will, Anna. Of that, I never had a doubt."

"You should probably leave now," I tell her. "I don't think Lorcan will be in a very good mood for the rest of the evening."

Olivia laughs. "A very astute conclusion, my dear. I hope to see you again soon under better circumstances."

"So do I, Olivia."

Olivia teleports away, presumably back to Nacreous.

I turn to see that Desmond and Jered are now standing by Brutus and know they will take care of Kyna for me. I briefly search the crowd to find the man I saw right before the fight, but he's nowhere to be seen. Still, his presence intrigued me, but I don't know why.

"Let's go home and see what we can do about your injury," Malcolm says, placing his hand on the small of my back and phasing us to his bedroom in New Orleans.

When we get there, Malcolm tosses my sword onto his bed then leads me to the bathroom. He makes me sit down on the small chair there while he fills the sink with warm water and dampens a washcloth.

"I suppose a healing wand won't work on this wound," I say as I watch Malcolm carefully wash away the blood on my arm.

"No, it won't," Malcolm confirms. "In fact, it might even leave a scar since it will have to heal naturally."

"That's all right. I have a feeling it won't be the last battle wound I get from this fight."

"It will be if I have anything to say about it," Malcolm declares determinedly.

"I guess I shouldn't have taken the blindfold off so soon. But I wanted to see his face. I wanted to see him beaten. If you hadn't stopped me, I probably would have killed him, Malcolm. I wanted to do it more than I would like to admit."

"But you didn't," Malcolm reminds me.

"Only because you stopped me," I say, realizing it's the truth.

I would have killed Lorcan if Malcolm hadn't intervened when he did. My soul screamed for me to spill his blood while I had my hand around his throat and completely helpless to stop me. And…what would have been the harm in killing him? It probably would have saved us a lot of trouble later on. There wasn't a doubt in my mind that I could have snuffed out his puny little life like I would a bug under my shoe. He was nothing, and I could have turned him into that with just one thought. Perhaps I wasn't supposed to take pride in my newly acquired powers, but how could I not? I was becoming the most powerful person on Earth, and with each additional seal I retrieved that power would grow exponentially.

"Anna…"

Malcolm's simple calling of my name brings me out of my reverie. I look up at him and see the concern on his face.

"What were you just thinking about?" he asks me.

"I was thinking about how powerful I am," I admit. "And how powerful I will become."

"Being the most formidable person in the world means nothing if you don't keep control of it," Malcolm tells me. "My greatest worry is that it will slowly take control of you without you even realizing it."

"I can handle it," I say with confidence. "I won't let it manipulate me."

"I think it might already be testing you, Anna. Like you said, the only reason you didn't kill Lorcan was because I stopped you."

"And why did you?" I ask. "You know as well as I do that it's dangerous to have him in control of Stratus."

"And like you told him, we'll be keeping an eye on him and what he does."

"But it would have saved us a lot of trouble if I had just killed him then and allowed Kyna to rule Stratus."

"That time may come in the future, but for the moment we need to concentrate on your mission. Abaddon understands how powerful you are now. He won't try to go against you any time soon. Right now, he isn't a threat. If he becomes one, I won't stop you from killing him."

I sigh heavily because I'm becoming tired of the conversation.

"I should go see Kyna," I say, changing the subject.

"Not until I stitch up this gash," Malcolm says, pulling out a drawer in the vanity where a medical kit is stored.

It only takes Malcolm a few minutes to stitch up my wound and bandage it. We both change into casual clothing before heading downstairs to find Kyna. If I know Millie at all, I suspect she has Kyna in the kitchen eating freshly baked cookies and drinking a glass of cold milk. It was Millie's idea of comfort food, and I have to admit it always worked on me.

We do indeed find Kyna and the others down in the kitchen, enjoying milk and cookies. Kyna has taken off her gold feather jacket and veiled crown, allowing her wavy red hair to flow freely past her bare shoulders. Everyone is sitting with her at the table except for Brutus. For some reason he's keeping his distance from her, leaning up against the doorframe.

As Malcolm and I reach him, I touch his shoulder to draw his attention.

"Thank you for catching her," I tell him. "I should have known Lorcan would try to ruin the moment."

"I didn't keep my eyes off of her the entire fight," Brutus tells me. "With someone like him, you never know what he might do out of spite."

"Why aren't you sitting with her?" I ask in a whisper.

"It's too soon," he says with a small shake of his head. "She needs some time to get used to her new circumstances. I'm in no hurry."

"You angels and your self-restraint," I say with a smile of appreciation.

"Years of practice," Brutus replies with a grin.

I squeeze Brutus' arm for reassurance before walking over to the table.

When Kyna sees me, I see tears cloud her sparkling emerald green eyes. She stands from her chair, walks over to me, and wraps her arms around me with a strength I wouldn't have thought someone of her slight stature would possess.

"I don't know how to thank you," she says, a small sob in her voice. "No one else had the gumption to stand up to him even though they knew what he was trying to do was wrong."

I hug Kyna back, hoping the action will bring her some sense of security.

"There's no way I would have just stood back and let him do that to you, Kyna."

Kyna pulls back from me, and I see that her tears are falling freely now.

"But you don't even know me, Anna. We only met a couple of times in our lives. Why would you risk your life for me?"

"We could have never met before, and I would have acted the same way," I tell her. "Sometimes you just have to stand up for what you believe is right and fight those who would take advantage of their power over people. Lorcan was abusing his authority and had to be put in his place."

Kyna drops her arms from me and wipes away the tears on her face.

"I always knew you were strong," she says to me. "Even when we were children, you always held yourself in a way that made us all want to be around you."

"I did?" I ask. As an adult, I heard people mention the aura I have that naturally draws them to me, but I didn't realize it was present while I was a child.

Kyna nods. "Yes, you did. Jered and Desmond were telling me about your plans to reform how the cloud cities rule the down-world. I want to do what I can to help you, if you'll let me."

I smile. "Absolutely. We'll need all the help we can get to make a difference... Though it might take the rest of our lives to make it long-lasting."

"I'm in it for the long haul," Kyna pledges. "I've never approved of the way we've treated them."

"I know," I tell her. "Desmond told me you tried to send supplies to your own down-world when you could. Unfortunately, that can only do so much. We have to find a way to make sure they're able to keep what they need to have a better life, but still provide the people in the cloud cities what they need to survive, not just what they want. I think we should to do away with the law that prevents down-worlders from having access to our technology. I don't think it serves a purpose anymore. We need to help them learn how to use the technological advances we have to help improve their lives."

"I agree," Kyna says. "Just let me know what I can do to help."

"I will," I assure her.

I see Kyna glance in Brutus' direction behind me before she leans in towards me and whispers, "Why does your friend keep staring at me? He hasn't said much since he saved me from the fall."

S.J. West

"I think he might be a bit smitten with you," I whisper back.

I see a rosy hue dapple Kyna's cheeks at my remark.

"Really?" she says, glancing briefly at Brutus with renewed interest. "There *is* something about him, isn't there?"

"Yes, there is," I agree.

I still find it curious that Kyna simply acts interested in Brutus and not head over heels in love with him. I make a note to myself to ask Malcolm about the discrepancy between her reaction to her soulmate and mine.

"Do you happen to have some clothes I can borrow?" Kyna asks me. "I really don't want to wear this stupid dress Lorcan made me wear any longer than I have to."

"I'm sure we can find something for you to put on," I say, wrapping one of my arms around hers. "Let's go raid my wardrobe."

I begin to walk out of the room with Kyna by my side. When we pass Brutus, I see Kyna glance in his direction and bestow upon my friend a glorious smile. Brutus looks almost shy at her notice of him, and lowers his eyes for a second as a pleased grin stretches his lips, and he looks back at her.

I give Kyna a brief tour of the house while we make our way up to my old bedroom.

"I'll be moving my things into Malcolm's room now that we're married," I tell her. "So you can have this room for your own personal space while you stay with us."

"I don't want to be a burden," she begins to protest.

"Don't even think of it that way," I tell her. "You're our honored guest for as long as you want to be."

Kyna and I go through the clothes in my closet, and she settles on a dark blue V-neck sweater, a pair of dark grey slacks, and some comfortable slippers.

"We can get you some clothes of your own tomorrow," I tell her. "In the meantime, wear whatever you want of mine."

"Thank you," Kyna says, hugging me again before pulling back. "You know, this is the first time I've felt safe since my parents died."

"Were the rumors true?" I ask, curiosity getting the better of me. "Did Lorcan orchestrate their deaths? It seemed like a strange coincidence to all of us that they would die in a freak accident at the same exact time."

"I never found any definitive proof, but, yes, I believe he murdered them," Kyna says in disgust. "If I can prove it I can petition to have him imprisoned, and take control of Stratus like my parents wanted."

I want to tell Kyna that her brother isn't really her brother anymore, but I know now isn't the time to bring her into the fold of secrecy that we live under. I'm not sure when we will, but I know it's a decision we'll all need to make together. Right now, she just needs to adjust to the new circumstances of her life.

"I'm sorry he killed your parents," I tell her. "I grew up without a mother and now Auggie has banished my father. So, I sort of know what you're going through."

"I heard rumors that your mother died during childbirth here in the down-world. Is that true?"

I nod. "Yes. She did die giving birth to me."

"I'm so sorry," Kyna says. "My parents weren't the best, but they were mine. I can't imagine how different my life would have been without my mother's presence in my life. I'm sure if your mother could see you now she would be proud of the person you've become. You're a natural-born leader, Anna. You'll do great things during your reign."

"Thanks," I tell her. "I hope you're right."

"I don't have a single doubt," Kyna says with a lift of her chin. "And I plan to help you as much as you'll let me."

When Kyna is ready, we walk out of the room and see Brutus walking towards us down the hallway. I wondered how long he would make himself wait before coming after his woman. I understood the strength of the bond between soulmates. Honestly, I was surprised he held himself back for this long.

"Princess Kyna," Brutus says.

"Please, just call me Kyna, Brutus," Kyna says graciously. "I think you earned that right after saving my life. Thank you for that, by the way."

Brutus grins. "It was my pleasure, Kyna. I thought you might like to see the horses in the stables." Brutus looks over at me. "Malcolm and the others would like to have a word with you in the sitting room, Anna."

"Thank you for telling me." I turn to Kyna. "Why don't you go with Brutus? You can see the new Arabian Jered gave me for a wedding gift."

Kyna looks slightly confused. "I thought you were still married to Auggie? But you've mentioned being married to Malcolm twice now."

"Legally, I *am* still married to Auggie," I tell her. "Mostly just so I can keep my status as Empress of Cirrus. But my heart belongs to Malcolm, and we made our vows to each other last night in front of our friends and family. To me, he's my real husband."

"What happened to Auggie, Anna?" Kyna asks, looking baffled. "He used to be so kind."

"He used to be a totally different person," I say, not speaking a lie but unable to tell her the whole truth about the change in Auggie just yet. "He's a monster now, and I have to find a way to take control of Cirrus away from him."

"I wish you luck in that endeavor. I know from my own experience how hard it can be to do."

Kyna returns her attention to Brutus. When she does her face lights up with a smile, and there's a special twinkle in her eyes as she walks to stand beside him.

"I would love to see the horses now," she says to him.

Brutus holds out his arm for her to take, and they begin to walk down the hallway away from me.

I stand and watch them until they begin to descend the staircase to the first floor, hoping to give them a little space and private time with one another. I would love nothing more than to witness the two of them flourish in their new relationship.

As I walk down the hallway, something draws me to my mother's room. I stare at the painted door for a moment before I walk inside and find the person I expected to find there.

Lucifer stands by the window looking out towards the courtyard.

"I heard what you did to Abaddon," he says before turning to face me. "Did you really have to humiliate him like that in front of his people, Anna?"

I close the door to the room behind me and walk over to stand in front of him.

"He needed to be taught a lesson," I reply. "I doubt you would have even given him a chance to live if you had been in my position."

"No, I wouldn't have," Lucifer says succinctly. "I would have killed him. Now his hatred for you will fester, and he'll find a way to make you pay for what you did."

I sigh because I know he's right, but I really don't want to argue about it.

"Since you phased directly to her room, I assume you used to visit my mother here when she was still alive."

"I've been here before," he tells me, as his eyes are drawn to the bed. "The last time was the night you were born. I can still remember…"

Lucifer phases before he can finish his sentence. I can see by his phase trail that he went directly to Hell, but I know it wasn't of his own free will.

Within the blackness of his phase trail stands a solitary figure, Helena. Her mocking smile seems to be daring me to come find out what she's doing to Lucifer.

I really hate bullies.

And I'll be damned if I allow her to torture my father against his will.

CHAPTER SIXTEEN

When I phase into Hell I find Lucifer sitting on the bench, completely covered in a thin layer of snow that's just beginning to accumulate on him. His eyes look glazed over like his mind is locked inside a nightmare that he's unable to awaken from. I look over my shoulder to see what he's staring at, and see the exterior of a quaint two-story home with a façade composed of a mixture of river rocks and wood siding. I hear angry shouts come from the interior of the house and instantly recognize the voices as belonging to Lucifer and my mother. It's night-time, and I can see their silhouettes through the curtained window of one of the upstairs rooms.

"They're fighting about you, of course," I hear Helena say.

I look behind the bench and see her standing there, looking quite pleased with herself. She's still wearing her red sequined dress. Her long blond hair is perfectly coifed as it hangs over her right shoulder.

"Lucifer wanted Amalie to abort you when they figured out you were killing her," Helena tells me. "But your mother was stubborn and wouldn't even listen to his pleas for her to get rid of the monster growing inside her."

"I already know this," I say, not needing to be reminded of the fact that my birth killed my mother. It was a truth I had lived with all my life. Intellectually I understood there was nothing I could have done to prevent her death; but, emotionally, such guilt never quite leaves you even when reason says otherwise.

Helena smiles. "Well, here's your chance to learn the facts and not just what you were told."

"Lucifer," I hear my mother say behind me, forcing me to turn around to face the scene inside the house in living color.

My mother is lying in a bed, already looking on the edge of death. Her eyes are ringed with dark circles, and her skin is as pale as the white sheets she's laying underneath. She doesn't look that far along in her pregnancy because there's barely a bump on her belly. Lucifer is pacing back and forth beside the bed, clearly agitated.

"Lucifer," my mother says again, finally drawing his attention, "stop fighting me on this. There's no point."

Lucifer stops pacing, and stares at my mother like she's completely lost her mind.

"She's killing you, Amalie!" he shouts, as if the volume of what he's saying will help her understand his words better. "How can you just lie there and let it happen? We don't need a child to make us complete. We're perfect just the way we are."

"I will not murder my own baby," my mother says fiercely, even though I can see that each word is costing her precious energy to say. "You can't ask that of me, Lucifer. Not if you truly love me as much as you profess to. You of all people should understand me well enough to know I could never kill my own flesh and blood."

"I *can* ask it of you and I *will*!" Lucifer bellows. "You say you would be murdering her, but isn't that what she's doing to you? Every moment you let that thing grow inside you is a moment of life that you will never get back."

"She didn't ask to be born into this world," my mother argues. "We are the ones who created her. How can you even think about destroying a child who's half you and half me, Lucifer? She was conceived out of the greatest love I've ever known in my life. Why would you want to kill something so beautiful?"

Lucifer walks up to the bed and sits down beside my mother.

"I can ask because if I lose you I lose myself, Amalie," Lucifer says, looking on the edge of desperation. "You are dooming me to live in a world where you don't exist anymore. If you truly love me, you won't leave me to suffer the rest of my life without you."

"And if you truly love me you won't keep asking me to kill our baby for selfish reasons."

Lucifer takes one of my mother's frail hands into his, bringing it up to his lips.

"Please, Amalie. I'll find you a dozen babies to raise as your own. I'll do anything you ask. But, please, abort this child before she takes you away from me. I can't survive in this world without you."

"Lucifer," my mother says, tears streaming down her face. "I love you, but I love our child more."

After those words, Lucifer's expression changes almost instantaneously. It hardens into a mask of complete indifference. He drops my mother's hand and stands from the bed.

"If you don't love me enough to kill that thing," he says, "then…I release you from the vows you made to me on our wedding day."

"Lucifer, don't…" my mother begs, sobbing uncontrollably. "Don't do this to us. Not now."

Lucifer shakes his head at her. "I can't stand by and watch you die. That thing is only inside you because of me. I'm the one who's truly killing you, Amalie. If it wasn't for me, you would have lived a normal life."

"But I would have never known true happiness."

"How can this make you happy?" Lucifer asks scathingly. "Do you like being on the edge of death? You know you'll never survive that creature's birth!"

"But I will have brought a child into the world who is the best parts of us both. She's a gift that could have never been made if we hadn't fallen in love. She will be unlike anything this world has ever seen, Lucifer. She'll be perfect."

"A perfect abomination," Lucifer spits out. "And I refuse to have anything to do with her."

"You're her father," my mother says, as if trying to drive the truth of that simple fact home. "She'll need you after I'm gone."

"She won't even know I exist if I have anything to say about it," Lucifer says. "And if I know your bleeding-heart Watchers, they'll raise her and make sure she knows nothing about me."

"But that's not what I want," my mother cries. "I want her to know you! You're her father whether you want to be or not!"

"I will not love her," Lucifer says ,with so much conviction and hatred I feel his words sting my heart. "She will be nothing to me. I refuse to care for something that takes the only person I've ever loved away from me. You can't force me to love something like that!"

"She's your daughter," my mother says reproachfully. "She isn't a thing!"

"She's nothing to me," Lucifer says resolutely. "And that's exactly the way I'll treat her."

"Lucifer," my mother says, stretching out a hand towards him, "please don't do this to me."

"You've given me no other choice," Lucifer says, keeping his voice emotionless. "Goodbye, Amalie."

Lucifer phases and the scene goes black. All I hear are my mother's plaintive cries.

I swallow hard, trying to contain my own tears after watching the scene. I turn around to find that Helena has moved to stand right behind me.

"There's no need to hide your pain," she croons, closing her eyes and smiling as if she's experiencing a moment of ecstasy. "Your sorrow is almost as deep as your father's. Why do you still feel guilt over your birth?"

"Who wouldn't feel sad that their birth was the cause of their mother's death?"

Helena opens her eyes and smiles. Her gaze is drawn to something over my shoulder, and I know she's conjured up yet another scene. I brace myself because I know which of Lucifer's memories she's about show me.

When I turn around, I see my mother's room in Malcolm's house. Positioned in the room like statues are my papa, Lucifer, Desmond, Brutus, Daniel, Jered, and Millie. Lucifer is standing off in the farthest dark corner while the others are around the bed. Papa is sitting on the bed beside my mother, holding one of her hands while Millie is standing on the other side, holding her other hand. My mother appears to be in mid-push, considering the strained expression on her face. Desmond is situated on the far end of the bed, acting as my mother's doctor. The others are busy tending to preparations for my entry into the world.

Brutus is readying a wooden cradle with blankets. Jered is laying out towels and what looks like some of Desmond's medical equipment on a table. Daniel is walking into the room with a bowl of steaming water and extra towels draped across one arm.

"Is this the moment you most dread to watch?" Helena whispers in my ear. "The moment you killed your mother."

I remain silent because I don't want to give Helena any more pleasure than she's already taking from me. I refuse to let her taunts provoke a reaction inside me.

Instantly, the room comes alive with action. It's almost like a switch was flipped to set the scene into motion.

"Push, Amalie," Desmond encourages my mother. "Just one more and I think we'll have her."

My mother squeezes my papa's hand tightly and screams as she pushes with all the strength she has left in her body.

I watch as my body slides head-first out of my mother and into Desmond's awaiting hands. After being so rudely thrust into the cold world, I begin to cry. Desmond hands me to Millie and she rocks me in her arms, trying to bring me some comfort. Millie quickly hands me off to Jered, who lays me on the towels on the table. Daniel quickly washes the evidence of my birth off my skin before Desmond comes over to examine me.

"You did it," Papa tells my mother, lovingly moving sweat-soaked strands of hair off her emaciated face.

My mother's breathing is labored, and I think everyone in the room knows she doesn't have much longer to live. She opens her eyes and anxiously searches the room until she finds Lucifer still standing alone in his corner.

"And here she is," Desmond says, bringing me to my mother, swaddled in a pink blanket. He lays me in the crook of her right arm, on the bed.

"Oh my," my mother says, tears streaming down her face. "She's even more beautiful than I could have imagined."

My mother looks back over at Lucifer.

"Lucifer, come meet your daughter," my mother begs, holding out a weak, shaky hand, urging him to come closer.

Everyone in the room watches to see what Lucifer will do.

Finally, he pushes away from his spot in the corner and walks over to my mother and me. The others move away to allow them a small bit of privacy.

Lucifer sits down on the side of the bed and stares at me as I rest against my mother's side.

"Lucifer," my mother says, drawing his gaze to her face. "I want you to do something for me."

"You know I would do anything for you."

"Raise our child," my mother begs. "Let her get to know the side of you that you've only shown to me. There's so much goodness inside you, but you refuse to let anyone see it."

"You're the only one who ever bothered to look."

"You know that's not true," she tells him. "Your father has always known it was there. I think He sent me to you so that you would remember who you once were. Let go of your hatred and jealousy towards humanity. Love our child and show her what a beautiful person you are on the inside. There's so much you have to offer and teach her. Please, promise me you'll keep her with you, keep her safe."

"I can't do that," Lucifer says, wiping at the tears that have fallen across his cheeks. "I wouldn't even know where to start, Amalie. She'll be better off staying here with your friends."

"But I don't want that," my mother sobs. "I want her to grow up with you. She deserves to know how much her mother and father love her. Don't take that opportunity away from her."

"But you're leaving us," Lucifer says as tears continue to stream down his face. "How are we supposed to go on without you? How am I supposed to live without you, Amalie?"

My mother looks down at me. "A part of me will always be here for you to love, Lucifer. Look at her," my mother urges. "How can you not see me in her?"

Lucifer looks down at me but says nothing.

My mother reaches a hand out and grabs hold of Lucifer's arm.

"Please," she begs, crying. "Please tell me you'll look after our child. Tell me you can show her the love you've shown me."

Lucifer remains silent as he stares at me. Finally, he raises his eyes to look at my mother's face.

"All right," he says, sounding defeated. "I'll do it for you."

My mother smiles wanly, and I can tell she knows he's lying to her.

"Oh, Lucifer," she says weakly, on the precipice of death. "If only you knew…"

My mother goes completely limp as death claims her body.

Lucifer stands up. He continues to stare at my mother for a long while. When I finally begin to cry, he reaches down and picks me up. Even though I know what will happen next, a part of me hopes he will take me and do as my mother asked.

Instead, he turns to the others in the room and asks, "Which of you is willing to take on the responsibility of raising Amalie's child?"

My papa steps forward before anyone else has a chance.

"I will," he says to Lucifer. "I will raise her as if she were my own."

Lucifer hands me over to my papa and stares at me for a moment before saying, "She would never find true happiness with me like Amalie thought. And I refuse to corrupt Amalie's last gift to this world."

"I understand," my papa says, not judging Lucifer in the slightest for his decision. "I promise she will always know that she's loved by me and those around her. You don't have to worry about her physical or emotional well-being."

Lucifer nods, accepting that my papa's words are true.

He phases away and the scene fades to black.

"Poor Lucifer," Helena utters mockingly.

I turn to see her bent at the waist, looking into Lucifer's face. Tears of sorrow cascade freely from Lucifer's eyes, yet he still looks frozen into place, completely lost in his last memory of my mother. Helena reaches out a hand and follows a trail of tears down one of his cheeks with her index finger. She brings the tip of her finger to her mouth and spreads his tears on her ruby red lips like it's lipstick. She smiles before standing back up and turning to face me.

"There's nothing quite as sweet as the taste of pure sorrow," she says to me. "I've tasted it quite often over the years from Lucifer's tears. Yet I can never seem to get enough of them."

Her heartless words awaken something dark inside me. It's a hatred so vile I feel on the verge of losing control of it. I grab Helena by the throat and lift her off the ground, my hands burst into blue flames.

"Stop torturing him," I order her, through clenched teeth.

Helena begins to laugh, and I squeeze her throat even harder, making her laughs turn to gurgles. I hold her in place like that for a long while before I loosen my grip a little to allow her to speak.

"Like father like daughter, I see. Do you think you're actually hurting me?" she taunts viciously. "You're simply feeding me, making me into something greater with your loathing. I live for hate. I live for pain. I live to make your world a living Hell. So do your worst to me, my dear, because it only makes me stronger."

I let go of Helena. She lands on her feet, looking unfazed by my actions. If anything, she looks even more pleased with herself.

"Release him from your spell," I tell her.

"No," she says succinctly. "And don't bother to come up with more threats. There's nothing you can do to truly harm me. I'm not something you can simply kill, Anna. Your puny little monkey brain can't possibly comprehend what I am. There's only one way I will ever let Lucifer go-- if *you* take his place."

"No!" Lucifer shouts.

Helena looks startled by Lucifer's outburst. I get the feeling she didn't think he was able to hear our exchange. Perhaps her hold on him isn't as strong as she believes.

"Anna," Lucifer says, standing to his feet, dislodging the snow on his body with his movements, "leave this place and never return. I'll handle this thing."

Helena begins to laugh, but it comes out sounding more like an insane person's cackle.

"Handle me?" she asks incredulously. "You act as though you still have control down here, Lucifer. It's been years since you did. I am the master of this domain now, not you."

Lucifer looks over at me. "Leave. Let me handle this."

"We would be stronger together," I argue.

Lucifer shakes his head. "I don't need your help. Just leave."

I stay, hoping he'll change his mind.

"Leave!" he shouts at me.

I phase back to the actual courtyard at Malcolm's house. I sit down on the snow-covered bench and think through everything I just witnessed in Hell. The remorse I've felt over my mother's death bubbles over, and I begin to cry uncontrollably from the breaking of my heart. Before I know it, Malcolm is drawing me into his arms, holding me against his chest. He phases us to the couch in his study, presumably to get me out of the cold. I cry against his chest, letting all of my pent-up sorrow from years of guilt finally find release.

Once I'm able to stop crying and pull myself together, I tell Malcolm everything that happened. He patiently listens to what I say, even though I can tell he's disappointed to hear that I made another trip to Hell.

"I hope you listen to Lucifer this time. It's obvious you won't listen to me," Malcolm says, sounding slightly frustrated. "You should never go back there, Anna. She's just goading you into giving into your hate. It's what she wants. The more she can make you hate her, the more power she can siphon from you. She's like a leech whose only purpose is to cause discord and loathing."

"I know," I say. "And I understand that, but I couldn't just let her torture Lucifer with his own memories. I had to try to save him."

"You can't protect everyone," Malcolm tells me gently, "Lucifer least of all. Hell is only as powerful as it is because he made it that way. He's simply become a victim of his own creation, Anna. There's nothing you can do for him."

I sit up straighter and look at Malcolm.

"Do you really believe that?" I ask. "Do you believe he's beyond saving? Because I refuse to think that way. I think he can be saved. I think he wants to be saved, Malcolm."

"Don't project your own desires onto him," Malcolm warns. "If you go down that path, you might lose yourself in the process. Lucifer made his choice a long time ago, Anna. When he defied our father and brought war to Heaven, he built a wall so high around himself that not even God Himself can breach it."

"But don't you think Lucifer has learned from his mistakes after all these years? Don't you think a person can find himself again and realize how wrong he's been?"

"Of course I do. It happened to me after I met Lilly."

"Then why don't you think it could happen to Lucifer, too? Malcolm," I say, grabbing his hand because I want to make sure he understands my position on the subject, "I believe Lucifer can be saved. In a way, I feel like I was born to show him his true self again. When we're together it's almost like he's able to let his guard down a little. He may not have wanted my birth to happen, but now I think he understands why it had to. I think God sent me down here to save him from himself."

Malcolm shakes his head. "I truly don't believe Lucifer can care for anyone more than he does himself, Anna. I mean, look at what he did to Amalie. He loved her more than anyone yet he turned his back on her when she needed his strength the most. He lied to her on her deathbed about agreeing to raise you. I think you're letting your empathy for him cloud your better judgment where he's concerned."

"And I think you're letting your hatred of him cloud yours, Malcolm."

"Perhaps," Malcolm concedes, absently rubbing his injured leg. "I just have a hard time imagining he can be the person you want him to be."

I lean against Malcolm again, resting my head on his chest and drawing strength from his warmth. I feel cold inside after my visit to Hell and confrontation with Helena, but Malcolm's natural warmth, something he's commented on before, is like a healing balm, mending my soul until it's whole again.

"I don't know how you put up with me," I tell him. "You keep asking me not to go there but I keep going."

"I understand it's just your nature to want to help people," Malcolm says, gliding a hand up and down my arm as he holds me close. "And I fear the pain you'll feel when Lucifer ends up disappointing you."

I don't say anything. I understand Malcolm's point of view. I simply don't agree with it.

I believe Lucifer can change. I just have to find a way to make both him and Malcolm believe it, too.

CHAPTER SEVENTEEN

For almost two weeks, Malcolm and I live in a state of marital bliss. Our mornings start with us making love and our evenings end in the same fashion. During the day, we spend quality time with our son and watch him flourish under our tutelage. We decide that it's a good idea for Lucas to not only learn how to master a sword, but also how to fight in hand-to-hand combat. Lucas' human frailties worry me greatly, considering the world Malcolm and I live in and the creatures that we deal with. He will never be as strong as us or most of our enemies, but that doesn't mean we should leave him completely defenseless.

With this fact in mind, I have Giles go to town to buy me something special for Lucas. One day, after his physical combat lesson with Malcolm, I present him with it.

"Come here, little man," I say to him, bending down on one knee so we are at eye level with one another. "I have a gift for you."

Lucas runs over to me from his father's side. The smile on his face is irresistible, and I can't help but smile, too.

"What is it?" he asks eagerly. "Are you going to have the babies?"

I laugh at Lucas' continued eagerness for his little sister and brother to be brought into the world. But I'm still wearing the necklace Malcolm gave me on our wedding night to prevent me from conceiving our children just yet. Becoming pregnant right now simply isn't the best idea, considering the circumstances. Although we decided to delay children, it didn't prevent us from practicing very vigorously for the day when we would be free to have them. I feel sure we can't

S.J. West

work at it much harder than we are, but that's not exactly something I can tell our son.

"Not that I know of," I tell him instead. "But I hope you like this gift just the same."

I pull out a brown leather belted holster from the blue velvet bag in my hands. I hold it by the sheath and pull out the small silver dagger I retrieved from Levi the last time he and I fought. It may have been foolhardy for me to go to Cirrus to retrieve the first wedding dress Millie made me, but at least I came back with a useful souvenir.

"This dagger is very special," I tell Lucas. "It was forged by Uncle Brutus a long time ago, and it's made out of silver that came straight from Heaven."

Lucas' eyes grow large in wonder and his mouth forms a little 'O' in surprise.

"I want you to always wear it," I tell him, strapping the belt around his slim hips. "And if anyone ever tries to hurt you, you have our permission to use it on them. Just stab them with it and run as fast as you can away from them. Do you understand?"

Lucas nods. "Yes, Mommy."

"Having a weapon is a great responsibility," I tell him. "It's not a toy. Only use it in defense of yourself or someone else who is in danger. Is that also understood?"

Lucas nods again. "I promise I won't take it out unless I need to use it."

239

I bring Lucas into my arms and hug him tight, silently praying he never has to draw the dagger out of its sheath.

As I stand back up to my feet, I hear Kyna's lilting laughter in the hallway outside the training room. It makes me smile to hear her so happy, and I know exactly why she is.

During the past two weeks, Brutus has become a mainstay in our home as he slowly started to woo the Princess of Stratus. When the courtship first began, I asked Malcolm why it seemed that Kyna hadn't been immediately struck by the 'love at first sight' soulmate syndrome that I had fallen victim to.

"She's human," he answered, like this was explanation enough for the discrepancy.

"I'm human, too," I said at the time, not seeing his response as a clear answer to my question.

"Yes, but you're also part angel," Malcolm went on to say. "If a human is lucky enough to meet their soulmate, they don't sense it right away. Take Jess for example. When she first met Mason, she didn't exactly feel the earth beneath her feet give way. She was attracted to him, but her love for him wasn't an immediate reaction. For those of us with angelic traits, like you, you know when you meet your soulmate the instant you see them. Brutus knew the moment he saw Kyna that she was meant for him, but for her it's taken a bit longer to feel the connection."

"Doesn't seem quite fair," I admitted.

"Meeting your true soulmate is something that doesn't happen very often between humans," Malcolm said. "If every human waited until they met their soulmate, the species might have died out a long time ago. People can love someone just as much without their souls being perfect matches to one another. Look at Daniel and Linn. He loves her just as fiercely as he would have his soulmate. They have a beautiful life together without that particular connection between them."

As I watch Kyna and Brutus walk hand in hand by the open door, I feel blessed to know I could help them share this time together. I doubt Kyna has had much in her life to be happy about and am thankful that Brutus has been given his chance at love. Desmond and Jered enter my thoughts, and I wonder how long it will take them to find their soulmates. After I complete my God-given task, their long mission will also be complete. Perhaps God will see fit to present them with their own soulmates. I hope I get to see them as happy as Brutus is before I die, but know that such a thing might not happen. But I can hope…

Malcolm and I follow Lucas out of the training room, holding hands. I see Vala walk towards us down the hall.

"You have visitors," she tells us. "Barlow and Gladson are here to see you. They said they're ready to broadcast the video today."

"I was wondering how much longer it would take," I say, feeling a sense of relief that the day of reckoning for the cloud cities has finally arrived.

"I think they want to give you the honor of uploading it to the satellites," Vala tells me.

"Then let's go."

Vala leads us to the sitting room where Barlow and Gladson are waiting.

"Well, I have to say married life seems to agree with you, Anna," Gladson tells me when we walk into the room. "I don't think I've ever seen you look more beautiful. You're practically glowing with happiness."

"Thank you," I say. "I don't think I've ever been this content with my life, to tell you the truth."

"Hopefully," Barlow joins in, "we can add to it today. Travis has the video ready to broadcast. All we need for you to do is push the button to start this little revolution of ours."

"Then let's go, gentlemen. I'm ready to bring change to the world."

We all phase to Travis Stoke's hideout. I still wasn't quite sure what part of the world his workshop was located, but figured the less I knew the better. Vala and Lucas come with us. It seems that their last trip to Travis' place was a memorable one, allowing them to form a friendship with our brilliant young friend. After the visit, Lucas proclaimed that he wanted to be an engineer when he grew up. Vala said it seemed like Lucas had a natural skill with the things Travis showed him. I was just glad they'd both made a friend. Neither of them had many opportunities to meet new people, since we rarely ever left our home.

I had a feeling Malcolm kept me out of the city of New Orleans because he didn't want me to have to face the poverty of the down-worlders. I understood his need to keep me inside our happy bubble, but he would have to learn that in order for me to change what was wrong with the world I would have to see what needed to be altered first-hand. I didn't push him on the issue because I knew we had enough to deal with. I would have to rely on Gladson and Barlow to be the flag-bearers of our revolution until I quelled the threat the princes presented.

For the past two weeks, the other Watchers had been collecting information on the princes for me. It would have been foolhardy for us to simply go in and kill them. We had to consider the political ramifications of depriving each cloud city of their leaders. Lucifer placed them in positions of power that made it almost impossible for me to reach them. We all knew they had to die. It was just a matter of figuring out the best way to go about it. Although their deaths would have ended the threat they represented, leaving the cities without rulers would be a more serious problem.

However, I did make one request.

Seeing Olivia Ravensdale in Stratus made me even more determined to find a way to execute Botis for the murder of her husband. The only problem was Belphagor masquerading himself in the body of Empress Zhin. If I killed Belphagor to retrieve his seal, that would leave Botis in power, since he was now wearing the skin of Emperor Rui. It was a no-win situation that didn't seem to have a practical solution.

When we reach Travis' place, we find him skate-dancing around his workshop to some industrial music. After he sees us, he stops dancing and claps his hands twice to lower the volume.

"Sorry!" he calls out, looking a little embarrassed at being caught. "I was just celebrating a little. You don't know what it took to hack into all the communication satellites needed to transmit this video simultaneously to every cloud city."

"I appreciate all your hard work," I tell Travis as we walk over to the holographic display he's standing in front of. "What do I need to do to get this started?"

Travis turns around to face the controls.

"I have everything set up," he tells me. "All you have to do is hit this button."

Travis points to a red button on the display, and I wonder if he made it red so I couldn't possibly miss it.

I place my hand over the button and hesitate.

Once this door is opened, there's no going back. The citizens of every cloud city will see the price their lives of luxury cost the down-worlders. They'll no longer be able to turn a blind eye to what's going on around them. It's what I want, but it's also like throwing cold water on a person who's been asleep for hundreds of years. The people living in the clouds have literally ignored what was happening to the humans who live below them. Now, they will have to come to terms with their own complacency. No one likes being forced to face his or her shortcomings, least of all people of privilege.

"Here we go," I say to those around me, pressing the button.

The display goes completely black.

"Did I break something?" I ask in worry.

"No," Gladson says, coming to stand beside me. "Just watch."

"Citizens of Cirrus, Cirro, Stratus, Nimbo, Alto, Virga, and Nacreous," a voice says, one I immediately recognize as belonging to Gladson. "For far too long you have lived a life of luxury and excess," he says as the video flashes images of parties where food is plentiful and wine flows freely. More pictures of citizens within each cloud city flashes on the screen. Some of them are enjoying lunch at sidewalk cafes. Some are playing with their children in parks. Still others shop for the latest fashions in the posh stores available to them.

"How many of you know exactly where the things you take for granted come from? Do you know the man, woman, or child who provides them for you?"

The video on the screen shows the poor seaside town I visited with Desmond. It's of a woman sitting inside a ramshackle dwelling, rocking herself back and forth as she cries and holds a dead child in her arms.

"Do you know whose blood was spilt just so you could have bread on your tables?"

Another video plays, showing a man being whipped by an overlord from Nimbo as he harvests wheat from a field. Snippets of videos showing similar abuse by overlords in the other down-worlds, including Cirrus, also play.

"Do you know the price that was paid just so your clothes can be made of the finest silks?"

A factory filled with children working several looms is shown. Some of the kids aren't much older than Lucas.

"Did you know that those who grow the grapes for the wine you drink and for the food you eat aren't even able to feed their own families?"

A video of a family sitting in a lean-to shack appears. The mother is giving her children small portions of bread, but sits down and takes none for herself because there simply isn't enough to spare.

The screen turns black again, but you can see Gladson's shadowy figure in the background.

"We've all been guilty of forgetting the multitude of less fortunate who live below us," Gladson's voice says. "But now is the time to raise your voice and make the rulers of our cities and the overlords who control the down-world listen. We must no longer cower in the complacency of our lives, in the shadows of our wealth, and allow the atrocities occurring in the down-world to continue. Join me," Gladson says as his figure emerges out of the dark to be plainly seen, "and maybe together we can bring an end to the price being paid by the down-worlders just so we can continue to live in decadence. Rise up…be heard…help me bring forth a new beginning for all of us."

The screen goes black, and I turn to Gladson.

"Well, if you didn't have a target on your back before, you certainly do now," I tell him, surprised he showed his face in the video so directly.

"Everyone knows my political views anyway," Gladson says with a nonchalant shrug. "Our movement needed a spokesperson, and I was the best choice."

"As soon as I've completed my mission," I tell him. "I'll be standing right beside you."

"No," Gladson says with a small shake of his head. "It will be I who stands beside you as your supporter. You're the real leader of this movement, Anna. When the time comes, you'll take the reins and lead us where we need to go. I'm simply your placeholder for now."

"It won't be too much longer," I promise him. "But as it is, I don't think you should go back to Cirrus anytime soon."

"Agreed," Gladson says. "Even if Levi doesn't try to kill me, some of the overlords in the video might. No one wants their dirty laundry made public."

"Where will you stay?" I ask.

"He'll be bunking with my people for a while," Barlow says. "He has a place with us for as long as he wants."

I look at Gladson's right hand. "What about your personal transporter? They'll be able to track you with it."

"Which is where our brilliant engineer here comes in," Gladson says, looking over at Travis. "He'll be removing it from me today so I can go into exile. But I have people stationed in all the cloud cities to watch for any new supporters. Hopefully people will demand change, and I won't have to stay hidden for very long."

"I think we should run this video at noon every day until something positive is done," I tell them. "People have short memories. We might even need to make more videos and let them hear from real down-worlders about the conditions they live in."

"It might be hard to find down-worlders who would come out and speak directly against their overlords," Gladson says.

"If we have to," Barlow says, "we can just use my people in their place. They can act out the parts. It's only a small lie to protect those who can't protect themselves."

"It sounds like you have it all figured out then," I say, wishing I could do more to help bring about reform in the way the down-worlders are treated. "As soon as I gain complete control over Cirrus, we can show the other cloud cities what they should be doing to change things. It will take some time to bring them up to speed with our technology, but I think most of them are up for the challenge. In the end, it should help production of almost everything down here. The more we prosper, the more likely the other cloud cities will follow our lead."

Malcolm and I soon return home with Lucas and Vala, leaving Gladson and the Stokeses to handle what needs to be done for the beginning of our restructuring of the down-world.

Since it's lunchtime, we all head to the kitchen. We find Jered sitting at the table with Luna in his arms. Since Lucifer gave her to me, Luna has grown to almost twice her size. I knew it wouldn't be too much longer before she was a full-grown hellhound, and wondered what people would think of me having such a pet. As soon as I returned to Cirrus to take back control, I planned to change the law that forbade people from having real animals as pets. Such a disconnect with nature simply wasn't healthy.

"I saw the video while I was in Cirro," Jered tells us. "It caused quite an uproar."

"Good," I say, sitting down at the table with him while Malcolm goes to see if Millie needs help preparing lunch. "That's the sort of reaction we wanted to provoke."

"I guess we'll see what happens," Jered says absently as he strokes Luna's fur.

"What's on your mind?" I ask him, sensing he's not here just to have lunch with us or chitchat about the uprising I hope the video instigates.

"I think I might have a way for you to take care of Botis and still get what you need from Belphagor," Jered says unexpectedly.

I sit up straighter in my chair at this news.

"How?" I ask eagerly.

"I think we should exploit Belphagor's weakness," he says as Malcolm comes to stand near the table to listen to Jered's proposal. "He's always been the most cowardly of the princes and not particularly smart. Since we know they can give you the seals voluntarily, I say we make a deal with him."

"What kind of deal?" Malcolm asks stiffly, already sounding skeptical about such a plan before Jered can even explain his intentions.

"Botis obviously knows that you want to do away with him," Jered tells me, glancing in Lucas' direction. It's obvious he didn't want to say 'kill' in front of my son. We hadn't really told Lucas what was going on. We didn't want to frighten him, and he was simply too young to fully understand the ramifications of the situation. "Botis has surrounded himself with so many guards that it's almost impossible to get to him. Even if you did, you would end up having witnesses. Belphagor is the only one who can get him alone and have it not look suspicious."

"Why would he help us?" I ask.

"Because he wants to be sole ruler of Cirro. It's why he took over Empress Zhin's body. Rui was practically dead, and the people of Cirro wanted Zhin to assume power. It was a perfect situation for him. He would have had sole rule over Cirro and not have to deal with a spouse or a child. Now with Botis inhabiting Rui's body he has to relinquish power to someone he considers lower in rank to him. I have a feeling if we go to him with this offer he'll accept."

"And what if he double-crosses us?" Malcolm asks. "What if Anna gets rid of Botis, but Belphagor doesn't live up to his end of the bargain and decides to keep the seal?"

"Then I'll take it from him," I say.

"I think Belphagor will agree," Jered says more to Malcolm than me. "You know he's always been the weakest link among the princes. If he can save his own skin and gain more power without much effort, I don't see any reason that he would refuse."

"What about Lucifer?" I ask. "He won't be happy with Belphagor if he helps us."

"I suppose that's a risk Belphagor will have to take. It's either face Lucifer or you. If he has any sense at all, he won't choose to go against you."

I look up at Malcolm. "I think we should at least try it. We won't be losing much, and could possibly gain everything. I would like to be able to keep my promise to Olivia and take care of the person who harmed her husband."

Malcolm sighs heavily. "I don't like making deals with someone who isn't trustworthy. But it does sound like our best way to deal with both of them."

"So, should I set up a meeting between Anna and Belphagor?" Jered asks.

Malcolm nods. "Yes. Set it up for tomorrow in the desert. I don't want that thing in my home, and we're not going to step foot inside Cirro until a firm deal is made."

Jered sets Luna on the floor and stands from his chair.

"I'll go make the arrangements. Any particular time tomorrow?"

"In the morning," Malcolm says. "The sooner we get this done the better."

"I'll come back after I talk to him," Jered tells us just before he phases.

Malcolm walks behind my chair and rests his hands on my shoulders, massaging the tension that's suddenly developed there.

"Well I don't know about any of you," Millie says, turning to the table with a platter full of thinly cut meat, "but I'll be glad when this whole mess is over with."

"Amen," I say, closing my eyes as I enjoy Malcolm's touch.

"How come I can't know what's going on?" Lucas asks. "I'm a big kid now, you know. I can take it."

"Not just yet," Malcolm says to him. "We'll tell you when the time is right. I promise."

Lucas doesn't look pacified by Malcolm's promise, but it just isn't in his nature to argue with his father.

Just then, Kyna waltzes into the room on the arm of her beau. Brutus looks so happy, it brings a smile to my face. Their love for one another is naked for anyone near them to see.

"Well I guess we don't need to ask how the two of you are doing today," Malcolm says to them knowingly.

Kyna smiles shyly, glancing over at Brutus out of the corner of her eye.

"We're doing quite well, thank you very much," she replies. "But I'm starving. What's for lunch?"

"You sure do eat a lot for someone so small," Lucas comments innocently.

Kyna laughs. "I've always had a high metabolism. My father used to say I was lucky he had so much money, otherwise I would starve to death."

"Well there's plenty here to eat," Millie says, setting down a loaf of freshly baked and sliced bread.

We soon have plenty on the table to make sandwiches for our meal. While we eat, Kyna tells us about Brutus trying to teach her how to be a blacksmith. Something she's obviously not adept at, at least not yet.

Honestly, I was only listening to half the conversation. For the past few days, my thoughts kept returning to the last of Lucifer's memories. By the end of the meal, I know what I have to do. I lean over to whisper in Malcolm's ear.

"Do you know where my parents lived?" I ask him.

Malcolm immediately looks troubled by my question but nods slowly. He seems to already know what my next question will be.

"Would you take me there?" I ask.

"Are you sure you want to go?"

I nod. "Yes."

Malcolm sighs in resignation.

"Then finish up your lunch," he says to me. "And I'll take you."

I place one hand on Malcolm's thigh and squeeze it gently.

"Thank you."

Malcolm nods, accepting my thanks, and continues to finish his meal.

I'm not really sure what I expect to find at my parents' home, except for a sense of who they were when they were together. All I know is that I need to feel closer to them, and there isn't any place better than the home they built together…

CHAPTER EIGHTEEN

After lunch, Brutus and Kyna volunteer to take care of Lucas while Malcolm and I are gone. I don't want to take him with us because I'm not sure what effect being in my parents' home will have on me. If it makes me emotional, I don't want him to see me break down.

"Are you sure about this?" Malcolm asks me, looking worried about taking me where I want to go.

I grab a purple wool coat with a fur collar and shoulder cape out of the walk-in closet in our room, knowing that anywhere we go in the down-world will be cold this time of year.

"I saw a little bit of the home while I watched Lucifer's memory," I tell him, pulling my hair out of the back of the coat to let it fall freely around my shoulders. "I just want to see it for myself."

"I haven't been there since before you were born. The last time I went there was to get your mother after Lucifer abandoned her. I didn't want Amalie to be all alone while she was pregnant with you," Malcolm says. "I'm not sure what sort of shape the house will be in after all these years."

"As long as it doesn't look like it will fall on our heads, I would still like to see it."

Malcolm holds his hand out to me, and I take it.

I soon find myself standing in front of the two-story home that once belonged to my parents. It's built deep within a forested area where I can't imagine many people would just wander across it. The exterior is overgrown with vegetation after being abandoned for so many years. A thin layer of newly fallen snow covers it, giving the house an ethereal appearance. With Malcolm holding my hand, we walk up the path to the front door. I reach out and grab the brass doorknob, to find it unlocked. I gently push the door open, letting it swing inward the rest of the way on its own.

Sun filters through a naturally made skylight, and the interior is dusted with a blanket of newly fallen snow. We walk in and see that sometime over the years a tree has fallen on the house, breaking through the roof and second floor to land in the middle of the entryway on the ground floor. The house is completely silent, bringing a sad and empty quality to the surroundings. I look over to my left and see a space that was once a living room. The few pieces of furniture left there have decayed from exposure to the elements over time, and most likely animals looking for a warm place to stay.

I let go of Malcolm's hand and walk over to the room. There's a fireplace with a mantel on the outside wall facing the front of the house. I walk over to it and run my hand through the snow that's accumulated on top of it.

"Ouch!" I cry out, as the palm of my hand runs across something sharp hidden beneath the snow. Droplets of my blood spill onto the object. Malcolm is by my side in less than a second, taking my hand to examine it.

"It's not too deep," he says, studying the cut. "Wait here. I'll be right back."

Malcolm phases and I return my attention to the mantel to see what was sharp enough to cut me.

Lying just underneath the snow is a shattered picture frame. Cautiously I reach out and pick it up, letting the broken glass fall out onto the mantel.

It's a picture of Lucifer and my mother, standing in front of this house in happier times. They're both smiling and look like the most content people in the world. Lucifer has his arms wrapped around my mother's waist with his hands splayed over her stomach. Her belly doesn't even have a bump showing that she was pregnant yet, but you can tell by their expressions I was already within her womb when this picture was taken. It had to have been before they understood my conception was a death sentence for my mother. Otherwise, they wouldn't look like they had the rest of their lives ahead of them.

I pull the picture out of the broken frame just as Malcolm comes back with a healing wand. I put the picture in the pocket of my coat as I hand Malcolm my injured hand.

"I don't like seeing you hurt," he tells me, running the wand over my hand to instantly heal the wound.

"Thank you," I tell him, leaning in to kiss him on the lips and wipe away the worry on his face.

"Have you seen enough here?" he asks, tucking the wand into one of his jacket pockets.

"I just want to walk through what's left for a little while longer."

Malcolm nods, and lets go of my hand to allow me to lead the way. He follows behind me, but not too closely, allowing me to soak in what remains of a home I'm sure was once filled with happiness, if the picture I found is any indication. I feel an immense sadness for my parents. Not only for losing the time they would have had here on Earth together if I hadn't been born, but also for the time they would never get to share with one another in Heaven.

I look over my shoulder at Malcolm. He's looking at something off to the side and doesn't see me studying him. My heart aches inside my chest at just the thought of us being separated from each other after death. I saw firsthand what such a divide was doing to my mother. She was an emotional wreck, even though she was in Heaven. Being in such a place was supposed to bring everlasting joy. For her it almost seemed like a prison sentence, because it meant an eternity without her soulmate and only being allowed to feel his pain after her loss.

Malcolm must sense my gaze. He looks at me and smiles, breaking my heart at the tenderness he holds for me in his eyes.

"I love you," I say.

"I love you, too," he says back.

A sudden movement behind a door to my right draws my attention. I walk over and swing the door open further to see what's inside.

As I stand in the threshold of the room, I'm caught off guard by what I see. A well of tears blur my vision as I look at what would have been my room once upon a time.

The sun shines through the large single-paned window behind a dilapidated crib. A white dove sits perched on top of what's left of the wood frame, but quickly flies past me out of the room. My gaze is drawn back to what's painted on the window. It's a mural composed of a beautiful tree with a plethora of leafy branches, but something looks odd about the branches. I walk further into the room to get a better look at it. As I study the tree, I soon discover what's unusual about it. The roots at the base of the trunk are painted in such a way that two names can be seen within their curls, Lilly and Brand. I follow what looks like natural bark lines on the trunk and see that they actually spell out two more names, Caylin and Aiden. I study the connecting branches and see a multitude of other names etched. I search the branches until I find the two names I'm looking for, Lucifer and Amalie. There is a branch stemming off it without a name, that should have had mine if my mother had named me before her death. I run the tips of my fingers over my parents' names. The instant I do, an array of colorful holographic butterflies surround me, kissing my skin.

I begin to cry.

I feel Malcolm wrap his arms around me from behind. I turn to bury my face against his chest finding comfort in his embrace. My husband simply holds me tight without saying a word. In this room, I feel the missed opportunity of another life. What would have happened if my mother had survived my birth? Would we have been a happy little family, living in this home where butterflies magically appear with just a touch? What other wonders would my parents have shown me if they had been given the opportunity?

It takes me a while to pull myself together. When I finally do, I lift my head and look up at Malcolm.

"Don't cry, my love," Malcolm says, wiping away my tears with the pads of his thumbs. "Every tear you shed tears a hole inside my heart."

Of course, this just makes me cry even harder.

I wrap my arms around Malcolm's neck.

"Take me home," I beg him.

Malcolm phases us back to our bedroom and simply holds me until I'm ready to let him go. I know what I want to do. I'm just not sure how well Malcolm will react to my idea.

I pull away slightly to speak.

"I would like to do something," I tell him, feeling nervous to give voice to my heartfelt wish.

Malcolm's eyes narrow on me, obviously sensing my reluctance to say what's on my mind.

"You act like this is going to make me mad."

I sigh. "It might."

Malcolm crosses his arms in front of him, as if he's bracing himself for my request.

"I would like to invite Lucifer to have dinner with us," I say quickly. So quickly, in fact, that I'm not completely sure it was intelligible.

But I can tell from the look of disbelief on Malcolm's face that he understood all too well.

"Are you serious?" he asks quietly. His calm, even tone is a little unnerving. It almost makes me wish he had yelled his question instead.

"I know you hate him," I say.

"For good reason," Malcolm states succinctly.

I reach out and place my hands on Malcolm's still crossed arms, hoping I can make him understand.

"I need this," I say on the verge of more tears. "I need to get to know him. If at all possible, I want him to become a part of my life. There's a side of him that I've only been able to get glimpses of so far, Malcolm. I think my mother was the only one he ever fully shared himself with. I don't think he'll be that open with me, but I have to try. I need to know there's a part of him that's still good. If he's

259

completely damned, then what chance do I have to fight what the seals will do to me? You don't know how close I came to killing Lorcan. I wanted to kill him. If you hadn't stopped me I would have, and that scares me, Malcolm."

"You don't know that for a fact," Malcolm tries to argue.

"I do know that," I tell him. "I felt so drunk with power when I held his life in my hands that I almost let it take control of me. Lucifer is my father, whether you want to admit that to yourself or not. I may physically look more like my mother, but I also have my father's blood coursing through my veins. I know you hate him. You have every right to from what I understand. But it doesn't mean I have to feel the same way about him. Maybe I have more empathy for Lucifer because I've seen how Helena is using his pain against him. I don't know. All I do know is that getting to know him allows me to know myself better. Before I take Belphagor's seal, I feel like I need as many ties to this life as I can get. We have no way of knowing what it will do to me, Malcolm. If I can have you both by my side, I feel like I have a better chance of surviving what comes next. Please try to understand. I need this."

I feel the tension in his posture dissipate as my words sink in. In a way I feel guilty. I know I'm using Malcolm's love for me to get what I want, but everything I said to him was true. I do feel that bringing Lucifer into my life will help me endure the rest of my mission. My request is a selfish one, and I know I'm asking Malcolm to be completely selfless. Malcolm's past with Lucifer seems to be a murky one filled with pain and deceit. In time, I hope they can come to some sort of understanding and use me as a bridge to mend their differences. But right now I'm allowing myself to be greedy in my request because it's what I need to do to survive.

"And when exactly would you want this dinner party to take place?" Malcolm asks, giving in to my demand with his question.

"As soon as possible," I say, dropping my hands from his arms. "We're supposed to meet with Belphagor tomorrow, and I don't know what's going to happen after that. Would tonight be all right?"

Malcolm sighs heavily and rubs his eyes with the heels of his hands, looking slightly frustrated.

"Fine," he finally says, placing his hands on his hips, not looking the least bit happy.

"Thank you," I tell him. I don't try to touch Malcolm because I feel like he's on edge. I know he's only doing this for me. I suddenly think of an idea that I hope will make the evening a little less tense.

"Why don't we invite everyone else?" I ask. "That way you won't feel the need to have to talk to him if you don't want to."

"Fine," Malcolm says curtly, looking away from me.

"And…I need your help with one more thing," I say, wondering if I'm pushing my luck with what I'm about to ask for next.

Malcolm looks back at me, his face completely blank as he waits for me to speak.

"I need your help finding him," I say. "I could go back to Hell to see if he's there, but I would rather check here on Earth first. Do you know of any places he might go to here?"

Malcolm just stares at me for a moment, before he shakes his head like he either thinks I'm crazy for asking, or *he* is for helping me. He holds one of his hands out for me to take.

"Only for you would I purposely go looking for Lucifer," he tells me. "I know of a few places we might be able to find him."

I place my hand in Malcolm's and squeeze it, making him look at me before I speak.

"And only someone who truly loves me would sacrifice so much," I tell him. "Every day we're together you do something that makes my love for you grow even stronger. I don't know what I would do without you in my life, and I never want to find out."

"You never will," Malcolm promises. "Now let's go find him and get this over with."

Malcolm phases us to a dozen different locations, including a spot in Antarctica and the hallway in the hospital where my mother and Lucifer first met. Yet we don't find Lucifer at any of them.

"Is there anywhere else he could be?" I ask Malcolm as we stand by the twisted metal wreckage of what was once the Eiffel Tower in Paris.

"There's one," Malcolm says. "But if he's not there I'm not sure where else he would be here on Earth."

Malcolm phases me to what looks like an empty field. Snow covers the ground like a white sheet. One solitary figure stands in the far distance.

"He's here," I say in relief at the sight of Lucifer. "But where are we?"

"Jess and Mason used to have a home here," Malcolm tells me. "When they were alive, it was a small community called Cypress Hollow. It was destroyed in the Great War and the homes here were demolished to make way for more fields. He's standing in the spot where Jess' front porch used to be."

"He really did care for her, didn't he?"

"More than he wanted to admit to at the time."

I stare at Lucifer's back for a moment. I'm certain he knows we're here, yet he doesn't turn around to acknowledge our presence.

"It might be easier if I speak to him alone," I tell Malcolm.

"You're probably right. Don't be long." Malcolm leans down and kisses me lightly on the lips before phasing back home.

As I walk up to Lucifer he says, "You know, Jess and I used to have our little heart to hearts here. Have you come to beg me to ask my father for forgiveness, too?"

"No," I tell him. "I actually just came to ask you over for dinner tonight."

Lucifer turns around to face me, looking completely caught off guard by my offer of hospitality.

"What on earth did you have to promise the big oaf to get him to agree to such a thing?"

"*Malcolm*," I say, stressing the name so Lucifer understands I don't appreciate him calling my husband derogatory names, "only wants to see me happy. He would do anything for me. Will you?"

Lucifer stares at me as if he's thinking over my question carefully.

"What time do you want me there?" he finally says.

"Six," I tell him. "And don't be late. I can't promise the meal I make will still be warm if you are."

Lucifer's face falls. "You're cooking? Is it too late to back out of this?"

I laugh at him.

"I'm a very good cook, thank you very much. But it looks like you'll just have to come see for yourself before you'll believe it."

"I lived with your mother. I'm fully aware of your family's track record for producing females who can't even boil water without burning the pot," Lucifer states matter-of-factly.

"Then come see what your miracle child can do," I tell him. "You won't be disappointed. I promise."

"You have me completely intrigued," Lucifer says, looking as such. "I will be there at exactly six, as you've requested."

"Good," I say. On impulse, I lean over and kiss him on the cheek. "I'll see you then."

Before Lucifer can fully get over his shock at my intimate contact, I phase straight to the kitchen back home. I didn't want to give him time to back out of his agreement to come to dinner.

I find Millie in the kitchen, peeling potatoes at the kitchen table.

"Hello, my sweet," she says. "Master Malcolm told me we would be having company this evening. I thought I should get started on it."

"Where *is* Malcolm?" I ask, not seeing him in the room.

"Oh, he went to invite your other guests. He told me to tell you he would be back soon and that he already misses you."

My heart fills with joy and I quickly take off my coat to get to work.

"I want to cook the meal myself," I tell Millie as I pull up the sleeves of my sweater, "but I wouldn't mind some help doing it."

"Simply consider me your assistant then," Millie replies.

I phase up to the bedroom and grab the recipe book Utha Mae and Tara gave me. When I return with it, Millie looks excited by the prospect of cooking new recipes.

"Oh, what shall we cook?" Millie says, looking at all the recipes as I flip through the book.

"Do you know if Lucifer has a favorite dish?" I ask.

"Oh now, let's see," Millie says, looking thoughtful. "I do seem to remember him having a fondness for barbecue. Ribs were his favorite."

I look at Millie and just start to laugh.

"What's so funny?" she asks, uncertain about why I'm laughing.

"Doesn't it seem a little ironic to you?" I ask, still giggling. "That barbecue is the devil's favorite dish."

I see realization dawn, and Millie laughs, too.

"Well," she says, "should we make it or not?"

"Absolutely," I say, flipping through Utha Mae's cookbook and finding her instructions to make a special barbecue sauce. "Let's get to work."

I tap the recipe and instantly hear Utha Mae begin her instructions.

"Ok, baby, first off you're gonna need to gather up the following. Find you some brown sugar, molasses, cayenne pepper...."

For the rest of the afternoon, Millie and I work feverishly at making the meal for that evening. About an hour after we get started, Malcolm comes back home and I immediately put him to work and place him in charge of making Utha Mae's deviled egg recipe. The irony of that particular dish isn't lost on me either, but they just sounded so good I had to have them. Millie makes a potato salad from the potatoes she already peeled. I find a recipe for a corn and black bean chopped salad and pan-fried cornbread. Malcolm flips through the book and finds a recipe for apple pie. He soon locates Lucas, who was with Kyna and Brutus, and puts him to work peeling the required apples and rolling out the dough to make two pies.

By five o'clock the meal is almost done, and Millie shoos me out of the kitchen, telling me to go get ready for my guests who are due to arrive at six.

Malcolm prepares my bath for me, but doesn't offer to join me in it. I think he can tell my nerves are frayed, and I simply need some time to myself to relax and mentally prepare for a possible disaster.

I know integrating Lucifer into my life will not be easy. For one, my husband hates him. Secondly, no one in my family seems to trust him, except for maybe Millie. During the years he secretly visited me on my birthdays they seemed to develop a relationship I'm not even sure I understand.

"Anna?" I look towards the doorway and see Vala peek around the door.

"Vala," I say in relief, "how did you know I needed someone to talk to?"

Vala pads into the room and comes to sit beside the tub.

"I didn't," she confesses. "But your husband did. He thought you might like someone impartial to speak with."

I sigh and lean my back against the tub.

"Am I being selfish for pushing this on Malcolm?" I ask her. "Lucifer's made him suffer through so much over the years. And now I'm asking him to welcome someone he thinks of as the enemy into our home."

"I think you need to do what's best for you right now," Vala answers. "Malcolm seems to understand you need to get to know your real father better. And yes, they have had their differences over the years, but it's you who they both love."

"Vala," I say, sitting up straighter as I suddenly realize something, "did you know that Lucifer used to visit me on my birthdays?"

"I did," she confesses reluctantly. "But I was sworn to secrecy and wasn't at liberty to mention it to you. It's how I know he loves you, Anna. I would see it in his eyes every year he came. When he stopped coming, it simply confirmed his feelings even more to me."

"Why?"

"Because I knew then that seeing you blossom into a young woman, and not being able to share in your experiences was tearing him apart. It hurt him more to see you than to stay away. I assumed he thought keeping his distance would make his love for you diminish, but I think the opposite happened. He needs you just as much as you need him, Anna. If the two of you are able to better understand one another and form a true connection, perhaps you can save each other in the end."

I smile wanly as I realize Vala has just spoken my own thoughts aloud. In a way, it makes me feel justified in my decision.

"Thank you, Vala."

"As far as Malcolm goes," Vala continues, "he loves you more than I've ever seen a man love a woman. He simply wants what's best for you. His relationship with Lucifer has been a tumultuous one up until now. It could be that you can act as a bridge between the two of them. You can be their common ground."

"That's exactly what I was thinking! I hope they can find a way to be civil to one another."

"I believe for you they will try," Vala says confidently. "There is no stronger love than that of a parent for a child. It's a forever love that can never be altered or taken away. I have faith that Lucifer will do what he can to keep you safe and happy. When he sees how happy Malcolm makes you, I don't believe he will be able to disapprove of your marriage any longer."

"I hope you're right," I say, relaxing again. "Otherwise this is going to be the most awkward dinner party in history."

CHAPTER NINETEEN

I dress casually in a black turtleneck sweater and slacks. This get-together isn't meant to be fancy, just a low-key affair with friends and family. My greatest hope is that this won't be the last time Lucifer comes to break bread with us. I want him to feel like he's a part of my life, and I want to feel like I'm a part of his, too.

"Don't be nervous," Malcolm says, buttoning the cuff of one of his sleeves as he walks up to me. "I promise to be on my best behavior tonight."

"I'm not expecting everything to go exactly like I want," I tell him. "I have no illusions that Lucifer will fit perfectly into our family, but I do want him to find a place in our lives. I want him to feel like he can come to me if he wants to, even if it's just to talk about my mother. He needs to share his memories of her with someone other than Helena. She's just using him to become stronger, and that's something I can't tolerate any longer."

Malcolm loops his arms around my waist.

"If anyone can help him see what she's doing to him, it's you, my love. You helped me see how stupid I was being when I tried to push you away. I'm sure you can work the same sort of miracle with Lucifer."

"He can't have a harder head than you, right?" I ask with a playful smile.

Malcolm grins and pulls me even closer. "It's possible but doubtful. Plus you've already claimed a small victory. He's coming to dinner, isn't he?"

"What did the others think about sitting down to share a meal with Lucifer?" I ask. "Do they think I'm insane?"

"I wouldn't necessarily say insane; an eternal optimist perhaps, but not insane. We all want what's best for you, Anna. If you think having Lucifer be part of your life is what's best, then we fully support your decision."

"Thank you," I say, laying my head on his partially-bare chest.

I had to admit that I liked Malcolm's hot-blooded nature. Every time he wore a button- down shirt, he always left the first four buttons undone for added ventilation. Honestly, if you had his chest, why wouldn't you show it off?

"Now let's go down," Malcolm says, pulling back and taking one of my hands in his. "They'll be here in a couple of minutes."

As we descend the staircase, I hear the voices of our friends already in the sitting room, talking to one another. The front door bell rings, and I know there is only one guest who would think he needed to do such a thing before entering our home. Malcolm stays close by my side as I answer the door.

Lucifer stands on the stoop, holding a bouquet of white and pink roses and a bottle of some sort of liquor. He's wearing a pair of smoky grey slacks and a dark grey cardigan sweater with a white button-down shirt underneath. His shoulder-length blond hair is pulled back into a ponytail, positioned at the nape of his neck. The expression on his face shows his uncertainty about tonight, but I feel an effortless smile stretch my lips in spite of it.

"Welcome to our home," I tell him, stepping away from the opening so he can enter.

Lucifer steps inside, and I close the door behind him.

"These are for you," he tells me, handing me the bouquet of flowers.

"Thank you," I say, taking them from him and smelling their sweet fragrance almost immediately.

Lucifer turns to face Malcolm and holds out the bottle of whatever it is he has.

"And this is for you," Lucifer tells Malcolm. "I thought you might need it either during tonight's little get-together or afterwards."

Malcolm looks at the label and actually smiles.

"Macallan M," Malcolm says almost reverently as he reads the label aloud. "How long have you been keeping this?"

"A long time," Lucifer admits. "I figured if you didn't need a drink of the best whiskey ever made, I might."

"I see no reason not to pop her open at the beginning of this evening," Malcolm says. "Might even help things a bit."

"I would have to agree."

"Oh, what beautiful flowers," Millie says, walking up from the back of the house towards us. "Let me take those, my sweet. I know just where to put them."

"Thank you, Millie."

"I came to tell you that dinner will be served in about ten minutes," Millie informs us.

"Thank you again."

Millie walks back towards the kitchen.

"Come on, Lucifer," Malcolm says, heading into the sitting room. "Let's see if this whiskey has held up over the years."

Malcolm takes the lead, and Lucifer and I walk side by side behind him.

"Thank you for not backing out," I whisper to him. "I know it's not easy for you to be here."

"It may end up being awkward for you, too," Lucifer says. "Your friends don't exactly like me very much."

"I'll be happy if you can all at least tolerate one another," I say, trying to keep my expectations about the evening extremely low.

"Tolerance I may be able to achieve," Lucifer comments dryly.

When we walk into the room, all eyes turn to us.

Desmond raises a skeptical eyebrow in our direction. Brutus looks brooding. Jered looks ambivalent, and Daniel looks neutral. Only Linn seems to remember her manners, and walks over to us.

"Lucifer, I would like to introduce you to Linn, Daniel's wife."

Linn holds out her hand to Lucifer, who in turn stares at it for a moment before accepting her polite gesture.

"It's so good to finally meet you," Linn says.

"Really?" Lucifer asks skeptically. "Most people would consider it a blessing never to meet me within their lifetime."

Linn smiles in spite of Lucifer's statement. "Well, I'm not one of them. You're important to Anna, which makes you important to the rest of us. I think we all realize you're only here for her sake. We're thankful for that. She needs all of the support she can get right now."

"Agreed," Malcolm says, walking over to us with two short glasses, filled a quarter of the way with the amber-colored whiskey Lucifer gave him.

Lucifer takes the glass and drinks it in one swig. He hands the empty tumbler back to Malcolm.

"I'll get you another one," Malcolm says, walking back to the small table behind the couch to retrieve the bottle and pour more whiskey into Lucifer's glass.

"Well, I can't just stand here and not get a glass of Macallan, too," Desmond says, walking over to the table.

"Help yourself," Malcolm encourages, bringing Lucifer his second serving of whiskey.

I begin to wonder if all the men will be drunk by the end of the evening. In fact, it was a brilliant idea to bring the whiskey and take the edge off all of them. I silently thank Lucifer for his forethought.

"We should probably go into the dining room," I tell everyone, noticing someone very important missing.

"Where is Lucas?" I ask no one in particular.

"He and Bai are in his room, playing," Linn tells me. "Vala is watching out for them while we have dinner."

It was a good idea. There was no telling what might transpire during the meal, and I didn't want Lucas anywhere nearby if things blew up in our faces.

Once we all reach the dining room, Malcolm takes his seat at the head of the table, and I sit on his right. Lucifer takes the seat right across from me, to Malcolm's left. Everyone else fills the remaining seats, and I catch myself smiling when I see Brutus hold out Kyna's chair for her.

Millie soon arrives in the room, carrying the flowers Lucifer brought me. She's arranged them beautifully in a crystal vase. She sets the vase behind Malcolm on the sideboard. Giles walks in, pushing the silver cart with the meal we prepared.

After everyone is served, the real test of the evening begins...small talk.

"Millie said barbecued ribs were your favorite," I tell Lucifer. "I was able to find a recipe in Utha Mae's recipe book. I hope you like them."

"Utha Mae?" Lucifer says, mulling the name over. "Why does that name sound so familiar?"

"She was Tara's grandmother and like a mother to Lilly," Malcolm reminds Lucifer. "You know... the nice old woman you scared into having a heart attack back when you were trying to destroy the universe."

And so it begins, I think to myself.

"Oh...yes," Lucifer answers. "I remember her now."

"I'm sure you've been responsible for the deaths of so many people over the years that you can't be bothered to remember them all."

"*Malcolm*," I admonish, seeing this evening take a turn for the worse before it's even been given a chance to start.

I watch as Lucifer's jaw muscles tighten and loosen, as if he's biting his tongue in order to give himself time to think about his response.

"There are things about my past and about me now that I cannot change," Lucifer finally says in a far calmer voice than I expected. "But I am here to try to let things from our shared history remain there for the time being, Malcolm. If you're going to dredge up everything that I've done since we've known each other, I might as well leave now. I can't change what I did. I'm only here to do what I can for Anna."

I place one hand on top of Malcolm's, giving him a silent plea to stop antagonizing Lucifer on purpose.

Malcolm looks away from Lucifer and down at his plate.

"You should know that Anna made most of this meal herself," Malcolm tells Lucifer, effectively changing the subject.

"How were you able to break the legacy of bad cooks in your family?" Lucifer asks me.

"Malcolm showed me how to cook," I say, leaving out the fact that Utha Mae's tutelage while I was in Heaven probably had more to do with it than anything. I didn't want to bruise Malcolm's ego in front of my father, and secretly hoped the accomplishment would make Lucifer see my husband with a newfound sense of respect.

"You should feel proud of yourself, Malcolm. I wish I could have taught Amalie, but I'm afraid she was a lost cause when it came to the culinary arts."

"Anna was a natural after I showed her a couple of things," Malcolm replies. "She just needed a little push in the right direction."

Lucifer takes a bite from one of the ribs on his plate, looking surprised by how good it tastes.

"What's in this sauce?" he asks me.

After that the meal goes by rather quietly. No major mishaps or arguments are instigated by anyone present. Lucifer speaks with me for the most part, which seems fine with everyone else. He's only there for me anyway. I don't think any of our guests take it as a slight that he doesn't readily start up friendly conversations with them.

By the end of the meal, I feel it's safe for the children to join us for dessert. I know Lucas would be upset if he wasn't able to eat some of the apple pie he helped prepare.

When they enter the room, Lucas immediately goes to sit on his father's lap, while Bai sits in her mother's lap.

"Did you and Bai have fun?" Malcolm asks Lucas, settling his son on one leg.

"Yes," Lucas says hesitantly, "but she sure is messy. I think I cleaned up after her more than we played."

Daniel can't help but laugh, and I can't prevent a giggle. I clearly remember how chaotic Bai's room was in her own house. If Lucas' vision comes true, I have a feeling he will be cleaning up after Bai for many more years to come.

When I glance over at Lucifer I see him staring at Lucas, like he's trying to figure something out about him. Apparently I'm not the only one who notices Lucifer's odd behavior.

"Are you staring at my son for any particular reason?" Malcolm asks, obviously not liking the attention Lucifer is giving him.

Lucifer drags his gaze away from Lucas and looks at Malcolm.

"No reason," he says, automatically wanting to drop the subject. "Now, where is this pie we're supposed to be having?"

After dessert, we all walk back to the sitting room. Lucifer pulls me aside as we pass by the front door.

"I think I should be leaving now," he tells me. "This evening has gone better than expected. I believe we would be pushing our luck if I stayed any longer."

"You don't know how happy you've made me by coming here tonight," I tell him. "I know it wasn't easy for you, and it means a great deal to me that you made the effort."

Lucifer looks uncomfortable with my expression of gratitude. It's obvious he isn't used to having someone thank him for doing something nice for them.

"I hope," I say, "that you will come and spend more time with us. It seems like the only quality time we've spent together before now has been in Hell."

"You must never go back there, Anna," Lucifer says forcefully. "It's too dangerous for you. Helena would keep you trapped down there if she could. Don't give her the opportunity."

"Are you saying that to keep me safe or to keep dominion over Hell for yourself?" I ask. "You know she wants me to become her new master."

"I know that," Lucifer says wearily. "If you stop collecting any more of the seals, I'm confident she'll leave you alone. It's imperative that you not absorb any more of their power. Do you understand?"

I remain silent, because I have every intention of completing my mission. From the disappointed look on Lucifer's face I can tell he understands my intent, even though I don't say it out loud.

"I should go," he tells me. "But I'll be close if you ever need me."

Lucifer phases, leaving me to wonder how violent his reaction will be after I collect the third seal from Belphagor.

When I walk into the sitting room, all conversation stops immediately.

"Where's Lucifer?" Malcolm asks.

"He left," I tell him.

"Just as well," Jered says, "we need to discuss the situation with Belphagor."

"Were you able to get him to agree to a deal?" I ask, taking a seat beside Malcolm on the sofa.

"Yes," Jered tells us. "Like I was telling Malcolm just now, Belphagor is all for you killing Botis to get him out of the way. But he won't give you the seal until after you kill him."

"That's not acceptable," I say. "I trust myself, but I do not trust a prince of Hell to keep his word."

"Maybe you can change his mind tomorrow when you meet in the desert," Jered says. "Perhaps after he meets you, he'll reconsider his position."

"How should I handle him?" I ask. "Be diplomatic or scare him into submission?"

"Scare him," Malcolm says without reservation. "Diplomacy will only make you look weak to Belphagor. Authority is the only thing he will respond to, because deep down he's a coward. If he knows you'll follow through with a threat, he won't stand up to you."

I nod, knowing exactly what I need to do.

After the rest of our guests leave, Malcolm and I take Lucas up to his room and help him clean up the remainder of the mess Bai left behind.

"And you're sure he said he was supposed to marry Bai?" Malcolm whispers to me as we're screwing the caps back onto the paint bottles.

"That's what he said he saw," I whisper back.

Malcolm shakes his head. "I might have to hire a person to just follow her around in their home and clean up after her. Lucas will never survive with someone who leaves a trail of destruction and chaos wherever she goes."

I giggle. "We'll do whatever is necessary to make sure he's happy."

We help Lucas change into his pajamas and tuck him into his bed. Luna goes to sleep above Lucas' head on his pillow while Vala curls up on the other side of him. She can no longer sleep with me since I now sleep with Malcolm. Obviously, there are things that go on in our bedroom that Vala does not need to witness.

When Malcolm and I go back to our own bedroom, he asks me, "So did tonight go as smoothly as you hoped?"

"It went better than I expected," I tell him, pulling off my sweater as I make my way to our bed.

I turn around to find Malcolm leaned with his back up against the door, watching me disrobe.

"And was there something else you were expecting to do this evening before we go to sleep?" he asks, sounding hopeful.

"Absolutely," I tell him, unbuttoning my slacks and letting them fall to the floor. I step out of them and kick them off to the side.

"Am I going to have to hire someone to follow you around and clean up your messes?" Malcolm teases, pulling his shirt out of his trousers as he heads over to me.

"Not when we're alone in this room," I tell him as he comes to stand in front of me. I place my hands on the belt around his waist and unbuckle it while he sheds his shirt.

"In a hurry?" Malcolm chuckles as he lets me unbutton his slacks and pull the zipper down.

I slide my hand down the front of his underwear to grab a hold of him.

"I'm as eager as you seem to be," I say, stroking him gently.

Before I can even think to tease him anymore, Malcolm grabs hold of my hair hanging loosely by my waist and yanks on it to make me look up at him.

The desire I see in his eyes to have me makes me lose my breath.

"Would you like to learn something new tonight?" he asks, lowering his head to mine and barely touching my lips with his kisses.

"I'm always interested in expanding my knowledge of things," I say breathlessly, as Malcolm trails feather-light kisses down one side of my neck.

"Then take the rest of your clothes off and get into bed, woman," Malcolm says, letting go of my hair and standing back from me to finish undressing himself.

I do as ordered, realizing Malcolm is the only one in the world I would accept such instructions from without question. That night Malcolm does indeed teach me new and very pleasurable things, even one dealing with hot wax from a white candle.

Afterwards I watch him fall asleep in my arms, and feel a sense of loss that I won't be able to enter his dream world with him. Finally the events of the day come crashing down on me, and I find rest in a dreamless sleep.

CHAPTER TWNETY

The next morning Malcolm and I make French toast for everyone's breakfast. Millie makes a big protest about us serving her, but I kindly tell her to stop fussing and sit at the table while we do all of the work. She huffs a bit, but I can tell she secretly likes us waiting on her. Jered joins us that morning because we're all supposed to meet Belphagor together. We have plenty of time to make, eat, and clean up breakfast before we have to go.

"Should I bring my sword?" I ask Malcolm.

"I don't think you'll need it for this," he replies. "You can kill him with one touch. He knows that. You've already proven it."

I grab my purple coat from the back of my chair at the kitchen table.

"Then let's go," I tell Jered and Malcolm. "I'd really like to get things settled today if we can."

Malcolm takes one of my hands and phases us directly to the desert.

Belphagor, in the disguise of Empress Zhin Liang, is already there.

Empress Zhin was a timeless beauty, exemplifying the true meaning of grace and poise. Her olive-colored skin, round face, and long dark brown, almost-black hair was classic. It sickened me to think that one of the princes stole her body. As I look at Zhin, I suddenly realize Lucifer commanded the princes to inhabit the bodies of the rulers of Earth, and that I was the reason he gave them such an order. In his misguided attempt to keep me safe, Zhin Liang lost her life. She would have had no way of knowing why Belphagor targeted her when she died, and I felt angry that she had to suffer through such a death just because of me.

Belphagor looks me up and down in a rather superior and appraising way.

"You don't look nearly as intimidating as I thought you would," he says, using the genteel and cultured voice he stole from Zhin.

"And you sound about as ignorant as I expected," I reply.

"Tsk, tsk," Belphagor says with a shake of his head, "should you really be talking to me with such disrespect? I thought you wanted my help."

"And I thought you wanted mine," I say, not about to let him think he has the upper hand in this situation. "As I see it, this meeting is simply you begging me to spare your life, Belphagor. Or do you doubt I can kill you with one touch? If you do, I would be happy to prove you wrong."

Belphagor doesn't look as cocky as he did at first.

"There's no need," he says. "I'm fully aware of what you can do. That's why I agreed to this meeting. I need you to do what I can't: kill Botis."

"Jered says that you won't give me your seal until after I kill him."

"That's right," Belphagor says, crossing his arms in front of him as if the act will cement his demand in stone. "Otherwise how do I know you'll uphold your end of the bargain?"

"I promised Empress Olivia that I would kill Botis for murdering her husband," I say. "And I always keep my promises. Unfortunately I can't say the same thing for you. I don't trust that you will willingly give me your seal afterwards. You do understand that I don't need you to be willing, right? I can take it from you anytime I wish, but that means killing you in the process."

"What guarantee do I have that you'll keep to your end of the agreement if I just give you my seal?" Belphagor asks.

"Because I promise you I will. I can kill Botis with or without your help, Belphagor. It would just be simpler if you helped me so no one witnesses his demise by my hands."

"And your plan is to simply kill him in cold blood?"

"I'll give him a chance to defend himself," I say. "But the outcome will be the same. He'll lose his life, but at least he'll die thinking he had a fighting chance. Either do it my way or lose your life, too, Belphagor. The choice is yours."

"And why would you leave me in charge of Cirro?" Belphagor asks, suspicious of my motives. "What's to prevent you from just killing me after you kill Botis?"

"I can't say I like the idea of you ruling Cirro very much," I admit. "But you know we'll be watching what you do there. If I see you mistreating the citizens of Cirro or the people of your down-world, I'll end your life without a second thought. That I also promise you."

"Are you the one responsible for that little video that was shown yesterday? There's a rumor circulating among the aristocracy of the cloud cities that it was instigated by you."

"Does it matter?" I say, becoming aggravated by his attempt to change the subject. "Are you going to give me your seal, or are you going to make me take it from you?"

Belphagor is completely mute for a while as he stands in front of us, thinking over his options, few though they are.

"I guess I'll have to rely on your honor to follow through with your end of this pact," Belphagor says, holding out his hand to me.

I walk the few steps towards him and take hold of his hand.

"Ready?" he asks.

I simply nod my head and brace myself for the pain I know is about to come my way.

Belphagor closes his eyes as though he's in deep thought.

The power of the seal hits me all at once. Oddly enough, the pain strikes me in the pit of my stomach first instead of my back, and courses from that epicenter to the rest of my body. I fall to my knees, but soon feel Malcolm lift me up into his strong arms. I faintly hear Jered speak to Belphagor before Malcolm phases me back home to our bedroom to lay me down on the bed. He lies down beside me and simply holds me as the pain from absorbing Belphagor's seal tears through my veins like molten lava. Only Malcolm's closeness makes it bearable enough to breathe. I begin to shiver like I have a fever, but I know it's simply my body's reaction to the added energy it's having to cope with.

"I love you, Anna," Malcolm says to me. "I love you."

Malcolm tells me repeatedly how much he loves me. He begins to tell me about all the things we'll do after I've completed my mission, and I let my mind drift along on his dreams for our future. I want nothing more than to live the life Malcolm sees for us. But in times like this, I begin to wonder if it will ever come to pass. Will I be able to survive this ordeal? And if I do survive physically will I remain the person I am, or become the monster Lucifer and Helena seem so certain the seals will transform me into? I refuse to give into doubt, and decide to stay true to myself for as long as I can.

After a while the pain subsides, and I'm able to pull away from Malcolm to look at his face.

He peers down at me. His expression is a perfect mirror of the helplessness he feels.

"I wish I could do more for you," he tells me, knowing he's powerless to save me from the torture I have to endure.

"You help me more than you know," I tell him. "You always have."

"I would bear the pain for you if I could."

"You have enough of your own to deal with," I say, letting him know I haven't forgotten the daily suffering he has to endure because of Lucifer's curse. "I'm strong. I can handle it."

"But for how long?" he asks worriedly. "It seemed like this seal caused you more pain than the others."

"It was a bit more...intense," I admit. "But it's passed now."

Malcolm kisses me on the forehead and holds me close. We rest in each other's arms until there's a soft knock at the door.

Malcolm kisses me on the forehead one more time before getting up to see who our visitor is.

"How is she?" I hear Jered ask anxiously.

"As well as can be expected," Malcolm says. "Did you make arrangements with Belphagor?"

"Yes, he said he would make sure Botis was alone during his morning bath. With the time difference, that's about seven hours from now. Will she be ready by then?"

I sit up in the bed.

"I'll be ready, Jered."

Malcolm turns slightly to look at me, giving Jered a chance to peer inside the room.

"You should wear your leather outfit. You'll need to go there invisible and wait for Belphagor to get rid of the guards."

"And how exactly does he plan to do that?" Malcolm asks.

"He's going to tell the guards beforehand that the empress wants to spend some intimate time alone with her husband. As soon as Botis gets comfortable in his bath, the guards will sneak out to give the royal couple an opportunity to be with one another."

"Botis will know something's up," I say.

"Yes, but probably not before you make your presence known to him and pick a fight."

"Do you think he'll stand and fight me?" I ask. "Or will he try to run away like he did in Nacreous?"

"Even if he does, it's not like you can't follow him this time," Jered says. "He'll know that. I have a feeling he'll take his chances and fight you rather than try to run. There's nowhere he could go where you wouldn't follow him."

"Good," I say. "I don't think I'll be in the mood to chase after him anyway. I only wish Olivia could witness the death of her husband's executioner."

"She'll be plenty satisfied to just know you've killed him," Malcolm tells me.

"I'll be back when it's time to go," Jered says to Malcolm. "Belphagor showed me where to take Anna so she can wait for Botis."

"I'll be ready," I promise.

Malcolm closes the door and crawls back into bed with me.

"You should get some rest," Malcolm tells me. "You look tired."

Even though I had just slept through the night, the ordeal of taking in the seal has indeed left me completely exhausted. I should have known Malcolm would notice it.

I curl myself against him and breathe deeply. In no time at all, I'm sound asleep.

When I awaken, I feel one of Malcom's hands gently glide up and down my hip as I lay with my back pressed firmly against him. I turn to lay flat on my back, to look up at his face as he slides his hand to rest on my thigh.

"Did you sleep well?" he asks.

"Yes. How long was I asleep?"

"A couple of hours."

"Have you been lying here all that time?"

"Where else would I want to be?"

I run my right hand over Malcolm's shoulder and bury my fingers in the hair at the nape of his neck. Malcolm doesn't need any more encouragement than that simple gesture. He lowers his mouth to mine, kissing my lips tenderly. I press my lips against his more forcefully, demanding a more penetrating kiss from him. I turn my body into Malcolm's and grab his shoulders with my hands as I wrap one leg around his waist, and press him onto his back without ever breaking the contact of our lips.

I reach down in between us and hastily yank his shirt out of his pants, popping the lower buttons free. Malcolm sits up, allowing me free access to slip his shirt off his shoulders. He quickly takes it the rest of the way off. Hastily, Malcolm helps me shed the shirt and bra I'm wearing, exposing my breasts to his undivided attention. Normally I would enjoy his tender teasing of my body, but gentle isn't what I'm craving. I take Malcolm's head in my hands and roughly push him back against the pillows.

He watches me as I float in the air to hover over him. I reach down and grab the waistband of his pants, ripping them down the middle and up the sides with brute force. Not feeling in the mood to waste any time, I do the same to his underwear until he's completely exposed to my touch. I quickly shed the rest of my own clothes until I'm finally naked, too.

I hover over Malcolm for a moment before settling myself down onto his hips to take the full length of him inside me. I watch his face as I begin to move against him. He closes his eyes and begins to murmur my name like a litany. The faster I move, the deeper his groans of pleasure grow. I lean down and grab the hair on either side of his head, forcing him to look at me.

For a moment, a confused expression passes over Malcolm's face as his eyes meet mine. I lean down and kiss him to wipe it away.

I feel Malcolm pull on my hair gently, forcing me to break the contact of our lips. He peers into my eyes, looking alarmed now.

"Anna," Malcolm says, breathing hard, "what are you doing?"

"What does it feel like I'm doing?" I ask, a bit aggravated by his question because there's really only one thing I want from him at the moment.

"Your eyes," he says staring into them. "They're glowing blue."

Malcolm's words act like a splash of cold water on my body. I sit upright on his hips.

"Glowing blue?" I ask, hoping I misunderstood what he said.

"Yes," he replies, continuing to stare at me.

It's only then that I realize what it is I'm really doing to Malcolm. I'm simply using him to satisfy a sexual hunger I feel. I wasn't viewing him as my lover, but simply a means to satisfy my physical urges.

"I'm sorry," I say, fully realizing what I was doing.

Malcolm reaches up and cups one side of my face tenderly. I close my eyes and try to reconnect to the real reason we make love. Before that moment, I was simply trying to gratify a baser need, but that wasn't right, not with the man who held my heart.

I open my eyes and look at the man I love again with a clearer perspective.

He smiles. "That's better."

Malcolm rolls me over onto my back.

Each kiss he plants on my face is a gentle reminder of how much he loves me. I ride the wave of his love to bring me back to who I really am.

"Malcolm," I say. "Make love to me."

I feel him smile against the base of my neck.

"I have every intension of doing just that," he assures me.

With every touch of his hands and his lips on my body, Malcolm reminds me that what we have with one another should never be reduced to just sex. The connection between us is so much deeper than that.

As Malcolm brings my body to the brink, I feel myself free-fall into the warmth of his love for me. Something I vow never to take advantage of again.

Afterwards I lie in Malcolm's arms, grateful for the comfort he selflessly gives me.

"I'm sorry," I tell him again. "I'm not sure what happened to me."

"I have to admit I found it pretty sexy at first," he says. "But I knew something was wrong. Your eyes simply confirmed it."

"I've heard people say that the eyes are the windows into the soul," I say. "Do you think it means mine is changing?"

"Absolutely not," Malcolm says with conviction, but it sounds more like he's trying to convince himself than me.

I don't make mention of my suspicions to him. I just hug my husband close and silently promise to keep hold of who I am for as long as I can.

I pull back and kiss his lips.

"I'll be right back," I tell him. "I just need to go to the bathroom."

I crawl out of bed and go into the bathroom. I immediately look at myself in the mirror just to confirm that no trace of my alternate persona is visible anymore. Thankfully, all I see are brown eyes that look familiar and all mine. I'm not sure what change Belphagor's seal has made in me, but I vow to fight against its effects. I turn my back towards the mirror so I can see the third seal there. When I turn my head to look at my reflection, I hear myself gasp in surprise right before a deep-set anger grabs hold of my heart.

I see no third seal on my back. Yet, the pain I felt when Belphagor supposedly gave me his seal was real. How did he cause such agony yet retain the seal for himself?

I feel angry, *and* I feel betrayed, two emotions that make for a dangerous combination.

When I look up into the mirror to face my reflection again, I find myself staring at blue glowing eyes.

CHAPTER TWENTY-ONE

I decide to keep Belphagor's treachery to myself for the time being. I don't want to cause Malcolm any more distress than I already have. He's dealt with enough of my drama for one day. I will myself to calm down and stay in the bathroom until my eyes go back to their natural color. When I do finally go back into the bedroom, Malcolm is already up and getting dressed.

"Are you hungry?" he asks me.

"I am actually," I say, feeling the gnaw of hunger in the pit of my stomach.

Malcolm walks over to me and pulls me to him.

"I'll go make us something. Would you rather eat up here or do you feel like being with everyone else?"

"I would rather have our family around me right now," I tell him.

"Then family time it is," he says, kissing me in a way that makes me think he would much rather we just stayed in the room alone the rest of the afternoon.

"Come down when you're ready," he says, forcing himself to leave me.

After Malcolm goes down to the kitchen, I go ahead and dress in my white leather outfit so I'm ready when Jered comes to get me. I grab my baldric and sword to have it close.

If I'm being honest with myself, I'm looking forward to the fight with Botis. I feel in need of the physical combat to get rid of some of my built-up anger before I confront Belphagor and force him to tell me what he really did to me. I have a feeling whatever he did is responsible for my behavior with Malcolm earlier. I can well imagine him laughing at me the whole time he worked his magic. He was able to deceive me once, but I would be damned if I would ever let it happen again. The more I think about his deception, the angrier I become.

Once I'm dressed, I go to the bathroom to check my eyes and see that they are glowing blue with anger. It takes me a good ten minutes to calm down enough to have them return to their normal color. I don't even bother to walk down to the kitchen. I simply phase there because I feel an overpowering need to have my family close around me. They're my tie to sanity in an insane world, and if there was ever a time I needed to keep a clear head, it's now.

"Just in time," Malcolm says when he sees me. He moves away from the stove with a bowl of soup in his hands and sets it on the table in front of my regular seat.

"Mommy!" Lucas yells, standing up from his spot on the floor where he was playing with Luna. He lunges at me and hugs me around the waist. It feels like the best medicine to soothe my growing ire towards Belphagor.

Luna comes up to me and nudges my leg with her muzzle, wanting attention, too.

I lean down and pick her up, realizing she's grown quite a bit since I last held her.

"How are you feeling, Anna?" Vala asks me from her spot near the table.

"A lot better now," I reassure her.

And it's the truth. I do feel better with my family near, more like my true self. I try to push the image of my eyes glowing blue to the back of my mind. I don't need to think about that right now. I need to concentrate on my family and gain clarity through their love for me.

Millie and Giles join us for lunch, making the table complete.

After we eat, Malcolm and I take Lucas and the dogs outside to play in the courtyard. Lucas and I build a snowman while Malcolm plays fetch with Luna. I can't help but smile at the sight of Malcolm playing with my little hellhound pup. Who would have thought such a miracle could happen? Considering Malcolm's track record with Luna's species, it was odd to watch him play with her like a person would any pet they cared about.

It had been a little over a month since Lucifer gave her to me, and in that time she had become an integral part of our lives, especially for Lucas. Where you saw one, you saw the other. They were practically inseparable. I wasn't sure if Luna's sweet temperament was due to nature or nurture, though. Lucifer did tell me hellhounds started out like all living creatures, innocent to the world. I had to believe the love Lucas lavished on her, and the strict code of behavior Vala imposed daily, was helping to shape her personality.

When Jered finds us that afternoon, I know playtime is over. There's work to be done that only I can do.

"Do you want me to come with you?" Malcolm asks.

I shake my head. "No. If I need to be invisible, I sincerely doubt there will be anywhere to hide someone as large as you. I'll be fine. He's no match for me. You know that."

I neglect to tell Malcolm I intend to confront Belphagor about his double-cross after I dispose of Botis. I don't want him to worry about me any more than he already is.

"Don't underestimate him," Malcolm warns. "He's an expert swordsman. And he has the ability to switch bodies almost instantaneously."

"What do you mean? He can transfer his soul to anyone at any time? Is that a special ability?"

"Most of the time it takes them a while to recover from forcing a soul out of its body. Botis has always been able to jump bodies at will. It's why he was able to assume Emperor Rui's form right after he left Horatio's body."

"Will he try to take my body?"

"You would be able to kill him before he could even try."

"Then we have nothing to worry about," I tell Malcolm, leaning up to kiss him on the lips. "I'll be home before dinner."

"You make it sound like you're going off to work," Malcolm says, looking like he finds it odd that I would take this particular battle so lightly.

"I am in a way," I tell him. "This is my job. It's what I was made to do. I'll be fine, Malcolm. You don't have to worry about me."

"And it's my job to do just that," he tells me. "Just be careful, Anna."

"I'll be back soon," I tell him, leaning up and kissing him before I join Jered.

"Just let me get my sword," I tell Jered, phasing to a now-empty kitchen to retrieve my sword from beside my chair.

I quickly return to Jered's side.

"Make yourself invisible," Jered tells me. "Then I'll phase you to where you need to go."

I wish myself to disappear from sight and take hold of Jered's arm, since he can't see where I am anymore.

Jered phases us into a large room made completely out of glass. A recessed pool of steaming clear water sits in the center of the room. The room seems to be situated at the top of the castle in Cirro, which is a modernized take on an ancient Chinese palace called the Forbidden City. White clouds can easily be seen outside the glass walls of the room, effectively shielding the occupants from prying eyes.

"As soon as Botis is settled in the bath for his daily soak," Jered tells me, "Belphagor will get the guards out. After that, you're welcome to pick a fight with him."

"Ok, Jered."

"Anna," Jered says, a tinge of worry in his voice, "be careful."

"I will be. You and Malcolm worry too much about me, when you really don't need to."

"We worry for good reason," he says. Jered hesitates, like he wants to ask me something. Curiosity seems to get the best of him. "Have you noticed anything different about yourself after absorbing Belphagor's seal? Any anger issues?"

I find it curious that Jered should ask such a question just then. My anger at Belphagor for deceiving me is slowly eating away at what little patience I have left.

"Why do you ask?"

"Because Belphagor's seal was torment. It makes sense you might feel some of each emotion or purpose the seals serve. Don't let your anger get the best of you in this fight. It's a sure way to lose focus."

"I've got it under control, Jered."

"All right," he says, not sounding the least bit convinced. "I'll go back to New Orleans and wait there for your return."

Jered phases and I simply stand and wait for Botis to show up. Thankfully, I'm not left twiddling my thumbs for very long. Botis swaggers in, looking rather arrogant about his own importance, with six armed guards flanking him on either side. As they enter the room, three of the guards split off to line the right wall while the other three line the left. Botis, now hiding within the imposing figure of Emperor Rui, casts off his red silk robe and steps into the steaming pool of water. I hear him sigh in delight as the water envelops him. He closes his eyes and smiles as he begins to luxuriate in his bath.

I see Belphagor quietly teleport into the room. In his disguise as Empress Zhin, Belphagor is wearing a transparent robe that leaves little for the imagination to conjure. With a seductive smile, Belphagor lifts a hand which acts as a signal to the guards. They immediately transport out of the room to leave their empress alone with her husband.

After the guards leave, I wish myself visible again. Belphagor sees me instantly and waves a hand towards Botis, as if offering him up for the slaughter to come. I don't give away my anger at Belphagor. I plan to unleash the full force of my wrath on him later. Right now, Botis needs to pay for what he did to Horatio Ravensdale.

I pull my sword from its sheath on my back, instantly igniting its flames.

Botis opens his eyes and sees me standing on the other side of the pool from him.

"I wondered how long it would take you to come after me," he says, not looking in the least bit startled by my presence. "I'm surprised you left me alive for this long."

"I was waiting for the right time," I tell him. "But I'm willing to give you a fighting chance. I won't just assassinate you, even though that's what you deserve."

"Well," Botis says, standing from the water completely naked, "isn't that sporting of you."

He steps out of the pool and puts his silky red robe back on. Botis looks over at Belphagor, who is all smiles, looking quite pleased with himself.

"I suppose this was your idea," Botis says knowingly.

"It's time for you to get out of my hair, Botis. Lucifer wouldn't do anything to get rid of you, but his daughter is more than capable of doing what he refused to."

Belphagor's choice of words bothers me. They make me sound like I'm more cold- hearted than Lucifer, which doesn't sit well with me given his past deeds.

Botis conjures up his large glowing blue broadsword, holding it in his left hand.

"I won't be as easy to kill as you might think," he tells me arrogantly. "I've had eons to practice wielding my sword. What have you had, a few measly years?"

"Skill makes you more proficient," I tell him. "Not time."

Botis raises his sword and charges me. I presume he hoped to catch me off guard, mistaking me for some amateur. I easily dodge his thrust and swing the edge of my sword across his back as he passes me, slicing it open from one shoulder blade to the other.

Botis turns around, wincing.

"You got lucky," he says, wounded physically and trying to salvage what's left of his pride.

"And you were overconfident," I reply. "That was a dim-witted move."

Apparently my words do nothing but anger Botis further, because he comes at me with a vengeance. I have to admit that he's stronger than I would have given him credit for, but not formidable enough to simply use his strength to force me into submission. After a while I finally back him into a corner, and he quickly realizes he doesn't have a chance of defeating me.

"I yield!" he says, throwing his sword to the floor.

"There is no yielding in this fight!" I yell at him. "Pick up your sword and die with at least a little bit of dignity."

"No," Botis says, looking confident that I won't kill an unarmed man. "If I pick it up, you'll just kill me. I don't believe you're a cold-blooded murderer. You're not simply going to stab me through the heart when I'm defenseless."

"It would be a justified execution," I tell him. "You killed Horatio Ravensdale and Emperor Rui. I made a promise to Horatio's widow that I would exact vengeance in her name and make you pay for killing her husband."

"Then do it," Botis taunts, lifting his arms to either side of him and raising his chin to bare his neck to my sword. "Kill me and be done with it."

I stare at his throat, knowing I could end his life with one swing of my sword. But in doing so I would be committing murder.

I lower my blade a notch, in dismay. Botis begins to laugh.

"Who would have thought the daughter of Lucifer would have a conscience? Too bad really; you could have ended this once and for all. Now you'll just have to wonder whose body I'll inhabit next."

His words sound like a warning and visions of him harming someone I love flit through my mind. The faces of Millie and Lucas being the most paramount.

The body of Emperor Rui falls to the floor, lifeless. I see a shimmering figure standing over it and know it's Botis in his true angelic form. He makes to phase away, but I drop my sword and grab hold of him with both of my hands to prevent him from leaving.

"You should have accepted an honorable death," I tell him, feeling my anger reach out like physical tentacles and wrap around his shimmering form. "Now, you'll always be remembered as a coward of the worst kind. I can't let you leave and end another innocent's life. Goodbye, Botis. Enjoy your time in the Void."

With a single thought, I reduce Botis to a pile of black ash on the floor at my feet.

I hear slow clapping behind me.

"Well done," Belphagor applauds. "For a moment there, I wasn't sure you had it in you."

I turn to face a smiling Belphagor and let loose the anger I've been keeping at bay up until this point. With one thought, I toss Belphagor's body up against the ceiling in the room, effectively wiping his smug little grin from his face. I hear his skull strike the glass, causing a long crack in it from the sudden impact. I release my hold on him and let his body fall to the floor naturally. I sense him about to phase away and hold out an open hand, curling it into a fist to hold him in place.

Obviously, my powers have grown to the point where I don't actually have to have physical contact anymore to stop someone from phasing.

"Did you really think I wouldn't know what you did?" I ask him, feeling my blood boil because of his deceit.

"What are you talking about?" Belphagor asks, looking confused as he tries to raise himself up onto his hands and knees.

"The seal, Belphagor!" I scream, feeling frustrated because he's making me explain something he already knows. "You didn't give it to me!"

Belphagor looks even more confused, showing an adeptness at acting which only makes me grow angrier. I lift him up and toss him against the left side of the room face first. A spray of blood blossoms against the wall before he slides to the floor, groaning.

Belphagor lifts himself up and spits out a mouthful of teeth and blood onto the floor before looking back at me.

"I did give it to you!" he professes, trying to sit upright on shaky limbs. "I kept my end of the bargain and now you've kept yours. We're even."

"You're lying!" I scream, feeling my anger break what self-control I had left.

I phase over to him and pick him up easily.

"Give me the seal now, or I'll tear it away from your soul," I promise him. "Trust me; you don't want me to do that."

"I swear to you," Belphagor says, looking feeble and weak. "I didn't double-cross you!"

"Yes, you did!" I say shaking him violently, almost snapping his neck. "I don't have it!"

"Neither do I!"

"Stop lying!" I yell, feeling a blind rage take control of me completely. I squeeze Belphagor's arms so tightly I break though his human skin, and rip through muscle until I feel the hardness of bone press against the palms of my hands. Blood gushes onto the floor around us.

Belphagor screams out in pain, feeding my rage to a point where I begin to enjoy hearing his agony. He continues to try to phase away, but I keep him put.

"I swear," he cries, looking at me with true fear in his eyes. "I gave you my seal!"

"No, you didn't," I say, shoving my face into his. "But you're about to."

I wish for Belphagor's death and watch without an ounce of remorse as he turns to black ash in front of me.

I wait for the power of his seal to incapacitate me, but nothing happens. Nothing at all.

"Anna... what have you done?"

I look up from Belphagor's ashes to see Lucifer standing a short distance away from me. The expression on his face as he looks at the blood around the room tells me exactly what I need to know. The realization of what I just did strikes my soul like a hammer on a nail.

Belphagor didn't double-cross me. He was telling me the truth.

"I thought he was lying," I say, trying to justify my torture and execution of the prince of Hell. "I thought he tricked me into thinking he gave me his seal earlier when he didn't, but..."

"You have the seal, Anna," Lucifer says quietly. "I can sense it inside you."

I look at the blood on my hands mixed with black ash.

"Oh, my God," I say, continuing to stare at my hands as if they don't belong to me. A well of tears blur my vision as I stumble away from the pools of blood on the floor.

I feel my world begin to spin out of control. Have I become the monster I was warned I would transform into? I tortured Belphagor because I thought it would make him give me what I wanted. At least that's what I tell myself. But if I'm being truthful, there was a part of me that enjoyed watching him suffer. Somewhere deep inside I gained pleasure in his torment.

As I look back at the blood splattered across the room, I suddenly feel sick to my stomach, and vomit.

Lucifer walks over to me and places a comforting hand on my back.

When I stand back up, I feel lost. Who am I now? What am I?

"What do I do now?" I ask as I turn towards my father, my body trembling uncontrollably from shock.

"You leave this behind you," Lucifer says, using the cuff of his shirtsleeve to wipe Belphagor's blood off my face. "You need to let this go and never think about it again."

"I can't do that," I say, knowing what I did will haunt me until my dying days.

Lucifer pulls me into his arms, trying to bring me some comfort. I begin to sob hysterically, and no matter what Lucifer says to try to comfort me I can't stop myself from crying.

I'm not only weeping for what I did to Belphagor. I'm also mourning the damage I've inflicted on my soul. How will I ever be able to live through this? How will I be able to even look at myself in a mirror again, knowing the horror I'm capable of?

"Come on," Lucifer says, gently pulling back from me. He takes hold of one of my bloodstained hands with his. "I know where you need to be."

Lucifer phases us and I soon find myself standing in the sitting room of Malcolm's New Orleans home.

"Malcolm!" Lucifer yells urgently.

Malcolm quickly appears in the doorway of the room. He immediately walks over to me and takes me into his arms. Within the safety of his embrace, I feel the full force of the horrifying things I did to Belphagor. I completely break down and begin to cry as my soul screams out in pain.

"What happened?" Malcolm asks Lucifer.

Lucifer tells Malcolm what he knows. Of course, only I can tell him the full story.

"Thank you for bringing her home," Malcolm tells Lucifer. It's probably the first time Malcolm has ever thanked Lucifer for anything.

"She needs you," Lucifer says, sounding as if he's finally realizing how important Malcolm is to my mental well-being. "She lost control of who she is. You need to help her cope with what she did and find a way to put it behind her. She's going to have to forgive herself or her guilt will eat her up and do more damage than good. It will leave her vulnerable."

"Like yours did you?" Malcolm asks knowingly.

"Just help her," Lucifer says, not arguing against what Malcolm said but not agreeing with it either. "I'll leave the two of you alone."

Malcolm continues to hold me while I grieve for the part of my soul I lost that day.

"Anna," Malcolm says gently. "You need to tell me why you thought Belphagor lied about giving you his seal earlier."

I take a deep breath and say, "Because I don't have the seal on my back like I do the other two."

"But you felt the power you received from it after the transfer, right?"

"I thought he did something to make me think he gave it to me," I say, sniffling. "I thought he tricked me so he could keep the seal for himself."

"Oh, Anna, I wish you had come to me with your suspicions. We could have found a way to discover the truth together."

I grab the front of Malcolm's shirt, like a child holding onto a parent because she's afraid she might drown otherwise. And that's exactly how I feel. I feel like I'm about to drown in what the seals are transforming me into, and I desperately need him to help me keep my head above water.

Malcolm pulls away from me slightly and cups my face in the palms of his hands, forcing me to look into his eyes.

"Don't let this destroy you," he tells me. "We'll find a way to make it through this, my love."

"How can you call me that after what I just did?" I ask, sobbing.

"Because you are the love of my life. You are the love I was always meant to find and you're mine. I won't let the princes of Hell or the seals steal you away from me. I'll fight them all to keep you safe, not only from them but also from yourself. I won't let you turn into a monster, Anna. I'll die before I let that happen."

Malcolm pulls me back into his arms, trying to keep me safe in his small way.

But deep down inside, I know not even his love can save me from what I've already become.

Author's Note

I hope you all enjoyed reading *Lucifer*! The last book of The Redemption Series is called *Redemption*, and is now available.

Thanks for reading!

S.J. West

Made in the USA
Charleston, SC
22 April 2016